Deadlier Rhymes

Book 2 in the Deadly Rhymes Trilogy

Deadlier Rhymes

Evil doesn't stay dead forever

Cory Blystone

Kwirk Publishing
Vancouver

For my sister Kassidie, the bravest person I know.

Deadlier Rhymes

Prologue
Sky

Contrary to popular belief, the world did not end in 1999. However, for one girl it certainly felt like it.

Sky Hawkins rolled into the broad main hall of Ravenwood High School in Ravenwood, Washington, glad to be out of the bitter cold winter winds and very much thankful for the gloves her grandma got her for Christmas, even though she was horribly embarrassed about the cuddly kitten and heart pattern because her grandma also saw her as a perpetual six-year-old. She was also glad to be in school again. Only now she was at a different school, a different town, a different place than she was used to. She was different too.

She wasn't herself anymore.

Couldn't be.

Never again.

It was late January in the year 2000, and although Sky was looking forward to getting back to her studies, she was fearful of what people would think of her. Desperately she wanted to make new friends and meet new people, but she knew that was going to be difficult. The naturally outgoing, fun-loving, risk-taking adventurer was gone, replaced with a hermit who wanted nothing more than to be left with her thoughts most days. So much for new millenniums bringing new beginnings. This millennium was already doomed from the start.

If only that accident never happened. If only she would have left that frat house party earlier. If only… if only she wasn't in a wheelchair.

Two girls in cheer uniforms ran down the hall with their books in hand. One of them stared at Sky with evil, uncaring eyes. The other pulled her closer and whispered something into her ear, covering her mouth over it. They giggled.

I know what they're saying. I know they're talking about me. Why? Why can't I be normal? Why did this happen? I hate this school already! And I hate cheerleaders! CHEER THIS! Sky screamed in her head before flipping them off. The effect may have worked better had her middle finger not been covered with a fluffy white kitten chasing a floating red heart.

Sky was furious.

Why shouldn't she be?

The larger wheels on her wheelchair were dirty and wet, caking her brand new gloves with unidentifiable filth as she pushed and pushed with them. The accident was so recent and her family didn't have the money at the time, so she was unable to get a motorized unit. But she was hoping that would change. Soon.

Stopped midway in the long hall, she brushed her soft, wavy brown hair out of her celestial eyes with her hands. She reached into her backpack that was placed in a basket behind the backrest, and pulled out her schedule.

"Room two-oh-seven? Where's that?" she asked aloud.

Nobody was near her. She was alone in the empty hall. All alone.

Sky looked at the nearest door. 713.

"Great," she said, waving the schedule in the air. "I'm nowhere near it."

Lost.

That's what she felt like. Lost in her own little lonely world, apart from everyone....

C-C-CLICK

An angry buzz followed by the sound of a heavy metal rock song invaded her head. It sounded like old Metallica, buy Sky wasn't quite awake to know for sure if it was or not before she turned the alarm clock off with a slam. It was time to get up. Time to get ready for school. Time to face the people of Ravenwood again.

I wish I could just sleep all day. Not have to worry what people think, or look at their curious, staring, rejecting eyes. Just dream.

Dream of what it would be like to walk again. Dream of having friends again. Dream, dream, dream…

Before she realized it, she was in her wheelchair and strolling into the kitchen with the Everly Brothers stuck in her brain. Her mother was at the stove making scrambled eggs and sausage. There was a heavy, greasy smell wafting through the air, accompanied by spindly smoke from whatever was left burning in the toaster.

"Good morning Sky. Are you hungry?" Mrs. Hawkins asked her daughter, turning away from the crackling sound of the sausage frying.

"I wish it was good," Sky muttered, pushing herself to the dining room table where the chairs that would normally be in place were off to the side against a wall.

"What do you mean by that?" Mrs. Hawkins inquired, staring at her through fogged glasses, hands on her hips, and holding a spatula in the left.

Looking up from her lap, Sky told her mom, "Everybody stares at me like I'm a freak. Nobody will even give me the time of day, literally, they won't even tell me what time it is because that is what I am, a freak. Look at me! I have become a useless waste of space! Why am I even here? I hate this town! Why did we have to move?" Her voice escalated with her anger.

"You know very well why we had to move," Mrs. Hawkins told her, turning back and attending to the eggs again, which now were almost the same color as the Brown N' Serve sausage links though decidedly not as black as the toast smoking and making Sky wonder if their smoke alarms had batteries in them because they should've gone off already. "Your father got a job here. And by the looks of it, this might be the last time we have to move."

"Yeah but…"

"Things take time, you know. It will probably be a while before you make some new friends. Just wait. You'll see."

"But…" Sky stopped herself. What was the use in arguing with her mom? Mother always wins; daughter always loses. That's the way it's always been. In this family anyway.

Mrs. Hawkins scooped up a large spoonful of scrambled eggs and placed them on a plate. Sky looked at them and started poking it with her fork, half expecting some evil chicken monster to hatch out of it, but knowing that could never happen. The eggs were far too cooked for that.

"How many pieces of sausage do you want?" Mrs. Hawkins asked while she buttered the toast that had just popped up from the toaster, the blackness sucking in the creamy butter as if it were a sponge.

"I'll just have one, Mom," Sky answered as she stared at the lumpy browned yellow pile in front of her.

A greasy link of sausage plopped on her plate along with a slice of burnt toast that had too much butter on it.

"Make that two, no, five links," Sky said, figuring why not, she'd already had a crappy few months. A few extra pounds won't hurt either.

Dropping a few more sausages onto Sky's plate, splattering fat in every direction, her mother asked, "Do you want all of them? I can nuke another package for your dad, he won't notice the difference."

Sky had a much-needed laugh. "No thanks, I'm already having second thoughts about the extras."

"Don't," her mom told her, giving her a kiss on the forehead, and a smile before heading back into the kitchen to plate up the remaining breakfast for herself and her husband as she licked her lips of the sausage grease she'd picked up from her daughter's face.

After breakfast, Sky wheeled herself to her bedroom to change for school. She was about to open the door when a loud *CRASH!* came from inside like someone dropped a pile of dishes.

Is there someone in my room? The only people here are Mom and Dad and me... Sky's thoughts trailed off.

An unwanted thought entered her mind.

There's a thief in my room.

Suddenly the image of a man with a dark ski mask covering his face and rummaging through her dresser drawers for valuables ran through her mind. Then, without warning, the intruder took the mask off and grinned an evil smile. So evil, his eyes full of fiery hate, the twisted smile making the hatred emanating from his face almost unbearable to witness. But she recognized the face, twisted smile and all, as one of the many students at Ravenwood High School who would stare at her, mock her, taunt her, and laugh at her as she struggled her way through the halls.

Shaking her head as she blinked, the image faded away. "Wait, why would a burglar try to steal my crap? We're poor as shit right now!" Wishing she could kick in the door, she succumbed to using all her upper body strength to mimic it with her arms. Peering in, the room looked empty at first glance. Nobody was there.

"Merrrooooooow!"

A cat leapt from the other side of her bed and jumped onto her lap, claws digging into her immobile legs as it landed.

"Oh!" Sky gasped as the creature continued to make itself comfortable. "Hi, Mr. Fluffy!" she said as she pet the animal's long, soft, white fur that reminded her of angora sweaters and those damned gloves from her grandmother.

It took a few moments for her heart to stop pounding as if it would burst from her chest, and once it did, she noticed what had crashed onto the floor. There, next to her oak dresser was a ballerina, broken in two and surrounded by dozens of tiny pieces of ceramic. A desperate sounding tune escaped from the shattered figure's music box. It was faint and only lasted four notes, thus ending its last hymn. It was her favorite porcelain figure.

"Now you're crippled, just like I am." Sky's head slumped down.

Mrs. Hawkins walked down the hall to Sky's room. "I heard a crash and… oh!" She saw the damaged ballerina beside her daughter's dresser. "I'll go get something to clean it up," she said calmly, turning around, starting to leave the room.

"No, Mom. I'll get it," Sky told her, head still flaccid and looking at the cat in her lap who knocked it over and yet obviously had no remorseful feelings about it. She wished she had the same guiltlessness as felines.

"That's okay, I'll…"

"I said that I will pick it up!" Sky said sharply, giving her mother a piercing glare almost as shrill as her words.

With that, Mrs. Hawkins left Sky alone, mumbling something nondescript, but Sky swore she heard something about extra sausages. She knew that particular figure was her daughter's favorite, a gift from her own dad. The last thing he gave her before he passed away.

Surveying the sea of pink shards scattered across the hard wood floor, Sky couldn't help but think that if they hadn't taken the carpet out when they moved in, this tragedy wouldn't have happened. Alas, the carpet was removed to make it easier for her to get around in a wheelchair. Her old bedroom was huge by comparison to this tiny and poor excuse for one. Well, a bed and dresser was about all that could fit into the space. Back in Chancellor, the town just south of Ravenwood, there were no houses, only estates, and theirs was amazing. Their current house was the size of the guest house or the stable where her horses were kept… her horses she'd never again be able to ride and had to sell, just like the house because the accident that nearly killed her ate up every last bit of savings the family had, timed perfectly right after her father lost his job.

The face of the figurine looked Sky in the eyes. It looked lonely and sad. Her eyes were deep and her expression was of sorrow. She looked like she was going to cry, as if she had failed. The last dance of the ballerina had sent her to her death. Wheeling closer, Sky bent down and slowly picked up the pieces off the floor as well as the bottle of anti-depressants that had gone along for the fall as a solitary tear slid down her cheek.

Before Sky realized it, a depressing week had gone by. She still hadn't made any friends, and she still was looked down upon as if she was an abhorrent creature by some poor excuses of the human race. As if they had room to judge, with their obvious lack of fashion sense and basic hygiene! Even some of the teachers treated her the same as most of her fellow classmates she came into contact with. As educators, how could they? However, with Sky's overly dramatic imagination, it could just be that they were too busy doing their job to accommodate her emotional distress she kept hidden to herself and expected everyone to pick up on. Well, except for one particular teacher, Mrs. O'Hurley.

The week before, Sky was struggling up the breezeway, an open-air hallway from one building to the next and perfect for the Northwest where it is not uncommon to have horizontal rain. Because of the terrain the school was built on, the angle was slanted in such a way that maneuvering a wheelchair up it took superhuman strength, something Sky lacked. Students laughed as they passed her by, not even bothering to conceal their thoughts as they casually mocked her amongst one another; mimicking her hand motions with exaggeration; making rude gestures; being just plain mean. All she wanted to do was magically transport to her second period class. Oh, how she wished certain aspects of *Star Trek* were real right here and right now!

"Speed up! You're holding up the line back here!"

"Can't you go any faster?!"

"Why don't you wait until the hall is empty before going up it?

"Move it, retard!"

She couldn't bear to hear them talk about her the way they were. Why couldn't they just leave here alone? Why did they have to be so cruel? So uncaring? So unthoughtful?

Feeling the rage build up inside her, the scalding blood turning her cheeks and ears red, she closed her eyes and just concentrated on regulating her breath. It was all too much for her to handle, so she stopped. Right in the middle of the hallway, she stopped. Everyone passed her on the sides, looking back at her with hateful eyes. Hot tears sped down her cheeks uncontrollably. They just came. And she shivered. It wasn't cold outside even though it was January, but her body shivered as if it were, probably from the anger and frustration that had just about reached the boiling point in her body.

"C'mon, I'll give you a push. Where are you heading to?" a soft voice from behind her asked.

Sky opened her eyes, the air stinging them from all the tears she'd just cried as she turned her head to see who had spoken. A small, slightly round woman stood behind her, holding the handles of her wheelchair. Thick, blue-framed glasses encircled her emerald eyes, covered slightly by her loosely curled chestnut hair. Her bright floral dress matched the flowery perfume she was wearing.

"Thank you!" Sky said gratefully, covering her mouth before wiping the tears from her red, swollen eyes and cheeks. "I'm trying to get to room one-oh-five."

As the teacher pushed her up the hall, she introduced herself. "My name is Mrs. O'Hurley."

Craning her neck to look Mrs. O'Hurley in the eyes, she said back, "I'm Sky. Sky Hawkins."

They had just entered the 100 Wing when Mrs. O'Hurley said, "That's a beautiful name. It fits you perfectly. Some names don't match people at all, and some names are obvious just by the way the person looks and acts. Isn't that weird?"

"Uh, yeah?" Sky question-answered, as she was unsure of where the conversation was going, but the more she thought about it, the more she understood what Mrs. O'Hurley was talking about.

"Hawkins… why does that sound familiar? Oh! Sadie Hawkins! Like the dance!" Mrs. O'Hurley blurted out rather loudly, her voice echoing off the walls.

"Yeah, like the dance. And the comic strip. And my mom," Sky said, embarrassed.

"Your mom?" Mrs. O'Hurley asked as they approached room 105.

"Her name is Sadie, so you can imagine how much my dad's parents love to tease her about that one."

"Well, I think it's great!" Mrs. O'Hurley's face showed no signs of feigned enthusiasm. She was genuine.

"She likes to throw that out at cocktail parties for conversation starters, telling everyone they throw dances in high schools across the country in honor of her."

"I would, too, if that was my name! Sky, you have a fantastic day!" Mrs. O'Hurley said with such force as she opened the door, it silenced the classroom Sky was entering.

"Thank you," Sky said back quietly with a small smile imposing its way onto her usually stoic face.

But that was last week, and Sky had only seen Mrs. O'Hurley once since then. However, she didn't even glance at her, just walked right past her without a smile or anything, almost as if she was purposefully trying to ignore her.

The lunch bell rang, which meant that third period Algebra was finally over. Students pushed and shoved their way out the door and through the halls to get to the cafeteria. Taking a cue from the previous week's Breezeway Incident, Sky waited for everyone to leave so she wouldn't get yelled at for slowing them down. With her head staring at her useless legs, she wheeled herself out of the room to follow the herd. She had decided it was easier to simply eat her lunch outside her fourth period class so she wouldn't have to fight the crowd after lunch was over. It was the usual suspects: peanut butter and strawberry preserves with a low-fat blackberry yogurt.

When school let out for the day, Sky wandered through the main hall when out of the corner of her eye, a bright yellow poster caught her attention, drawing her in to find out what it was all about. She stared at it intently, but it was too far away for her to make out what it said—making her fear she also needed glasses and adding to the freak show that was already on display—so she rolled over to where it hung on the brick wall.

"A talent show? Ugh!" Sky said loudly with disgust, rolling her eyes.

But then her mind started going at hyper-speed. *What is it like? Is it fun? Exciting? What kinds of things do people do in a talent show? Chancellor didn't have a talent show. Why didn't Chancellor have a talent show? Probably because everyone is plain boring vanilla pudding there. No talent except sports. Sports. Football jerseys. Basketball shorts. Baseball butts.*

"Hmmm… a talent show," she repeated, then went out the double doors that led to the parking lot in front of the school and waited for her mom to pick her up, being sure to stay out of the way of students walking to their busses or cars or home.

Later that night as she was at the dining room table doing her English homework, Sky looked up as her mom entered the kitchen to pour herself yet another cup of coffee and said, "Guess what?"

"Monkeys," her mother responded, taking a sip from the mug her hands were enveloping.

Giving her mother a rather disapproving look before rolling her eyes, Sky told her, "It's not monkeys. It will never be monkeys."

"It could be. You don't know. One day we may just go to the zoo and you'll say 'guess what' and I'll say 'monkeys' and lo and behold, there they will be, in all their monkey glory," Mrs. Hawkins said matter-of-factly, before taking another swig of coffee.

"Fine, Mother. Perhaps just that once I may amuse you, but I was going to say that the school is having a talent show."

"That's nice. Do you know someone who is going to be in it?" The mug was strategically placed, never more than an inch or two from her awaiting mouth.

"Well, no…" Sky shifted her eyes slowly to look away and avoid seeing her mother's response in case it was unforgiveable. "I was thinking of doing something for it."

Sky suddenly felt nervous. *What the hell are you thinking?*

"You?" her mother said, nearly choking on the coffee she had just chugged, her face twisting. "That sounds like a good idea.

It might be, uh, fun? Maybe it will give you a little confidence in yourself!"

"Confidence? Thanks, Mom!" Sky shouted, throwing her pencil into the air. It landed just on the other side of the dining room table and bounced under a chair where her cat picked it up and snuck off with it.

"In my defense, I said a little," her mother told her. "Besides, do you even have a talent?"

Dropping her head below her shoulders, Sky said, "Thanks for the deflating pep talk. I'm just going to go to my room and take another pill."

"I'm being serious. What would you do?" her mother asked, setting the coffee cup onto the table and taking a seat next to her to avoid any mishaps.

"That is a very good question," Sky said shaking her head in agreement as she fumbled through her book bag for another pencil since the one she was using mysteriously went missing.

⁂

"Move it, Sky! You're blocking the hallway!" a fat kid with an unfortunately exorbitant amount of acne and body odor that made him seem like a cranberry Stilton left out for too long bellowed from behind her wheelchair.

She obediently parked herself as close to the wall as she could, scraping her elbows against the exposed brick. Her head seemed to be perpetually stuck in slump-mode when she was at school. Nobody cared. Nobody cared about her feelings, her thoughts, or her frustrations. Nobody wanted her there, at *their* school and in *their* classes and in *their* halls. They all wished she would leave. Just disappear and never return, like the smell that suddenly made her hungry for cheese.

Even with a slumped view, she could not escape seeing the fat kid with a bad case of acne and body odor also wore two obviously different over-the-calf socks; yellow and green on the left, red and blue on the right. The only parts that matched were the dingy "white" portion that disappeared at his ankles into shoes that had been glued and duct taped one too many times.

"Hi, Sky. Need a push to class?" a voice asked from behind, startling her.

It sounded so soft, caring and understanding; all that cliché nonsense she'd been dreaming of since her first day at Ravenwood High. She turned her head over the backrest of her wheelchair and saw a familiar face, but why it was so familiar was escaping her brain.

"We have Advanced Algebra together, remember? I'm Sheree. Sheree Hollins," the familiar face said, with her golden hair flowing just past her shoulders, tinted with a hint of orange and wavy. She smelled like strawberries. Her aquamarine eyes looked straight into Sky's as she introduced herself, wearing a black and purple Ravenwood High sweatshirt over a hot pink T-shirt that was barely visible except for the collar.

Even in something as frumpy as a sweatshirt, she looks like one of those models you see in the magazines. Ugh. I hate her and love her all at once. "Um…" Sky was speechless. So far, Sheree was the only student who had ever offered her any help whatsoever. And now she was offering to push her to class instead of just out of the way.

"I'll take that as a yes!" Sheree said with a smile over her perfect face, and with a swift motion they were on their way to Algebra together. "So, Sky, how do you like Ravenwood so far?"

"Honestly, I don't," Sky told her coldly. "It's kinda weird, you know? Of course, being in a new school after going through a lot doesn't help my circumstances any."

"I know how you feel. Everyone staring at you. All those scary new faces. This school still frightens me sometimes," Sheree told her.

"How long have you been going here?" Sky asked curiously, hoping Sheree wouldn't mind her imposing.

"Since the beginning of the school year. My family moved here from Seattle. They say kids have a culture shock moving from a rural town to the big city, but seriously, I think it's just as bad with the roles reversed!" she said, laughing as if it were the funniest thing she'd ever heard herself say.

"Oh… you're only a freshman?"

"Yep."

"You just seem, well, please don't take this the wrong way, but you seem older."

"I am. I'm sixteen."

"Can you drive?"

"Yep. Got my own wheels and everything."

"The only wheels I'll probably ever have you're pushing!"

Sheree let out another boisterous laugh that seemed to bounce off everyone they were passing in the hallway, smacking them in the face as they stared back at the sight of the popular new girl pushing the wheelchair of the unpopular new girl. "Sorry, I don't know why I found that so amusing. I'm just glad you've got a sense of humor about your situation."

"Trust me, this is new," Sky said as they entered the class together while the bell rang. She could feel the heat of thirty sets of eyes glaring at her.

"We'll talk more at lunch, okay?" Sheree told her quietly and not waiting for a response before taking her seat.

Wow, Sky thought with amazement. *It's been so long since I've talked to someone like a friend, I almost forgot how!*

Before she knew it, it was lunchtime. Hopefully whatever they went over in class wasn't important because she couldn't recall anything. And now she was panicky and fidgety.

Sheree picked her books up from the desk and rushed over to Sky. "You want to go to the cafeteria?"

"No, not really," Sky told her.

She felt scared. She didn't know how to react. This sudden change where someone actually talked *with* her instead of just *at* her made her a bit uneasy.

"Are you sure? I could introduce you to some of my friends?" Sheree asked.

"I don't know." Sky could feel her clothes start to stick to her skin as nervous sweat spilled out of her pores.

"You don't have to. I mean, I don't want to be the one responsible for you giving into peer pressure or anything! We can do lunch another time if you want, okay?"

"I've got to do my Spanish homework. There was an assignment I had last night, but I forgot my book. I was sort of planning on doing it during lunch," Sky confessed, even though it was a lie.

"Oh my gawd, isn't Mr. Santos a frickin' hotty?" Sheree squealed, and then suddenly realized they were still in a classroom with a teacher. "Let's move this outside."

With that, they left the classroom and entered the nearly empty hall. "I don't know. He's not my type," Sky told her.

"What?! Oh, are you a lesbian?" Sheree asked as if that would be the next logical step for someone not thinking the Spanish teacher was attractive.

"No, I'm not a lesbian!" Sky shouted, which managed to garner a response from the end of the hall of someone announcing that she wasn't either and another from the opposite side that she was indeed a lesbian.

"Cool!" Sheree yelled back. "Now that we've got that out of the way, I'm gonna go catch some lunch before they run out of whatever food-like surprise they're serving up today. Talk to you later!"

With a swift motion, Sheree was running down the breezeway towards the cafeteria.

Why did I do that? Why didn't I go to the cafeteria with her? Why, Sky? Why?! she scolded herself, almost wanting to take her book and hit herself over the head over and over and call herself an idiot each time.

After wheeling to her usual spot in front of her fourth period class, she ate her lunch with guilt for not going to the cafeteria with Sheree and guilt for lying about it. Guilt guilt guilt. Why couldn't she be more like her asshole of a cat? Relenting to her own fear and stupid conscience both insisting she wasn't good enough to be a real girl, she chewed on a bite of her peanut butter and jelly sandwich. Halfway through it, she realized she forgot to pack a spoon for her yogurt.

"Are you kidding me?!" she said louder than anticipating, but decided that since nobody was around to witness, she would attempt to test Einstein's Theory of General Relativity.

When school was out, Sky was headed towards the front doors when she heard, "Sky! Don't leave yet!"

It was Sheree, so she stopped and turned around, amazing herself at just how good she was getting at this whole wheelchair thing. As Sheree ran towards her, Sky thought, *She looks like a penguin when she runs. I wonder if anyone's ever told her that?* "Hi, Sheree! Sorry again about lunch. Stupid homework."

"That's okay, we can do lunch anytime," Sheree told her, quite out of breath from her quick jaunt. Being off any athletics was certainly beginning to take its toll.

"No it's not. I lied. I didn't have homework."

"I know. I just didn't want to push it."

"You knew and you didn't call me out on it? Bitch!" Sky said, shocked at the words coming out of her mouth.

Sheree's face lit up. "I knew there was something I liked about you! Want a lift home?"

This is amazing! I can't believe this is happening. "Really?" *Really? Was that all I could say? Really?*

"Yeah. C'mon, we can talk in the car," Sheree said, motioning for her to follow.

"Thanks! I've gotta call my mom first to let her know I've gotta ride, okay?" Sky asked, stopping just outside the school office.

"Okay. I'll be right here," Sheree told her.

This is so weird. Why all of a sudden does she want to be my friend? I hope it's not because she feels sorry for me? I don't want that to be the reason. But how am I supposed to find out? Ask? 'Excuse me, Sheree, but are you only being nice to me because I'm paralyzed from the ass down?'

Sky asked one of the ladies in the office if she could use the phone to call her mom, and she told her to use the one next to her and dial 9 first. After punching in the numbers, she waited for her mother to pick up on the other end, praying she hadn't already left the house to pick her up from school.

"Oh! Uh… Hello?" a peppy voice asked in a somewhat out-of-breath way.

"Hi, Mom," Sky responded, her face suddenly green.

"I was just on my way to pick you up! Sorry, I didn't realize I was running that late!" She sounded frazzled.

"That's okay. I've got a ride," Sky told her excitedly.

"Oh, well then we'll see you soon!" her mother said.

"Okay, bye Mom."

"Bye!"

Sky thanked the nice office lady before rolling back into the hall where Sheree was pretending not to listen in on the conversation. The sun gleaming through the double doors behind Sheree created an aura around her made Sky think she looked like an angel.

"Ready?" Sheree asked, beaming a smile full of sunshine.

"Yes, but we may want to give my parents a few more minutes to, um, make themselves presentable?" Sky told her new friend with a look of utter disgust.

"Oh, you caught them in the middle of having sex, didn't you?" Sheree asked sympathetically.

"I'm like ninety-nine percent positive," Sky said, trying not to vomit.

"At least they're coy about it. My parents would have been like, 'We're having sex, can you call back in, like, ten minutes?' or some shit like that," Sheree said matter-of-factly.

Sky burst into laughter, which caused Sheree to do the same.

"Damn, we have time to kill. I guess that means we have to get ice cream," Sheree said with monotony, staring at her wrist and nonexistent watch.

"Damn! I would kill for some Death by Chocolate right now!" Sky announced, her eyes lighting up like fireworks on the Fourth of July.

"Girl, it's like we're long lost sisters!"

They strolled out into the afternoon towards Sheree's car. It was windy, and it felt good against Sky's face, also making her chocolate hair seem to fly from her head in an organized chaos. Unlocking the passenger side to her little blue sedan, Sheree helped Sky into the front seat before folding up her wheelchair and putting it into the back. After Sheree got into the driver's seat, she started the car and headed to the grocery store to procure their required sustenance.

"So, where do you live?" Sheree inquired nonchalantly, casually glancing at Sky as she asked, trying not to stare too much at the pimple starting to form on her chin but failing to take her eyes off of it.

"Baker Street. Do you know where that's at?"

"Yeah, my best friend lives there. What's your address?"

Sky told her

Sheree said, "Shut up! You live only a couple houses down. Do you know Jennifer Hoang?"

"Uh, no?"

"She's Asian."

"Oh, yes. Her mom's crazy."

"Probably. Tried to buy the hair off my head for twenty bucks last month."

"Really? Mom says I should stay away from her. Pretty sure that makes us racist."

"Probably," Sheree told her, but smiled and winked.

They started laughing.

"Sorry I lied about having Spanish homework. I was just being chickenshit because someone was actually talking to me." Sky stared straight ahead at the road as they approached their first destination, too afraid to look at Sheree.

"No problem," Sheree said as she parked her car into a space at the grocery store. "Now let's go get that ice cream!"

After picking up the ice cream, along with accompaniments, they headed to Sky's house to, in theory, work on homework. Of course, they were about to get chocolate wasted, so the chances of said homework actually getting done was somewhere between slim and none.

"Hi, Mom and Dad!" Sky said loudly, announcing her arrival as she burst through the front door in case they were still busy doing it.

Mrs. Hawkins walked into the hallway to greet her daughter, her hair slightly disheveled but showing signs that she had tried to remedy the situation, though unsuccessfully. "Oh, is this your ride?"

"Yeah, this is Sheree Hollins," Sky said as she pushed herself into the kitchen, Sheree following close behind with a grocery bag filled with goodies they were about to partake in.

"Well, hello, Sheree. It's a pleasure to meet you," her mother said, eyeing the container of chocolate ice cream, chocolate syrup, brownies, and a can of whipped cream as Sheree placed them onto the counter in that order.

"Nice to meet you, too!" Sheree said in her usual bubbly voice. "What's your name?"

"Sadie," Sky's mom told her.

"Sadie? That makes you Sadie Hawkins, like the dance!"

"Yes. Yes it does," Sky's mom said proudly, letting a slight grin form on her scant lips that needed cleaned and refinished and had a slight sheen in places that Sky prayed was just saliva.

"Sky, are you home?" a man's voice asked.

"Yes, Dad. I'm in the kitchen," Sky answered.

Sky's dad was a tall man with short salt and pepper hair, and a bit overweight in his midsection who was tucking his shirt into his pants as he walked into the kitchen. "Oh! Sorry, I didn't realize we had company!" he said, embarrassed that he had his hand down the front of his pants as he entered.

"I'm Sky's friend, Sheree," she said, extending her hand and having second thoughts afterward because of where his hand had just been, but not wanting to be rude and take it back, so she left it out there.

"Hi, Sheree. I'm Jack," he said, shaking her hand with the one he'd just had on his crotch.

"Nice to meet you, Jack. Now, if you don't mind, Sky and I have some ice cream that is melting and needs to be eaten rather quickly, so if you could please point me into the direction of bowls, spoons, and a scoop, that'd be great."

Both Sadie and Jack pointed in different directions, so Sheree checked both and found bowls in one direction and spoons and the ice cream scoop in another. She simply flashed a smile at them both in response, and proceeded to build the most extravagant chocolate ice cream creation imaginable. Brownies drowned in ice cream piled so high, Sky wondered if that gravitational theory she'd tested earlier on her yogurt was in retrograde. Sky's parents simply stared in awe.

"I don't suppose you want me to make you both one as well, do you?" Sheree asked.

"Well, since you offered!" Sadie said, grabbing the two that were already made and giving one to her husband, exiting the kitchen as they both exclaimed, "Thanks!"

Sky held her head in her hands as she said, "I apologize for my parents. I'm pretty sure they both grew up in caves. With wolves."

"Don't worry about it," Sheree assured her. "I went a little skimpy on those two anyway!"

"That was skimpy?! Good Lord!" Sky shouted.

And sure enough, Sheree really outdid herself on the ones she prepared for herself and Sky, using up the brownies, remaining ice cream in the half-gallon container, and covering it with so much whipped cream and chocolate sauce they would surely be in a coma for a week after consuming so much chocolaty goodness. However, neither of them spent much time devouring their bowls before heading into the living room to study.

"That has to be the best thing I've ever put in my mouth!" Sky told Sheree. "But I think I'm going to throw up now!"

Sheree's eyes bulged out in horror. "No! You can't waste chocolate! It is the most unholy of sins!"

They laughed heartily, but quickly stopped for fear that they might actually vomit from the belly shaking and commit the sin. Sky even let out a burp she tried to gracefully hide by keeping her mouth closed, but her body had other plans and she involuntarily opened her mouth to release a gaseous belch loud enough for the neighbors to hear.

"Excuse me!" Sky said apologetically, covering her mouth.

"Don't be, I'm about to do the same!" Sheree assured her, letting out a burp that put Sky's to shame.

Sheree took a seat on the sofa, and then realized her book bag was still in the car. "Damn it. How are we supposed to study if I didn't bring in my books?"

"Damn it. That is so sad," Sky said back. "I think I left mine in your car as well."

With a defeated look, Sheree said, "We can study in a few minutes. Did you hear about the talent show coming up?"

Sky shifted in her seat. "Yeah, I heard."

"Doesn't that sound like the lamest thing ever?" Sheree asked, scrunching up her nose.

Sky shifted in her seat again. "Yeah, I was thinking about entering it."

Sheree's mouth dropped. "I meant lame for other people. What were you thinking of doing? I remember at my middle school back in Seattle we had one and this one guy did a stand-up comedy routine that was full of crude sex jokes and had to be hauled off the stage, some girl did a really offensive dance, and another sang *The Rose* by Bette Midler with disastrous results."

"Crap! Those were my top three choices!" Sky said, throwing up her hands.

"Well, that sucks," Sheree said rather unapologetically.

Sky shifted in her seat yet again. "Actually, I was thinking about singing *The Rose*."

"Shit, seriously?" Sheree asked, a little freaked out by the coincidence.

"Yeah, it was mine and my boyfriend Chad's song," Sky told her.

"Was? Did you guy's break up?" Sheree asked, her sarcasm completely gone.

Trying to choke back tears, Sky said, "No, he died."

But it was no use. The tears started pouring anyway, no matter how hard Sky tried to fight them. Sheree searched the room for a box of Kleenex and, after spotting one, handed it to Sky. Half its contents were removed in one fell swoop towards her face.

"It was a car accident a few months ago that left me in a wheelchair and him in the grave," Sky managed to get out, furiously trying to keep her face dry with the tissues in her hand but failing miserably.

Goosebumps started crawling all over Sheree's skin, pricking up like a crowd doing the wave at a baseball game. Could it be? Could Sky have been the girl in the other car? Was it possible she's the one who survived the accident that killed Sheree's boyfriend too?

"That was on the main road, wasn't it?"

"Yes, it was," Sky confirmed.

Sheree couldn't hold back the tears any longer. "My boyfriend was in the other car!" she informed Sky.

Covering her mouth, Sky's eyes were sorrow-filled as she said, "I'm so sorry! It's my fault! That accident was my fault!"

The news came as a shock. All this time Sheree had assumed it was the ghost of her dead sister that caused the accident. She'd even told her so. And now to find out it was someone else, someone she'd befriended no less.

"I had been drinking at a friend's house in Portland who was having a party, and on the way home I started to get sick. I threw up all over Chad while he was driving, and as he was wiping his eyes from the vomit and pineapple chunks that had landed on his face, a bright bluish-green light flashed and the next thing I knew I was in the ditch, my legs crushed under the car, and his open eyes just stared at me in horror, his dead body suspended by the seat belt. It's all so vivid still, like it just happened!" Sky said, shaking uncontrollably.

The blue-green light was a dead giveaway to Sheree. It was Kayla, her sister who only last month was finally allowed to enter the next world in peace after being in limbo for years. Her sister, whose anger and hate were all she had to hold onto when she died, and took two innocent lives with her before crossing over.

"It wasn't your fault, Sky," Sheree assured her, putting a hand on her knee.

But Sky couldn't take it, and pushed her hand away and screamed, "It is! I killed him! I killed both of them!"

At this point, Sky's parents had entered the room, wondering what was going on. Sheree tried to explain the situation, but their worried faces were not going to be consoled by what she was saying. It took Sky, after settling down from the hysterics she succumbed to, telling her parents she was okay; that she felt so much better getting all those pent up emotions out in the open, even if they were painful. They didn't look convinced.

"Mom, Dad, I'm okay. Promise," Sky assured them, forcing a smile onto her blotchy face.

"Are you sure?" Mrs. Hawkins asked. "Sheree, honey, perhaps you should go."

"No! Sheree, stay, please. I really need someone to talk to about this." Sky's voice was sincere, her eyes desperate.

"It's okay, Mr. and Mrs. Hawkins," Sheree told Sky's parents. "We've got a lot to talk about."

And talk they did.

Sky had never poured her heart out to anyone like she was doing now, not even to the therapist she'd been seeing for the past couple months. She couldn't understand how it was so easy to talk to this person who only this morning didn't even know existed, but with every word she spoke she could feel the burden she'd been carrying for far too long being lifted. Sheree told Sky about the tremendous sense of loss she felt after Jeff died, talking about stuff she never even told her best friend, Jennifer. She was tempted to let her in on the events of last year, but decided against it. Besides, they were so unbelievable, so incomprehensible, that there would have been no way for Sky to fully understand anyway. No way to understand unless she was there to experience it herself, that is.

"I can't ever thank you enough for just listening," Sky told Sheree as they hugged.

"The same for you," Sheree said, not ready to let go from their embrace, but she could tell Sky was uncomfortable from her stance, so she slowly released her arms as Sky did the same. "So, we were talking about you doing something for the talent show before we got all hormonal. You really want to sing?"

Laughing as she raked her hair behind her ear, Sky responded, "Yes, I think I do."

"Well, can you sing?" Sheree asked, bracing herself for an answer that might very well be one of insult.

"Yes, I can sing. I was in choir at Chancellor High my freshman year and sophomore year until, well, this happened," she said, gesturing her hands towards the wheelchair she was sitting in, letting them rest on the immobile extremities that required it.

"Wait, what? You're a sophomore?" Sheree asked, surprised.

"Yep. I even celebrated my sixteenth birthday last week, and by celebrate I mean we had soggy pizza delivered and watched *Sixteen Candles*. And yes, I know how pathetic it sounds," Sky said, anticipating Sheree's response.

"Happy birthday last week!" Sheree exclaimed, throwing her hands up in the air waving them to show her excitement.

"Thanks," Sky said, flushing with embarrassment, though she did not know why.

Then Sheree asked her what she'd almost been dreading since she brought it up. "When are you going to sing for me?"

"Crap. Do I have to?" Sky asked, looking rather deflated like a five-day-old helium balloon from the dollar store.

"Uh, yeah! You can't just tell someone you plan on singing for the school talent show and then, oh, I don't know, not sing!" Sheree said rather loudly, enough so that Sky's parents overheard from the bedroom with the door closed and the TV on.

"Fine, but it's been a while so be gentle," Sky told her before starting.

The next words that came out of Sky's mouth were so unbelievably amazing that Sheree just sat on the sofa stunned, listening to every nuance and all the emotion behind the lyrics coming through almost effortlessly. Her parents had walked into the living room when they heard her start singing for the first time in months. They had almost forgotten just how powerful and soul-touchingly beautiful her voice was.

As Sky sang, she watched the reactions of her audience of three, and knew that things were about to change. She was not going to allow others to trample on her anymore. Sky was back, and she was going to make the most of what life had thrown at her.

Chapter 1
Be Aggressive

"Be aggressive! Be, be aggressive!" could be heard throughout the gymnasium at Ravenwood High School as the cheerleading squad shouted the chant in front of hundreds of spectators towards the basketball players, clapping their hands in rhythm. The black shells of the cheerleader uniforms were blazoned with RHS in purple outlined in white, and a stylized version of a crow, the rather unoriginal yet recent replacement mascot of Ravenwood High. Furthermore, the girls wore purple spankies with crows on their asses, which I suppose is better than the original face of Chief Ravenwood, the Native American leader for which the town was named, to which some girls would joke about an old man riding up their ass all day. The male cheerleaders didn't have to be bothered with such indignities, except for the fact that they were male cheerleaders. However, most of the male cheerleader mockery came from opposing teams, as Ravenwood's cheerleading squad was consistently in the top five during regional competitions, making them a source of school pride.

"That's my boyfriend!" Jennifer Hoang shouted excitedly from her seat in the front row of the bleachers to her friends Sheree Hollins and Sky Hawkins, pointing toward a cute blond guy with a perfectly white toothy grin and remarkably clear blue eyes that sparkled like the midday sun on the sea.

"I know, Jen! You've been going out for months!" Sheree shouted back as she pulled her strawberry blond hair behind her ears, and showing off her freshly manicured nails at the same time, making Jennifer twinge with jealousy. "Well, except for that week during winter break that you decided to break up with him."

Jennifer didn't seem to hear that last remark. Or it didn't bother her.

Sky, while only a few feet from the other two found it difficult to hear them so she had been leaning to one side of her wheelchair, shouted back, "He's hot, Jennifer! Can I have him when you're done?" She was only half joking.

Jennifer gave her a perplexed look. "You do know he's gay, right?"

"What?!" Sky screamed in something that could only be described as in the pitch of a banshee. "Then why are you dating him?"

"Because he's an amazing kisser!" Jennifer said, positively glowing as she continued to stare at her boyfriend and imagining the make-out session they'd be having after the game.

Sheree leaned over towards Sky and said, "Don't try to think about it too long, you'll give yourself an aneurism."

Sky simply flashed a confirmatory grin in acknowledgment. Making herself as comfortable as she could, she continued to watch the game, which, quite honestly, was more fun than she was expecting it to be. Of course, she knew a big part of that was her new friends, her only friends so far at Ravenwood High, who were so easy to get along with and didn't make her feel like a freak for having wheels instead of working legs.

The score was already twenty-one to sixteen at only four minutes into the first quarter, with Chancellor in the lead. Chancellor; the school Sky had to transfer from after the accident that took away her ability to walk and her boyfriend's life, who would be on the opposing team had he not been killed; the school she spent her freshman year and one short month into her sophomore before ending up in a hospital; the school she thought she would graduate from. But all that is part of her past, and now she's a Crow. She recognized all of the Chancellor players and knew many of the people in the bleachers supporting them, however she felt uncomfortable even attempting a hello, let alone a conversation, all thanks to her recent mobility issues.

"Hey, Sky! I think that guy is trying to get your attention," Sheree said, touching her shoulder.

The words broke her out of the trance she had found herself in while reminiscing about her past and contemplating the challenges of her future. Looking in the direction Sheree was pointing, she saw Tom, her late boyfriend's best friend waving at her, and gave him a half-hearted smile and matching wave back.

Don't start crying, damn it! Don't do it!

Noticing Sky's eyes start to water, Sheree suggested, "Let's go get something to eat at the snack bar!"

Sky nodded her approval before asking, "Want us to bring you back anything, Jennifer?"

As if she was thinking long and hard, with overly exaggerated expressions on her slightly round yet petite Vietnamese face, Jennifer responded with, "Yeah, I want a hot dog real bad!"

"I wonder why?" Sheree said playfully, pointing toward the male cheerleader eye candy only a few yards away, making Sky chuckle.

Jennifer's face was full of resentment. "Not everything I say has sexual innuendo, you know? Granted, a disproportionate amount is, but not everything!"

As Sky wheeled out of the gym with Sheree by her side, she said, "Thanks. I don't know why, but seeing Tom again just brought out the emotional basket case in me."

Assuming Tom was the guy waving at Sky, Sheree responded, "After my boyfriend Jeff died, I was a zombie for weeks. Of course, it didn't help that I'd stare at the graveyard he's buried at every day from my bedroom window."

"Oh, that's healthy!" Sky said with a bizarre laugh, making Sheree cringe slightly as it reminded her of another person's laugh who had caused her so much grief and pain and agony... her twin sister, Kayla.

Kayla, who was taken so young, yet allowed to wander aimlessly as a ghost, haunting her in such nightmarish ways. What would she have done if the roles were reversed, if she had been killed instead? Would she haunt? Would she torment? Would she kill?

"I know we need a hot dog," Sky said, causing Sheree to come back to reality. "I think I will have nachos with extra jalapeños. What do you want?"

"Um, uh…" Sheree fumbled around for words, but seemed to be having difficulty getting anything out until from somewhere deep inside her, buried and clawing its way out, she said, "Your soul!" with a gravelly voice she knew was not hers.

"Huh?" Sky didn't know if she heard right, but played along anyway. "I don't know if they serve souls here. How about some French fries instead?"

Embarrassed and shocked at what came out of her mouth, Sheree covered it with her hand, her face turning scarlet. "I'm sorry! I have no idea where that came from!"

The volunteer basketball mother behind the counter looked like she was getting annoyed, along with the few people in line behind them. "Is that it, or do you want anything else?" she snapped.

"Yeah, French fries and three Cokes, please!" Sheree said quickly.

Sky turned to Sheree and said quietly, "I drink diet."

"Urrgkuh!" Sheree gagged loud enough for everyone around them to hear. "Not tonight!"

After paying for the snacks, Sheree grabbed a Coke and the nachos and handed them to Sky before picking up the remaining two drinks, hot dog and fries to take back to the gymnasium. When they returned, the crowd was cheering raucously and it didn't take long to realize why after looking at the scoreboard. Ravenwood was ahead by twelve points. When they got to their seats, Sheree asked Jennifer as she handed her a drink and the hot dog she hadn't realized was naked, "What the hell did we miss?"

"The most amazing two minutes of play I've ever seen!" Jennifer said, squealing with delight. "Oh, thank Buddha you didn't put anything on my hot dog! I almost forgot to tell you plain." Jennifer sat back down, put her Coke next to her, reached into her purse and pulled out a full-size bottle of Sriracha. "I never leave home without it!" she said, grinning goofily at an imaginary camera before squirting the hot sauce onto her hot dog.

It was all too much for Sheree, who just could not let the metaphor continue to go unspoken. "Really? You're putting cock sauce on your hot dog?"

Nearly choking out a laugh with the hot dog firmly lodged into her mouth, Jennifer accidentally spit some of the chili sauce onto Sheree's shirt, cheek, and her left eye. Her own eyes were full of apology as she stared at the red stained one of her friend, and couldn't say anything with the giant bite of hot dog she'd just taken still rather unchewed and definitely not ready for swallowing.

"It burns!" Sheree screamed, dropping her fries into Sky's lap.

Sky quickly grabbed the drink cup from her hand before that also had a chance to spill on her, placed it on the bleacher, opened up a packet of mayonnaise Sheree had grabbed for the fries (Yes, mayonnaise. Don't judge.), and held it up to Sheree to place in her left eye to ease the burning, to which Jennifer told her to open a packet of ketchup instead, so Sky did as she said and handed the opened packet to Jennifer, who carefully squeezed its contents onto her friend's left eye.

Sheree could feel the fiery stares of a dozen kids around them and shouted, "Seriously, this is more interesting than the game?" as ketchup oozed off her eye, down her cheek, and onto her heather grey zip-up hooded sweatshirt splattered with red.

"Well, in their defense, you did just get shot in the eye with cock sauce at a high school basketball game. It's not like this sort of thing happens everyday," Jennifer pointed out before bursting into hysterical laughter, which caused Sheree and Sky to do the same.

Taking a napkin from one of the pockets in her hoodie, Sheree wiped off the remaining ketchup from her face and shirt before sitting down, grabbing the French fries which had landed so elegantly into Sky's lap that only one had escaped the confines of the food tray. Sky handed her the packets of mayo and ketchup, including the opened mayo, and Sheree squeezed every last bit from all of them on the fries before taking three at a time and shoveling them into her mouth.

As Sheree was busy stuffing her face, she felt a tingling sensation dancing across her tongue. At first she attributed it to possibly getting some of the Sriracha sauce in her mouth, but this wasn't hot, but more like less intensive Pop-Rocks. Brushing it off as just a figment of her imagination, she reached for another handful of fries, but before she could eat them Jennifer grabbed her hand. "What the hell, Jen?"

"Sheree, you need to drop the fries now," Jennifer said quietly, trying to keep calm but showing the fear in her eyes.

Looking at her hand, she saw why.

Spiders.

Lots of spiders.

Little. Black. Spiders.

She dropped the container onto the floor of the gymnasium and saw that they had not only invaded her French fry tray, but were surrounding her feet. Moving about like soldiers marching, Sheree could swear they looked like they were starting to form words. Behind the spiders, the cheerleading squad was forming a Wolf Wall during a timeout, but she and Jennifer couldn't take their eyes off the arachnids, no matter how impressive the stunt was. The audience was in an uproar, many of them getting to their feet to cheer on the cheerleaders, when the double doors leading outside burst open, letting in a ferocious whistling wind that seemed filled with what sounded like faint laughter.

Two loud *THUNKS!* echoed off the walls almost simultaneously. It took a few moments for everyone to realize just what had happened. But after a horrified scream shot out, all eyes were on the cheerleaders. Specifically two cheerleaders, who were on the floor in twisted, mangled, unnatural positions.

Blood.

Lots of blood.

Growing puddles of thick, red blood.

But all Sheree and Jennifer could focus on were the spiders, which were now making their escape through the open doors out into the frigid night. Sky on the other hand, couldn't take her eyes off the broken girls on the floor. Part of her was filled with a great sense of satisfaction, something that surprised her until she thought about it. Those two girls had been so merciless in their bullying, so mean spirited and hateful towards her that she felt no sadness for the awful accident they'd had. Instead, she was thankful for karma.

Suddenly, and with a violent force, Sheree vomited all over the floor, adding partially chewed fries to the mess in front of her. She felt another tickle in her throat, but instinctively swallowed before she could stop herself. She knew that it was one of the spiders, but at this point, her focus was on the two cheerleaders lying on the floor. They looked so awkward, so out of place, so broken, that she had to hold herself back from getting up to put them back together. Like Humpty Dumpty, they'd fallen off the wall. And like Humpty Dumpty, nobody was going to be able to put them back together again.

"They're dead!" Courtney, one of the girls on the squad yelled, collapsing onto the wood floor and causing the chatter all around them to silence.

Sheree turned to her left to find Jennifer hugging Chad, tears streaming down his cheek as he cried in disbelief, "How could this happen?"

Then she turned to her right to find Sky, staring at the dead girls surrounded by pools of blood and their saddened and shocked teammates and parents, with a smile on her face. An evil, pleased smile. It was almost enough to make her throw up again.

How could she be happy two people are dead?

Sky's eyes locked onto Sheree's as she said coldly, "Isn't it a tragedy?" She was still smiling. "They never got to finish the routine… and now they never will."

The room began to spin.

Noises began to slur together.

The lights got brighter and brighter and brighter until suddenly everything went black.

Silent darkness.

"Sheree, can you hear me?" she heard. The voice sounded so far away. Her head and right elbow were throbbing with pain. Slowly, she opened her eyes and was flooded with such harsh light she immediately closed them again, hoping that the nightmare that had happened in the gymnasium was just that, a nightmare.

You only wish it were a nightmare, but I guarantee that I am the only nightmare you should fear!

Her eyes shot open, filled with horror as she thought, *She's back!*

I know, another voice said in her head.

And with that, she knew that the psychic connection she had with Jennifer was back; the one that was only made possible by the presence of pure evil. After taking a mere month hiatus off, Kayla was back to haunt them, and she obviously had more power than ever.

Chapter 2
Revelations

Sitting in her usual spot at the dining room table, surrounded by the night's dinner of meatloaf, mashed potatoes, gravy, braised carrots, and a mixed greens salad covered in crumbled blue cheese and lightly dressed with olive oil and balsamic vinegar, Sheree was in awe. It was her favorite meal and it wasn't even her birthday.

"What is the special occasion?" she asked, but nobody responded. It was as if her family's lips were sealed. Literally.

Without hesitation, she began piling the meal onto her plate and eating. She was halfway through when she realized her father, mother, and brother were all still seated with empty plates in front of them, staring at her with unblinking eyes. Opening her mouth to speak, she couldn't get any words out. Then, without warning, a wave of nausea came over her so abruptly she felt as though she was going to explode. It was as if she had no control over her own body as it thrust back and forth and finally threw itself onto the table with her back flat on it, landing on her half-eaten plate and the remaining meatloaf now firmly planted in her golden hair. Staring at the gaudy brass chandelier, Sheree suddenly forgot about the pain and wondered when they were going to update the fixtures in the old house. But the thought was only a passing one as she felt her heart beating so fiercely and the queasiness returned with a vengeance, making her clench her teeth so hard she swore they were cracking and chipping from the pressure.

So much pain.

Make it stop.

Please.

A low growl came from her stomach. She looked at it, noticing movement through her shirt like a gopher burrowing close to the surface of the earth or one of those tiny moles her father hated with a fiery passion. She looked all around her and saw the upside down faces of her family, still staring at her. Couldn't they see she was obviously in need of their help?

Then, just when she thought the object in her gut was finally settling down, it burst through her chest. She let out a scream so loud and forceful the whole house shook. Standing on top of her was a large, black spider with razor sharp yellow teeth and very human eyes looking right into hers. And it had a knife dripping with blood. Reaching behind its back, it pulled out a top hat and started to sing and dance.

"Hello my baby
Hello my honey
Hello my living sister pal

Send me a kiss by wire
Baby my heart's on fire!
If you refuse me
Sister you lose me
And you'll be left alone
So will I rejoin you?
Will you reject me?
Or force me to put you
In a grave of your own!"

Sheree awoke suddenly, heart racing, sweat pouring down her face as her eyes adjusted to the early morning moonset beginning to pour through her window in mottled patterns as it tried to break through the usual clouds that clung to the city like flies on fly paper. She prayed the events from the night before were just a nightmare, a figment of her wild imagination she sometimes wished she didn't have. Of course, she could pray all she wanted to, but it happened. Two people were dead. Two more killed by the hands of a ghost, as preposterous as that was to comprehend.

A noise came from the doorway, the sound of floorboards being pressed on, and she knew instantly it was her little brother, Brendon; his silhouette framed with light coming in from behind him in the hallway.

"Kayla's back, isn't she?" he said so quietly it was barely a whisper, clutching his left arm as if it was suddenly in pain again from when he was pushed out of a tree last September.

"It's the only explanation. She has to be," Sheree told him, knowing he was hoping for any answer other than that.

For a few moments there was silence between them. Nothing to hear but a slight creak where Brendon stood as his feet rocked back and forth from ball to heel.

"I'm scared."

He looked so small. He sounded so fragile. He was, after all, just a kid, and shouldn't have to go through yet another horror story. Pulling over the covers on the right side of her bed, she told Brendon in a sympathetic voice, "Come on. We've still got a chance to get a couple hours of sleep."

Brendon hesitated about turning the light off in the hallway, deciding it would be best for his sense of security to leave it on, even if it was a false one. Without another word between them, he crawled into bed with his older sister, pulling the covers up as far as he could without suffocating under them. As if she knew what he would need, she scooped his head up under her arm and held him, nestling her head into his soft brown hair. She selfishly never wanted a brother when she was little, as it took away much of the attention she was used to receiving, but she couldn't imagine not having him in her life now. He somehow managed to find sleep again, but Sheree could not, spending the rest of the night alternating her gaze between her brother and the bay window in her bedroom that looked out onto the cemetery.

As dawn began to break, Sheree decided to head downstairs and start some coffee. She felt like a zombie as she fumbled with the measuring spoon for the coffee beans as she poured them into the grinder, managing to spill about half of them onto the counter with each scoop.

"Shit, Sheree! Get it together!" she said aloud, sweeping the beans into her hand and adding them to the grinder.

"No shit, Sheree! Those are expensive beans!" a man's voice said from behind her, causing her to jump and drop a few on the floor, scattering into the most hard to reach areas possible under the cabinets and refrigerator and somehow even under the dining room table where a lone shriveled up mushroom could still be found lurking in the shadows.

Turning around to find her young looking father in a red flannel robe and gray pajama bottoms, Sheree simply gave him a don't-mess-with-me look as she pushed the pulse button on the coffee grinder. "I've been awake since three, so I'm not in the mood for your sarcastic wit, Dad."

Deciding to put his sarcastic comeback away, he opted instead for "Yeah, I noticed the hall light on, and Brendon wasn't in his room. Is he sleeping in yours?"

Her dad looked genuinely concerned. However, Sheree knew she couldn't tell him the truth. She couldn't tell him that his dead daughter is haunting them and trying to take her place in the family. She couldn't tell him about all the awful things that Kayla had done, all the people she had killed, and that she wasn't through spreading her wrath upon the citizens of Ravenwood. "He had a bad dream."

Nodding that he understood, he responded, "I'm glad you two are close like that. Of course, it only seems to be when your mother and I aren't around!"

"Yeah, that's true," Sheree agreed as she filled the carafe full of tap water to add to the coffee maker's reservoir.

"I mean, Billy and I are close," he said, referring to his younger brother, "but Tami and I are practically like strangers, and she's my twin sister!"

"I always forget that you and Aunt Tami are twins. You are both so different from each other." Then, with a bit of curiosity and morbidity and the fact that her sister was unfortunately on her mind, she asked, "I wonder what it'd be like if Kayla was still alive?"

A chill ran down Mr. Hollins's spine as she asked the question, but as he wondered why, he realized it was simply the mentioning of Kayla's name. "Well, you two were extremely close, inseparable even. But I'm pretty sure that would have changed."

"Why?" Sheree wondered, casually glancing at the coffee maker to see where it was at in the brew cycle.

"For starters, you two had absolutely nothing in common except for your looks," he said, also casually glancing at the coffee maker to see where it was at in the brew cycle. "And secondly, why the hell is that thing taking so long?"

Looking at the kitchen clock and seeing that it was only five-thirty, Sheree concluded, "Maybe because it isn't used to being woken up this early?"

"That could be. It's only five-thirty? Damn, why the hell am I awake? Oh, that's right, I heard a noise, got up to investigate, saw the hall light on, and found you in the kitchen spilling ten dollar a pound coffee beans all over the place!" The sarcastic comeback he'd put away had finally been released. The satisfaction on his face was glorious.

"I told you I wasn't in the mood for, well, you know, you," Sheree told her father.

"Well, I wasn't in the mood to be awake, but now I am and we've got an hour before your mother will be up, so we're talking," Frank told his daughter.

The drip had fizzled, signaling the coffee was ready to be consumed. Sheree poured each of them a cup and sat down on the barstools pushed up against the counter on the side closest to the dining room table. After they had both taken a sip, she said, "Talk."

Giving his daughter a look of disappointment, Mr. Hollins said, "I was hoping this would be more of a dialogue and less of a monologue."

"What? We don't talk like regular people. Oh my gawd, it's bad news, isn't it? Are you and Mom getting a divorce? Really, a divorce at your age? Shit, it isn't cancer, is it? It is. It's cancer… and a divorce."

"Yes, Sheree, you figured it out. Your mom has cancer so we're getting a divorce," her father said with his typical sarcasm, showing no facial expressions whatsoever.

"I knew it," Sheree said, squinting her eyes slightly as she gave her dad a sideways glance while taking another sip of her coffee, wondering when she suddenly felt comfortable enough to start cussing in front of him.

"In all honesty, I was hoping we could talk about, you know, stuff."

"Thanks for clarifying that up, Dad."

"You know what I mean. We don't ever really just talk. Not like you and your mom do."

"Okay. Hopefully this won't turn weird."

"Thanks for your vote of confidence," her dad said, rolling his eyes. He took another sip of his black coffee and noticed that Sheree hadn't put any creamer or sugar into hers. "When I was your age, I couldn't drink it black. I had to add so much sugar and cream to it that it barely resembled its former self."

"Well, in your defense, I'm sure grandma and grandpa bought whatever cheap store brand generic ground coffee in a can they found on sale while grocery shopping at the Five and Dime, so I'm sure it was the only way to choke down that crap," Sheree offered, thankful her parents only bought premium coffee beans.

"True," her father said, raising his eyebrows, causing his forehead to wrinkle and make his face start to resemble his age rather than the much younger looking version of himself most people saw.

Feeling like he was stalling, like he was having second thoughts about this whole father-daughter conversation thing, Sheree asked, "So, what was it that you really wanted to talk about?"

"Kayla."

This time the chills were running down her spine. He actually said her name. She couldn't remember the last time he'd said it. "What about Kayla?"

"There are a lot of things about your sister you may not know," her father started to say, but felt a sudden choking sensation in his throat, as if it was tightening.

Noticing that he seemed to be struggling, she asked, "Are you all right?"

He gave her a reassuring smile as he forced out the word, "Yes." His eyes were obviously watering and about to form tears but he ignored them as he continued. "Your sister was… different."

Seeing that this was obviously difficult for her father to say out loud, she was hoping her psychic abilities she'd recently been gifted with would work on him, but it didn't appear to be so. Only Jennifer was able to exchange thoughts with her, while Brendon was tethered to her dreams. She was about to ask what made her different when her eyes caught something on the counter next to the refrigerator that shouldn't be there. "No! No no no no no! This can't be happening!" she said loudly, rushing over to the container of Death by Chocolate ice cream. Slowly, she opened the lid, revealing a thick chocolate puddle about two-thirds full. "Why, God? Why?!"

As Sheree mourned the death of her Death by Chocolate ice cream by means of room temperatureness, her father consoled her with one hand while refilling his coffee cup with the other. "There, there, honey. You had one perfect night together, but now it is time to part ways. Here, let's dump the contents into the sink and pour running water over it. It deserves a proper service after being shunned from the freezer all night long."

Sheree playfully punched her dad in the shoulder, tossed the container into the sink, and sat back down. When she felt composed again, she hardly had time to mourn the passing of her favorite ice cream with her father finally wanting to talk about the one person she needed to know more about. "How was Kayla different?"

Sitting down on the barstool next to his daughter, Mr. Hollins said, "I'm pretty certain… that… she was… a… witch." The words seemed to take a lifetime to escape his mouth.

Not surprised by this revelation, Sheree responded with, "Mom told me that a few months ago, but assured me that she was joking."

"She wasn't."

"She called me gullible."

"You are."

"So, she wasn't a witch?"

"No, she was."

Rolling her eyes in disbelief, not at her sister being a witch because she was already privy to the fact that even in death, she was quite a powerful witch indeed, but that her parents seemed to revel in confusing the hell out of her. "And why do you say that?"

"One day, I caught her talking to someone in her room. Assuming she was just talking to some imaginary friend, I asked who it was. I don't know, maybe I was expecting some random, silly name, but when she told me, 'I'm talking to Gramma Jessica,' I was taken aback," her father said, adjusting his posture in the seat to get more comfortable.

"Why? Who's Grandma Jessica?" Sheree asked, as the name was unfamiliar to her.

Clearing his throat, he told her, "Jessica was the name of your mom's great great grandmother who died in 1899."

"She could have just been making it up. I mean, Jessica is a pretty common name," she said, just before taking a huge gulp of coffee, saddened that it had gone cold so quickly.

"That was what I thought at first, but then Kayla started telling us all about her. Things that she couldn't have known because nobody ever talked about Grandma Jessica. Nobody. Not even your great grandma will speak her name, and she's the only living relative to have known her." He seemed so focused all of a sudden, like he was determined to tell her everything he could before something stopped him. That something, Sheree feared, was her mother.

"So Kayla could talk to ghosts?" Sheree asked, hoping that her being able to see and feel the presence of her own dead sister was somehow a family trait.

Her father seemed nervous, jittery even. Trying as best he could to steady his hands, he slowly took another drink of coffee. "The reason I know Kayla was a witch is because nearly all the women on your mom's side of the family are witches."

"Mom's a witch!" Sheree nearly shouted, her hand gesturing causing some of her cold coffee to splatter onto the counter.

"No, your mother is not a witch. She was the first girl born in generations without being gifted. And so she assumed that when you and Kayla were born, neither of you would be witches, but I guess I should back up because she assumed you would not be a witch. Kayla was a surprise nobody saw coming."

"Yeah, Mom told me about not even knowing she was carrying twins. And that Kayla clawed her way out of her hoo-ha. Thank you, Mom, for that image!"

Coffee spurted out of Mr. Hollins's nostrils and mouth, mostly spilling into his lap, but a few droplets managed to find themselves onto Sheree's nightgown. Of course, nightgown was a loose term, as it was really just one of her dad's old T-shirts.

"Sorry!" he said, getting up to grab a towel to wipe up the mess he'd created.

"It's okay, Dad. Keep talking," she begged, helping with the coffee spillage before refilling both their cups.

"Where was I? Oh yeah, so since your mom isn't a witch, she just assumed both of you weren't either. But after Kayla started talking with Jessica, your mom was convinced that she was. And that scared her more than anything," her dad said, looking back at the stairs to make sure his wife wasn't there overhearing everything he was telling their daughter.

"Mom doesn't want me to know any of this, does she?" Sheree gathered as she saw where his gaze was.

Shaking his head, he told her, "No. And for good reason, but with Kayla dead, I don't see the harm in telling you."

Of course, she's also a ghost and she's haunting me and Brendon and trying to kill us. "I understand, but why, if Kayla was able to convene with Jessica, would nobody else?"

"Because nobody else wants to. Jessica was, well, to put it mildly, she was evil. And from what your mom told me, she was a very powerful witch, too. You've heard of the phrase hell hath no fury like a woman scorned?" her dad asked, to which Sheree shook her head in agreement. "Now add magic to that mix. After your triple great grandpa was murdered, she just lost it, leaving a trail of blood in her path before she was hanged, shot, beheaded, and burned to ashes."

"Oh my gawd," Sheree said, horrified. "Where did all this take place?"

"Here in Ravenwood," he told her, taking another sip of coffee before adding, "Right outside the courthouse downtown."

Suddenly fearful, Sheree built up the courage to ask, "Where did Jessica live?"

Her dad looked hesitant to tell her.

Realizing the truth before he ever spoke it, she said, "Please don't tell me we are living in her old house."

Still, her father was silent.

The blood drained from her face as she became pale.

Pale as a ghost.

"Dad, what if she is still here?" she managed to ask, even though it took more effort than it should have.

"She's not," her father told her confidently. "Your grandma and aunts did some extensive banishing spells before we moved in to make sure Jessica's spirit couldn't inhabit this house any longer."

"Just Jessica? What about other spirits?" Sheree asked, curious as to whether the spell they cast actually did any good at all since she knew of at least one spirit that was still there.

"I don't know," he said, shaking his head. "I mean, who else would be haunting this house?"

"I don't know," Sheree lied, shrugging her shoulders.

She wanted so badly to tell her dad everything. She wanted to tell him about all the evil things Kayla had done. But she didn't. She couldn't. Kayla was his daughter, his little girl who was taken away so young. But he also knew about her abilities, and that she not only could talk to the dead, but to a murderous witch who could have bestowed more power than she ever would have gained on her own. An internal struggle was brewing inside her.

Tell him!

I can't!

You have to. He must know the truth.

Now is not the time.

Now is the perfect time!

Why?

Because he just revealed more to you in half an hour than he's said to you your entire life.

She was about to tell him everything when she heard her mother walking down the stairs and into the kitchen. It was a sign. Now was not the time.

"Good morning. What are you two doing up so early?" she asked, pouring herself the last cup of coffee before starting another pot, then looked at Sheree as she asked, "And why is Brendon sleeping in your room?"

"Brendon had a bad dream and asked to sleep in my bed with me," Sheree told her.

A smile formed on her mother's face as she responded with, "Oh, it just melts my heart that you two manage to get along so well when your father and I aren't in sight."

"Don't get too mushy. I apparently also left out the Death by Chocolate ice cream last night and had to dump it out," Sheree confessed before taking a sip.

The smile faded as a torrent of red rushed over Mrs. Hollins's face, "You ungrateful little bitch! I slave all day at that damned school to bring home a measly paycheck and buy you ice cream only to have you waste it! What the hell is wrong with you? When are you going to learn responsibility?"

"Calm down, Mom!" Sheree yelled. "What the hell, are you on your period?"

Mr. Hollins slowly crept off the barstool and into the den to avoid any oncoming wrath, taking his coffee with him.

Mrs. Hollins started to cry. "Yes. Yes I am! Or it's menopause! I don't know. I have to go see my gynecologist because this is getting ridiculous. And to think, all that chocolate gone! Wasted! Unused, unloved, and uneaten!"

Sheree knew this was going to be a long weekend.

Chapter 3
Tryouts and Talent Shows

Monday morning when Sheree arrived at school, she found that the cheerleaders were already holding tryouts to replace the two girls who died at Friday night's basketball game by means of a freshly painted poster hung up in the main hall.

"That is so tacky," Sheree said aloud, shaking her head.

"I know, right?" Jennifer said from behind her, nearly causing her to jump out of her own skin.

"Bitch, you shouldn't sneak up on me like that, you know I've got an Irish bladder!" Sheree squealed, holding back a punch aimed right for Jennifer's neck. "I think I peed a little. Hopefully it didn't seep through my pants." Upon further investigation, the coast seemed to be clear, at least where Sheree's crotch and wetness were involved. "Well, that was close."

Jennifer agreed, knowing full well how powerful Sheree's neck punches could be. Actually, just about any punch she threw could cause intense bodily damage. However, the ones she'd give due to a wardrobe mishap could possibly be deadly. "So, cheerleading?"

Sheree gave her an incredulous look back as she said, "Duh!"

"Oh my gawd, that is so tacky!" another voice said from behind them, causing them to jump in place and Jennifer to lose one of her books, which landed spine up on the ground, crinkling some of the pages. It was Sky.

After regaining composure, and rechecking for leakage, Sheree said, "Right? I mean it's only been two days!"

"What the hell?" Sky said, shrugging with her hands in the air, elbows on the armrests of her wheelchair. "So we're all totally trying out for the team, right?"

"Duh!" Sheree and Jennifer said in unison, with big goofy grins on their faces.

The three of them made a plan to tryout for the cheerleading team. The only problem was the date, which was Friday, the same day as the talent show. However, both Sheree and Jennifer assured Sky that she'd do fine.

"The tryouts are in the morning before school and the talent show is an end of day assembly," Jennifer told her.

"And besides," Sheree chimed in, "it's not like you need to practice for the talent show or anything. Your voice is amazing!"

"Is that it?" Sky said nonchalantly. "That's supposed to be my motivation? Thanks."

The warning bell rang, signaling that first period would be starting in five minutes, leaving the girls to depart ways. As

Sheree and Jennifer walked off in opposite directions from her, Sky headed up to her class and thought, *What am I doing? Cheerleading? Seriously? I'm in a frickin' wheelchair! Why did I agree to tryout with them?* "Ugh!"

Sky became more and more paranoid throughout the day, with the voices in her head pulling her in every which direction. *Do this. Do that. Don't do this. Don't do that. Don't screw up. Be a man. Take one for the team. Wait, be a man? I don't even have a dick! Don't be a dick.* She wouldn't even make eye contact with Sheree in Algebra for fear she'd bring it up again. By lunchtime, it was obvious to Sheree and Jennifer that something was bothering her.

"Honey, what's going on with this?" Jennifer asked Sky, moving her pointed finger in a zigzag motion across her face and hair to mimic her favorite sitcom character.

Deflating herself to be as small as possible and staring into her lap, Sky responded, "I don't know what the hell I was thinking agreeing to tryout for the cheerleading squad with you two."

"Uh… maybe because you would be amazing!" Sheree told her, utterly confounded she didn't see that as plainly obvious.

"Seriously, take all that teen angst hate-the-world attitude you've got and put a smile on it and you've got the makings of a perfect cheerleader," Jennifer added, nodding her head up and down.

Not believing her ears, Sky asked, "You're not just effing with me because I'm a cripple, are you?"

"Oh my gawd, you're crippled?!" Sheree and Jennifer said in unison, both making the same Macaulay-Culkin-Home-Alone-double-hands-on-cheeks-open-mouthed-surprise face.

"You two are creepy sometimes," Sky said with a grin.

Sheree and Jennifer looked at each other and appeared to have a conversation without words from Sky's perspective until Sheree piped up, "Jennifer and I were just thinking that the lunch line is getting long being Cheese Zombie day, so we better get in it now."

"Cheese Zombies?" Sky asked, genuinely confused.

"You've never heard of Cheese Zombies?!" Jennifer shrieked. "They are only the most delicious school lunch item ever!"

"Huh?" Sky asked, hoping for clarification.

Rolling her eyes, Sheree said, "It's like French bread dough flattened out and stuffed with cheddar cheese and baked to a perfect golden brown and topped with an insane amount of butter that you dip in tomato soup."

"Oh! So it's like a grilled cheese sandwich," Sky said, her face revealing she finally got it.

"No! It's so much more than that!" Sheree exclaimed wildly. "It's like manna from heaven on a melamine platter served straight from the hands of God!"

"Calm down!" Sky said.

"No, you just don't understand. You won't until you eat one, so get your ass in line with us now, Sky," Jennifer said, grabbing Sheree's hand and hurrying to the back of a fairly engorged herd of students and faculty all waiting for their delicious golden bounty to be plated by ladies in hair nets and loose-fitting plastic gloves.

And it was true. Words could not do justice to the oral pleasure Sky was experiencing as she savored every bite of cheesy goodness. She now understood. She now got it. She has now been initiated. She was now a believer. There was to be at least one day a month that school lunch could be tolerated, and Cheese Zombie day was it. But, oh, the agony of having to wait a whole month before being able to receive the food of the gods again!

Before lunch was over, Sheree asked, "So, where are we going to practice for tryouts tonight?"

Jennifer tsk-tsked before saying, "No can do tonight. Got thrown a major project today in Washington State History I have to finish for tomorrow."

"Liar. That project was handed out last week," Sheree told her friend.

"Okay, so I procrastinated!" Jennifer said loudly, brushing her tray to the side.

"Fine, Jen. What about you, Sky?"

Fumbling for words, Sky finally managed to get out, "I've got a History project I need to get working on, too. Oh, and some Spanish homework."

"Sí," Jennifer added. "Yo también."

"Bullshit, Jennifer!" Sheree yelled, then looking around to make sure there weren't any teachers around her. Then in a much quieter voice, she continued, "You don't even take Spanish, you're in Sign Language with me."

"Sheree, I have a confession to make," Jennifer said, looking quite serious.

Waiting for her confession, Sheree assumed she was just going to blurt it out, but apparently Jennifer was waiting for her to acknowledge her first. She rolled her eyes and shook her head. "Okay, what is it?"

Looking up towards the ceiling of the cafeteria and welling up like she was about to cry, Jennifer admitted, "I'm taking both! The only reason I'm in Sign Language was to have a class together. Mom and Dad would kill me if I stopped taking Spanish because they say that the world market will be dominated by China and Mexico since that is where most of our crap is made now! I'm already fluent in Mandarin, so that just left Spanish to master."

"Well, it won't hurt to be able to speak to deaf people too, will it?" Sheree asked, almost upset by the honesty her friend just relayed.

"No, I suppose that will look good on a résumé. Fluent in English, Vietnamese, Mandarin, French, Spanish and American Sign Language," Jennifer said, visualizing what that would look like on paper.

"Well thanks for making me look like shit!" Sky said, throwing her hands up in the air in defeat.

"You watch your mouth, young lady!" Mrs. O'Hurley said from behind her, walking off with a smirk on her face as she went to deposit her lunch tray in the designated area, causing Sky's face to light up redder than a hot coal.

"Fine. Be that way. I'll just sit at home and mope since apparently I am the only one who took the time this weekend to actually do her homework assignments." Sheree pouted with her arms folded across her chest, completely shocked at Jennifer's irresponsibility that was utterly out of character. Then she wondered if the tragic events of the game had affected her more than she was willing to admit. Or maybe she had to spend the weekend consoling Chad. She decided to drop it for the time being.

After school was out, Sheree reluctantly gathered her friends and dropped them off at their houses on Baker Street and cursed them both a long and tedious night of mind-numbing homework they could have worked on the day before but didn't, causing them to have to delay practicing for cheerleading tryouts until tomorrow afternoon. She decided it would be beneficial to go to the grocery store, grab a half-gallon container of Ravenwood Creamery's Death by Chocolate ice cream, and head home to eat it in peace before the rest of her family got home. She also decided it would be best to pick up an extra one to replace the container she left out on the counter Friday night, causing her mother to go into conniptions. And furthermore, she decided it would also be a good idea to leave a note on the ice cream before placing it back in the freezer:

"That should brighten her night!" Sheree squealed as she slammed the freezer door before pulling a spoon out of the drawer, ripping the lid off her personal Death by Chocolate container, and hungrily devouring the entire thing while she watched *The Oprah Winfrey Show*, which, ironically, was an episode about high school and whether it did more harm than good.

Brendon was the first intruder to walk in the door, dropping his backpack, coat, shoes, and lunchbox in a trail leading straight for the kitchen, where he poured himself the first of three bowls of cereal and began eating like there was no tomorrow. "Did your friends abandon you?" he asked, mouth full of sugar coated oat shapes and marshmallows.

Looking back from the television, she said, "Yes. They all have homework. And you better not eat all the Lucky Charms, because if I don't have any for breakfast tomorrow morning, you'll regret ever being born!"

Knowing that he had just emptied the box he'd been eating from, sweat started forming on his brow as he frantically checked the pantry. He was relieved to find two more unopened boxes of her magically delicious cereal within.

Minutes later, their mother walked through the door and nearly tripped on Brendon's discarded belongings, mumbled some nondescript curse words, and headed straight towards the downstairs bathroom to relieve herself. Upon exiting, she said, "I really hate holding it all day, but the alternative of using a middle school bathroom just isn't a viable option in my life."

"Good to know," Sheree said, not taking her eyes off the television as she continued to watch the last few minutes of the episode.

Curious, Mrs. Hollins asked, "What are you watching?"

"Oprah," Sheree told her. "It's entirely devoted to the question 'Does High School Do More Harm than Good?' "

Rolling her eyes, her mother responded, "Well, that's just preposterous!" then hopped up the stairs to change out of the skirt and blouse she was wearing and into a pair of sweatpants and old T-shirt before starting dinner.

As soon as Oprah signed off, her father walked through the front door, sat down on the couch next to Sheree in his puke-like shade of blue-green scrubs, grabbed the remote, and was about to change the channel to catch the five o'clock news when he realized it was already on the station he normally watched. "What was on Oprah that you were watching, Sheree?"

"It was about high school," Sheree told him.

"Well that sucks for you. Can't even escape it when class is out!" he said, chuckling.

"I've concluded it definitely does more harm than good," Sheree said before getting up and heading into the kitchen to throw away her empty ice cream container and get a glass of water. Her mother gave her the stink eye as she threw it into the trash. "Check the freezer, Mom."

Upon opening the freezer door, her mother squealed with delight and did a mildly amusing happy dance. "Thanks, Sheree! Was that to replace the one you so unceremoniously desecrated?"

"Oh my gawd, will you ever let that go?" Sheree snapped, but knew the answer before she ever let the words fall from her mouth: Never.

Annoyed at her friends for having homework, and annoyed at herself for having none, Sheree went to her room to read a book for a bit before dinner was ready. As usual, it was ready all too soon, as she barely had a chance to finish the first chapter when her mother yelled it was dinnertime. She looked into the mirror above her dresser and nearly jumped back from the disturbing image she saw reflected in it. Expecting to see herself in the reflection, she instead saw Kayla. Although they were identical, she could always tell the difference.

"What do you want, Kayla?" Sheree asked her reflection quietly through clenched teeth, barely able to contain the fear and anger that was boiling up inside her.

"You know what I want. Are you willing to give it to me?" her reflection asked back.

She was about to answer when Brendon walked in her bedroom and said in a muffled voice so as to not get the attention of their parents, "Sheree, you're scaring me. Why won't Kayla just leave us alone?"

Shaking her head, Sheree answered, "I don't know, Bren. I just don't know." Upon looking back into the mirror, it was back to just her own reflection. "Don't worry, we'll figure it out… again."

Giving him a forced smile, he forced one back, but each of them knew that this was just the beginning of things to come.

Neither of them would be prepared for what Kayla had in mind. And neither of them knew why Kayla was back, either.

The next three days were a blur, as Sheree, Jennifer, and Sky all practiced for hours after school for the cheerleading tryouts on Friday. Chad, being a cheerleader himself, helped them out with pointers and minor routines to try. While he was really hoping Jennifer would make the team so he could spend more time with her, he was rather impressed with Sheree's skills. However, he was especially surprised by Sky. Even though she obviously couldn't do anything that required the lower half of her body, her facial expression, hand gestures, and voice were all spot on. Of course, Jennifer picked up on this and hit him repeatedly in the arm, causing a bruise to form on his left bicep. Mr. Hollins checked out the wound for good measure, even though he usually dealt with the dead at the hospital.

Friday morning arrived, and Sheree picked her friends up and headed to school early for the tryouts. To their surprise, only a few other girls had shown up. Eyeing the competition, they pretty much knew that the choice was obviously going to be between the three of them. They weren't being vain, just real, since the other four girls just didn't have it. They didn't bring it. They brought frump and drama and way too much makeup and body odor, in that order.

Jennifer went first out of their group, and surprised both Sheree and Sky with her audition, showing moves she never showed them while they were practicing. Sky leaned over to Sheree and whispered, "Obviously Chad has been giving her private lessons."

"Obviously," Sheree whispered back. "But not with their privates, because, you know, he's gay."

"Obviously," Sky said, though she doubted that was the case. Of course, her main doubts stemmed from the growing crush she had on him and the way his smile tickled her nether regions.

Applause from the entire squad and a few onlookers sprang out when Jennifer finished. "Sky Hawkins?" the head cheerleader, a girl named Mandy who looked like she was an amateur MMA fighter, called out, not having a clue as to who it was until she wheeled out to the floor in front of the team. A few chuckles could be heard both from the squad and the small audience. It wasn't hard to make out who they were. "Shut up!" Mandy yelled, and everyone did just that. "Sorry, we've obviously got some real assholes here. Go ahead."

Clearing her throat, Sky got into a good starting position then began her chant.

> "Hey Crows, let's do it!
> Ravenwood can't be beat!
> Come on crowd, let's hear it now!
> RHS is number one!
> Yell it
> RHS is number one,
> Yeah!"

Before anyone had a chance to react, she started another one.

"Purple Power
Go RHS!
We got the ball,
We got the ball,
Ravenwood, go, go!
C-R-O-W-S
Crows [clap clap] are the Best!"

The audience and cheerleaders were all on their feet, clapping and cheering for her. Sky didn't know what to do. Shock spread over her as she just sat there, motionless until Chad ran up to her and told her, "That was amazing!"

"Uh, thanks!" she said back before wheeling over to where Jennifer and Sheree were giving her huge smiles and still clapping until she got close enough for a group hug.

"Seriously, you just nailed that!" Jennifer said with a twinge of jealousy, but genuine happiness for her friend.

"That was awesome! Thanks for letting me have to go after that. No matter how well I do it'll look like shit by comparison!" Sheree told her, still beaming her beautiful smile with words full of razor blades.

Talking over the noise still being made, Mandy yelled out the last name on the list. "Sheree Hollins!" to which Chad and Courtney (almost reluctantly because she "secretly" had a grudge against her) clapped and received death glares from their leader for doing.

After making her way out to the middle of the floor, Sheree took a deep breath, closed her eyes for a second, then opened them wide, put a huge smile over her face and started with an audience participation cheer, to which most of them participated.

"Give me a C!"
"C!"
"Give me an R!"
"R!"
"Give me an O!"
"O!"
"Give me a W!"
"W!"
"Give me a chance and I will kill you all you worthless pieces of shit!"

Sheree immediately covered her mouth in shock. The words were not hers and the voice was not hers, but they did come out of her and there was no way to explain what had just happened. Beyond embarrassed, she ran from the gym crying and went straight for the girl's restroom, locking herself in one of the stalls.

Everyone was still in shock over what they heard. The voice was so gravelly and shrill and evil, and brought with it a deathly chill in the air that tingled their spines and twisted their nerves. Chad and Courtney looked at each with horrified faces, though Courtney was "secretly" pleased that once again Sheree was obviously knocked out of the running for the cheerleading squad.

One of the first girls to audition, Body Odor, whispered to Frumpy, "Well that seems a little morbid for a high school game."

Jennifer looked like she was scared out of her mind when Sky asked, confused and genuinely concerned, "What happened?" but Jennifer didn't say a word. She just flashed a look of utter fear before running after her friend. Sky followed close behind.

"Sheree!" Jennifer yelled in the hallways as they started to fill up with students arriving for the start of school. Assuming she'd gone into the nearest bathroom, her and Sky entered it. There was only one closed stall, and Sheree's shoes were visible from behind the door. "Sheree, are you okay?"

They could hear her crying, the sound echoing off the tile walls and floor. "I can't deal with this right now," she managed to get out between sobs. "What the hell is happening to me?"

Looking at Sky and her perplexed but compassionate expression, Jennifer debated over how best to answer, or at least try to answer since she didn't know either. Deciding it would be best to not bring Sky into the mess, Jennifer decided the only way to communicate would be psychically.

We both know Kayla is back.

But how, Jen? How?!

I don't know.

We both saw her leave. We both saw Jeff take her to heaven. Why would she want to leave that? Does she hate me so much that not even the love of heaven could dissuade her from vengeance?

It doesn't make sense to me either, Sheree.

"Why don't we go play on the swings again, Jennifer?!" a child-like voice asked, laughing hysterically afterwards causing Sheree to scream, "Get out of my head!"

Jennifer was momentarily paralyzed as she flashed back to the events of last Christmas: the four year old ghost of Sheree's twin sister tormenting her like a marionette just to exact revenge on Sheree because she lived, because her life wasn't taken twelve years ago. "You have no power over me anymore, Kayla!" she screamed.

"Okay, someone needs to explain to me what the hell is going on here, because I am seriously freaking the fuck out!" Sky yelled, completely clueless.

Just then, the stall door opened and Sheree walked out, her eyes red and face wet from the tears. Jennifer looked like she was about to go into karate mode when Sheree said, "It's okay, Jen. It's just me. I think I've fended her off for now."

"Who? Who's this Kayla?" Sky asked, still confused and growing more and more frustrated that her two best friends seemed to be ignoring her.

Jennifer fell on the floor and leaned up against the wall, putting her head in her hands as Sheree put her hand on Sky's shoulder and told her. She told her everything. About how Kayla was her twin sister, how she died, and how she tried to kill her. "And one more thing," Sheree said, her throat clenching as she felt another wave of tears about to flood through her ducts, "she caused the crash that put you in that wheelchair."

"What?" Sky said quietly, still unsure she heard everything correctly.

"I'm so sorry!" Sheree sobbed, falling and landing on her knees, ignoring the pain as she continued to apologize.

It was almost too much to take in for Sky. She thought about leaving, pretending she didn't hear any of it and getting ready for first period, but how could she? How could she ignore her friend's confession? How could she ignore someone telling her the truth about the car crash that nearly killed her? And then, without warning, the memory of that night came rushing back to her...

"What do you mean you've never heard of a highway handjob?" Chad Miller asked his girlfriend, Sky Hawkins as she sat in the passenger seat of his car while they drove along the highway back to Chancellor.

Sky gave him a look of absolute astonishment as she responded, "Chad, you can't be serious?"

"I'm totally serious! It'll be great!" Chad said, smiling, followed by a chuckle.

"For you!" Sky shouted. "Besides, you've been drinking and I need you to stay focused on the road."

Giving her pouting lips, Chad told her, "It's hard to stay focused when, you know, it's hard."

"We just had sex, like, an hour ago. You can't possibly be ready again," Sky said in disbelief.

"Really? I'm sixteen. I'm always ready again," he said sarcastically, but his words were truth.

"Fine, just keep your eyes on the road, okay?" Sky told her boyfriend as she rolled her eyes and started to unzip his pants, but the car hit a pothole and the sudden motion was a little much for her, causing her to vomit all over Chad.

Just then, a bright flash of teal light suddenly appeared with what could only be described as a child's mischievous laughter. The next thing she knew, her head was touching broken glass and soft grass, she couldn't feel her legs, and her boyfriend was crushing her body as he lay motionless on top of her. "Chad, you're hurting me," Sky said trying to push him off, but he didn't respond. "Chad!" she screamed, shaking him as best she could. "Chad!"

Blank, lifeless, horrified eyes stared back at her.

Red lights flashed in the distance, getting brighter and brighter. Sirens sang their cautionary tune, getting louder and louder. It seemed to take a lifetime to reach their destination, when in reality it was a matter of minutes since the crash.

The emergency team exited the ambulance just as a fire truck arrived and she heard someone exclaim, "Oh my God! That's Jeff Mains!"

Who is Jeff Mains? What about me? Why aren't they helping me?

Sky was about to scream when someone approached the car, which had landed on its side in a ditch just off the main road. "Don't worry, we'll get you out of there," the woman assured her.

"I can't move my legs," Sky said, crying. "And Chad won't wake up!"

Sky composed herself in the bathroom, Sheree by her side still on the floor, and Jennifer across from her against the wall. "It's okay, Sheree. It wasn't your fault."

Trying her best, Sheree forced a smile on her face.

"Gawd, I hate you, Sheree!" Sky spat out. "Even when you cry you look hot!"

They both started laughing about that when Jennifer asked, still crying, "What about me?" to which Sheree responded, "Honestly, you scare the shit out of me when you cry. You've got this look like, man, I don't even know how to describe!"

"I do," Sky informed them. "You don't look sad, you look like you're angry, I mean, like, so angry you'd kill a puppy and throw it at the owner's face, and the owner is a little kid."

"What?!" Jennifer shouted. "Are you kidding me?"

Shaking her head, Sheree told her friend, "Honestly, I wish we were."

"You could have told me, jerks," Jennifer said, wiping the few tears that had managed to escape. "For some reason I feel like I have to exaggerate my facial expressions like you crazy ass white folks do."

Looking at her watch, Sky said, "We really should get ready for first period. I've got enough to worry about this afternoon at the talent show to be trying to explain to Jennifer that her cry face is whack."

Cocking her head to the side, Jennifer responded coolly with, "Bitch."

And with that, they went to the locker room to change into their school clothes. While Sheree felt it would be best to skip school altogether after the embarrassing mishap during cheerleading tryouts, she felt it was more important to be there for Sky. She was not looking forward to first period Biology, where she'd have to face Courtney and Chad, both of whom will want an explanation, even though she was certain Courtney was well-pleased with her outburst as it probably knocked her out of the running.

I wonder if they'd buy the excuse that my brother ate all my Lucky Charms?

So that was what Sheree told everyone who asked. Sadly, everyone seemed to buy it. In second period American Sign Language, she and Jennifer didn't say a word to each other, just half-hearted smiles. They didn't even sign anything to each other. In third period Advanced Algebra, Sky simply acknowledged her with a quick unemotional glance. Trying to ignore all the hurt and guilt she felt inside, she decided to let her mind wander, zoning out as letters and numbers began dancing together on the chalk board as if doing the tango.

"The itsy bitsy spider went up the waterspout…"

Sheree's eyes suddenly focused on everyone in the classroom, darting from one head to another. She didn't know why, but she was certain that the voice was coming from one of her classmates.

"Down came the rain and washed the spider out…"

Looking from one person to the next, nobody was saying a word except for the teacher, and the words coming out of his mouth did not match the ones she was hearing. It left her with the only logical conclusion: that the voice was completely and solely in her head. For a brief moment, that brought her some relief, but it was short lived.

"Sharing a body is just not the same,
But soon I'll be the only one in control again!"

Sheree shuddered before belching loudly. The entire class turned in her direction as she let out another burp. There was a tickle in her throat and she thought for sure vomit was going to follow, but instead she opened her mouth wide, releasing another eructation so violent, she had to hold onto her desk to steady herself from the earthquake centered at her core. Horrified gasps came from every direction as a large black spider jumped from her mouth, onto her desk, and scurried out the slightly open classroom door.

Leaving her books and bag behind, Sheree ran into the hallway, out the closest exit, and headed straight for the student parking lot towards her little blue sedan. Slowing down as she approached her car, she realized her keys were in her bag, and her bag was still in the classroom. Filled with rage and frustration, she growled into the air as she kicked one of the rear tires before leaning her back against the car and sliding towards the pavement. Covering her head with her hands, she began crying uncontrollably, the hot tears stinging her face against the frigid air as snowflakes slowly fell to the ground.

"You might need these," Sky said as she wheeled close to her, holding car keys in her hand and Sheree's book bag in her lap.

Looking up, Sheree merely mouthed "thanks" unintentionally, as her voice could not be found at that moment like it was on vacation or something. As she stood up, she saw Jennifer running towards her, picturesque as always.

"Are you okay?" Jennifer asked Sheree as she slackened pace upon approaching her friends, her scrunched and wrinkled face terrified and worried all at once.

"I don't think so," Sheree managed to get out after her voice took a redeye back home.

"What did Kayla mean?" Jennifer asked. "What was that about sharing a body?"

Confused and feeling out of the loop again, Sky said, "Huh?"

"I… I…" Sheree fumbled for an answer, but the record was stuck in a groove.

Looking at Sky as snow landed in her straight black hair, Jennifer told her, "Sheree and I, our minds are somehow linked to one another sometimes. I don't know how to explain it. All I know is that Kayla was singing in Sheree's head, and I need to know what it all means."

Sheree still looked like she was searching for her voice again as it had apparently caught a connecting flight.

Sky assessed what she was hearing. "Okay, so Sheree's sister's ghost was talking in her head, and you can also hear it?"

"Well, more like singing in her head," Jennifer clarified.

"Oh, well, that makes everything better," Sky said, her face twitching.

"She's inside me!" Sheree told her friends. "She's a part of me, and I don't understand how that is even possible."

Holding her left hand open to the clouds and shifting forward in her seat, Sky said, "The ghost of your dead twin sister put me in a wheelchair, has killed at least four people from what I've gathered between my Chad, your Jeff, and the two cheerleaders last week, and the part you can't believe is that she's in your head?"

A shocked laugh escaped Sheree as she said back, "Okay, when you put it that way, I suppose it is rather minor in the grand scheme of things!"

Not knowing what she could do to comfort her friend, Jennifer simply informed Sheree, "We'll keep an eye on you, won't we, Sky?"

"What do you mean?" Sheree asked, drying her face with her shirtsleeve.

"You can't control her, can you?" Sky asked, brushing the snowflakes that dotted her hair like dandruff. Bad dandruff. Like, you-need-to-see-a-dermatologist dandruff.

"No." Sheree wanted desperately for her answer to be yes, but knew that wasn't possible.

"Then we will do everything we can to keep you safe from her," Sky assured, a small smile forming on her face that would be imperceptible had any more distance been between them.

"I can't let you," Sheree told them while she stared at her shoes.

"You can't stop us," Jennifer told her as the bell rang, signaling that it was lunchtime, and that the last period for the day had ended as the talent show was starting immediately after lunch was over. Soon the parking lot would be filled with juniors and seniors ready to skip out on the rest of the school day. "We'd better figure out what we're doing for lunch. I mean, we can hang out here in the parking lot if you want, but I'm gonna need my coat if this snow keeps up because I'm practically fat free!"

"I'm anything but fat free and I'm freezing my ass off!" Sky said. "And I'm sitting on it!"

Sheree smiled and suggested, "We should head back inside and help Sky get ready for the talent show. The cold might break her voice."

When they reached the auditorium, it was already full of people practicing their random routines while hurriedly eating peanut butter and jelly sandwiches and washing them down with Snapples, so they found an empty hallway, sat down their stuff, and tried to confuse the hell out of Sky with the wrong lyrics to the song she already knew by heart. She playfully cursed Jennifer and Sheree before blurting out, "Just curious, what's up with your sister and spiders?"

The question caught Sheree off guard, something she wasn't used to despite the abundance of instances as of late. "Um," she started, adding a pause before continuing with, "The Itsy Bitsy Spider was her favorite nursery rhyme when we were little, and probably because she knows I'm terrified of spiders."

Sky shook her head in acknowledgment. "I get the nursery rhyme bit, but I don't understand your arachnophobia. I mean, what's so terrifying about spiders?"

Jennifer's lower jaw jutted out and her eyelids dropped with it as she told Sky, "Do you know how many different things come out of a spider's butthole? It's like fifteen!" which caused Sky and Sheree to both start gagging. "Seriously, it's disgusting. I've got a diagram," she informed her friends, digging into her book bag to retrieve the photocopy of everything that can come out of a spider's butt from a book she casually perused in the school library one day out of morbid curiosity.

The sound of vomit filled the air.

"Do you wash your jeans with Windex, because I can see myself in them!" a redheaded pockmarked boy said with a subtly slack-jawed snicker before being escorted off the stage by an unamused teacher.

Sheree turned to Jennifer and commented, "Seriously, that was the same joke someone told at my eighth grade talent show last year. Am I on Candid Camera?" Looking around, she concluded that it was just another random coincidence.

"I don't think so," Jennifer said, also looking around without any real conviction. "But just in case, what came after dumbass joke guy?"

"The Rose," Sheree told her, looking her straight in the eye with a deadpan expression as Sky wheeled out on stage.

"Next up is Sky Hawkings, I mean Hawkins!" a quite embarrassed yet still hot looking Mr. Santos announced to a mostly silent audience where only about a dozen people clapped. Sheree, Jennifer, and most of the cheerleading squad were among the clappers.

Sky stared out over the crowd of people, barely able to make out the shapes of faces and bodies because of the stage lights, and waited.

Silence.

Awkward silence.

Students started murmuring to each other.

Sky shifted in her seat and was about to ask where her accompanying music was when she remembered there wasn't any.

She forgot that she planned on singing it a cappella. *Crap! Here it goes.*

When she started singing, the audience went silent again. When she stopped singing, the audience was still silent until the fat pimple-faced boy with mismatched socks who had mocked her only days ago stood up and yelled, "That was so awesome!"

Applause.

Over the crowd of cheering and clapping voices, Sky quickly found Sheree and Jennifer who were screaming the loudest of all and beamed a huge smile in their direction that she found simply would not come off her face for the rest of the day.

Chapter 4
Practice

Sheree sat in the bleachers of the gymnasium not far from where she was sitting just over a week ago when two cheerleaders died of a horrible freak accident her dead ghost of a sister caused that has led to this very moment of being stuck watching her two best friends on the cheerleading squad practice without a shred of experience while she had plenty to spread around, along with a tad bit of jealousy and anger, who were seated on either side of her. Bad thoughts were running through her head like a private marathon.

Very. Bad. Thoughts.

Oh my gawd! How does Courtney's fro not move when she is doing those routines? Good night, one would think it would bounce around but then again too much bouncing with that thing might make it fall off. Ugh. I hate her. Hope that it does fall off. Shit! Does that make me racist for hating the only black girl in school? Fuuuck…

Will you please stop thinking so loud, Sheree! I am trying not to screw up on my first day with the squad! Jennifer communicated telepathically.

Confused, Sheree's face contorted to quite quizzical unnatural expressions. *What?! Jen, how can you hear me if Kayla isn't doing something bat-shit crazy?*

Because your wacko sister is stuck in your head, fool! STOP THINKING!!! Jennifer gave her a death glare with a phony smile while clapping to some random cheer about balls.

Okay. You look great. Your gay boyfriend even looks great. Hell, even Sky looks great. Sonofabitch! I should be out there with you. If only there was a way to make room on the...

Don't you even think about it! Before you know it, Kayla will take over and knock me or Chad or Sky or Courtney, who, by the way is really cool so you might not want to mess with her because she's also kinda badass, or someone else out or kill them and then I'll have to listen to you bitch and complain about how helpless you feel having a psychopath trapped in your head.

Excellent points. I will focus my thoughts on chocolate then.

I hate you.

And so for the rest of practice, Sheree thought of chocolate. While Chad and another male cheerleader were throwing Jennifer into the air, she thought of Death by Chocolate ice cream. When Jennifer was waving her pompoms like everyone else, she thought of sinking her teeth into a giant chocolate Easter bunny. And when Jennifer was trying to step in-sync with everyone else (except Sky who was really quite adept at doing the routines despite being bound to a wheelchair), she did the unthinkable: she thought of triple chocolate fudge brownies topped with Death by Chocolate ice cream and smothered in hot fudge sauce. Thinking of that amount of chocolate entering her oral portal created such a sensation that Sheree orgasmed right there on the gymnasium bleachers, startling herself, yes, but causing Jennifer to blurt out, "Oh my gawd! Really?"

"Jennifer, what the hell?" Sky shouted at her friend, looking furious as all get out. "Step back in line, bitch!" She looked angry. She was angry. She knew her friends were carrying on a conversation without anyone else and she felt alone. Left out. Even though she knew they couldn't control their psychic connection because of a restless hell-bent spirit, she was jealous and pissed all at once, both wanting and not wanting any part of it.

"Sorry, Sky!" Jennifer shouted back. "I didn't realize you were squad leader all of a sudden! Someone needs to take her chill pill!"

"Shit! I do!" Sky said, wheeling over to her book bag and taking out a prescription bottle and popping one of the pills inside and chugging it down with a quick swig of water from a plastic water bottle (that will remain on the Earth for at least the next million years) sitting next to it on the gym floor.

Everyone was looking at her wanly.

"They're anti-depressants. Lose your ability to walk and see how well you fare," she told her captive audience as she flipped them off.

A girl sitting a few bleachers up from Sheree snorted an uncontrolled laugh that sounded like something between a hyena cry and an elephant fart, high-pitched and hefty, which caused

Courtney to scream, "Shut it, Nikki!" to which the girl who answered to Nikki did just that, quietly, though with a smirk on her face, looking back at her History book. Sheree probably wouldn't have given her a second glance, but something about her sweater and body shape reminded her of an Easter egg and it made her angry to the point that she realized she needed to leave the gym right then or something bad would happen.

Something. Very. Bad.

You don't have to leave, Jennifer told Sheree using the Psychic Friends Network, of which only they were privy to as it was a private hotline.

Sheree shot a manic glare in Jennifer's direction, showing that her normally aquamarine eyes were a fiery red.

Leave now! I'll catch up with you later. We can pretend to study Math. I can tutor you and Sky for your Advanced Algebra test coming up.

Sky watched as Sheree grabbed her book bag, flashed a fake smile in her direction that disappeared as fast as it came on, along with a half-assed effort of a wave, and quickly stormed out of the gym. Wheeling herself toward Jennifer, she asked quietly, "What was that all about?"

"Anger management issues," Jennifer barely whispered to her.

"Like *Carrie* or Columbine?" Sky asked, not sure which would be the better option.

"Maybe a little of both," Jennifer said, trying not to sound alarmed that of all the comparisons Sky could have chosen, she chose those two.

"Well, is she planning on leaving the school? I hope not because she's my ride," Sky said, checking her polished nails for chips.

"Crap!" Jennifer shouted, regretting her outburst as all eyes in the gymnasium were on her. *Sheree, wait for us in the car. We're almost done.*

Almost there. Going to get it all nice and toasty so you bitches will feel like you're in hell! Sheree answered with an evil grin plastered to her face, such a stark contrast to her normal perky smile.

"All right maggots, listen up," Mandy, the redheaded cheerleading captain shouted. "We've got a big game against Hudson's Bay Friday, so I don't want you all preoccupied about what you are going to wear to the Valentine's Dance Saturday. Get your outfit together NOW! If you need help, Courtney has offered to give free fashion advice, being the chair of the Fashion Committee. And..."

Tuning out and rolling her eyes at the ridiculousness of the words coming out of Mandy's mouth, Sky said, "Oh my gawd, not everyone is going to the freakin' dance," then turned to look at Jennifer for a response, but she was busy giving googly eyes to Chad who was doing the same back with his perfect white-toothed smile and twinkling blue eyes and dimples that could fill up like swimming pools on a rainy day. *Ugh, I need a boyfriend. I'm already starting to mentally date my friend's guy.*

As Sheree waited for her friends, the car slowly began warming up to the point it was almost comfortable. Closing her eyes and breathing steadily, she tried to calm herself down, thinking only of puppies and rainbows. Puppies. Rainbows.

Puppies prancing over rainbows. Rainbow colored puppies. Puppy colored rainbows. Raining dogs. Raining cats and dogs. Rainbow fog. Teal fog. Teal mist filling her whole field of view. Teal mist enveloping the air and taking all the oxygen with it.

Suffocating.

Sheree opened her eyes to find that she was surrounded by a sea of blue-green fog-like mist that seemed most concentrated at the air vents, seeping through and swirling around her while taking her breath away… literally. She thought it would be ironic if "Take My Breath Away" was playing on the radio at the same time, but was thankful it wasn't because she hated that song. Since her nostrils seemed useless at breathing all of a sudden, she opened her mouth wide to take in a gulp but only inhaled a mouthful of the thick teal haze that burned her lungs and throat as if it was sulfur dioxide.

Must. Get. Out.

Reaching for the handle to open the door, she pulled but the door wouldn't budge. Her arms felt like boulders as she lifted them to pry the lock up, but it was already in the unlocked position. She could feel herself being pulled further down in her seat as her arms fell back down like bricks falling off a building during an earthquake.

Sinking.

Singing.

"The itsy bitsy spider went up the water spout…"

So this is how it ends, Kayla?

"Then came Jeff who tried to flush the spider out…"

Really? You had to say his name?

"But Jeff only got half and the other half will stay…"
And now for the big finish!
"As long as you simply stay out of the way!"

The supernatural fog disappeared through the air vents in reverse and they began blowing hot air again, bringing with it gas-flavored oxygen as Sheree filled up her lungs in large gulps that she knew would probably end up giving her the hiccups and cancer. When she finally felt like she could breath normally again, she asked herself, "What did I do to deserve a dead-sister-ghost-witch haunting me?" as Jennifer opened up the front passenger's side door for Sky to hop in before folding her wheelchair and putting it in the backseat.

"Be born," Sky offered, putting on her seatbelt.

"Live," Jennifer added as she pushed the chair over to the seat behind the driver's.

"I hate you both," Sheree said without looking at either of them.

Smiling a big goofy smile that made her eyes look like a televangelist after reaching her daily monetary goal, Sky turned to Sheree, grabbed her right arm, dug her head into her shoulder, and said, "I love you, Sunshine! Even the part that wants me dead!"

Then Jennifer leaned in, reaching her arms around Sheree's neck, and said, "I love you, too, Princess!"

Furious, Sheree shook her friends off of her and yelled, "You realize I have a very powerful witch trapped inside of me, right?! Why are you purposefully trying to piss me off?"

Sky laughed. "Oh no, Sunshine is angry. We should kill her with kindness!"

Jennifer laughed. "Princess needs love! Smother her with love!"

Then they proceeded to mockingly hug her and kiss her and make her feel all sorts of awkward until she couldn't handle it anymore and shouted, "Knock it off!"

"No, no! It's love!" Jennifer said in a small voice that vaguely sounded like Michael Jackson.

"Yeah, love!" Sky added in an eerily similar voice.

"Sweet Lord Jesus, I'm going to have to sneak into my parent's liquor cabinet when I get home because of you two," Sheree informed her friends.

An inordinately long pause followed. Then, without warning, all three girls started giggling uncontrollably to the point that Sky said she needed to stop before she peed herself.

After gathering her composure, Sheree asked, "So you said something about helping with our Algebra test, Miss Jennifer?"

Sky looked at her friends and said, "You have this magical psychic connection and you talk about homework? Oh my gawd, I need better friends. And a boyfriend. Or maybe just a guy to take me to the dance and then I can pawn him off on Frumpy or Body Odor or some other poor soul who couldn't get a date."

"The scary part is that everything you said makes total sense to me," Sheree said to Sky.

"Well, obviously I'm going with Chad," Jennifer said (to which both Sky and Sheree mouthed, "Obviously," to each other) before adding, "You could always ask Harry Wood from the squad!"

"Ew! Harry?" Sky said with her face twisting into a bunch like a wadded up T-shirt while at the same time Sheree said in total disgust as if being forced to eat a slimy mushroom, "Someone seriously named their child Harry Wood? That's unfortunate."

Shocked at both their reactions, Jennifer said, "C'mon! He's also a quarterback on the football team!" but by now she could no longer keep a straight face and burst into laughter as she tried to get out, "Give Harry Wood a chance!"

Chapter 5
Coming Out

"Yeah, everything was going great with my girlfriend and then all of a sudden she started talking about her feelings, and I was like, whatever," Brendon told his sister and mother after dinner Tuesday night while he loaded the last of the dishes into the dishwasher.

"Then what?" Sheree asked, leaning forward as she sat on a barstool next to her mother doing the same, though without a glass of wine in front of her to swirl around and stare into pensively.

"I dumped her," Brendon replied as if that was the most obvious thing to do.

"You dumped her?" Mrs. Hollins questioned to reaffirm, nearly spitting out the red wine she had just taken a drink of but quickly swallowing it instead as that would've been sacrilege.

"Uh, yeah. She was telling me about these feelings she was having in her stomach. I don't need to deal with that!" he said. "Besides, I know that I already got my flu shot for the year and all, but what if she had like meningococcal or some weird shhh…" – his eyes widened as he realized what he was about to say in front of his mother and quickly finished with – "…tuf like that!"

"That's harsh, Bren," Sheree told her littler brother, shaking her head ever so slightly that it barely moved her strawberry blond tresses that were shockingly not being strangled in a ponytail.

"No it isn't. Look at it this way…" He paused before his face lit up. "I was doing her a favor!"

"Huh?!" Sheree asked with a bewildered expression upon her face, arms up in the air. "How do you figure?"

"Well…" Brendon started before yelling out, "DAD!!!"

Mr. Hollins called out from the family room, "What do you want? I'm busy watching TV," to which Mrs. Hollins muttered under her breath, "You're always watching TV," which made Sheree burst out a short laugh she quickly smothered with the arm of her purple sweater she got for Christmas from Jennifer even though Jennifer is Buddhist and doesn't actually celebrate Christmas. Soft soft chenille, so lovely on the skin.

Rolling his eyes, Brendon told his father, "I've got something to tell you, all of you."

Getting up off the den couch, Mr. Hollins stated as he walked toward the kitchen, "Well it's a good thing my program went to commercial. Now what's so important?"

Brendon didn't waste any time. "Mom, Dad, Sheree… I'm gay."

"You're what?" Mrs. Hollins asked.

"Huh?" Sheree sputtered out.

"You're nine," Mr. Hollins told him.

"I'm gay, quit acting like you didn't know, and I'll be ten next week!" His eyes were wild.

"Okay, cool," Mr. Hollins said. "Do you need a hug or something?"

"No, but your show's back on," Brendon informed his father.

"Crap!" he yelled, running back to the couch and hoping he didn't miss anything important.

"You're what?" Mrs. Hollins repeated.

"Huh?" Sheree repeated.

"Oh dear gawd, people. Let me explain this to you as simply as possible. While my now ex-girlfriend says she had all these feeling in her stomach over me, I realized I didn't have them over her, but every time I see Tommy…" Brendon said, unable to finish as a goofy smile went over his face and his eyes began to glaze over as if he was suddenly daydreaming. "Tommy…" he said again. "He's so dreamy, with his chocolate donut eyes and swimming pool size dimples and adorable a… forementioned features!"

"Did I miss something about dimples suddenly becoming pool-sized?" Sheree asked with such innocence that the absurdity of her question was overlooked. "Because you are seriously the third person to use that phrase. Jennifer and Sky both commented on how Chad has swimming pool dimples."

"Oh, Chad…" Brendon said with a dreamy voice. "He's so cute, and yes, also has dimples that would fill up like swimming pools when it rains. Yeah, pretty sure he's gay too."

"Yeah, almost sure of it," Sheree confirmed.

"Amanda's pretty sure he is too," Mrs. Hollins said, cringing at her son talking about the neighbor kid, suddenly out of shock and taking another swig of wine to bite her tongue before she accidentally spilled out information they weren't yet in the know about. "That's Chad's mom. We're friends. We talk about our ungrateful children to each other at work. It's pathetic."

Putting his hand on his mom's shoulder, Brendon told her, "Mom, I think you've had enough wine for the night."

She said, "You're right," before finishing off the glass, getting up off the stool, giving Brendon a hug, then walking over to the den to cuddle with her husband while he watched some television show about some war that was very important.

Sheree grabbed the wine glass, went over to the sink to wash it off, and asked, "So, you're gay, huh?"

"Yep," Brendon responded.

"Then start dressing like it," she told him, staring at his uncoordinated outfit of mismatched socks, sweatpants with stains from Godknowswhat, and inside out and backwards T-Shirt that made him look like he had a white tongue on his throat just below a red tongue in his mouth.

"Stereotype much!" he snapped back with an actual snap.

Sheree couldn't help but laugh. "Wow, you are gay for like a minute and already got the sassy thing going. Give it a week and you'll be flamingly fabulous!" she said, singing the last two words with a high-pitched falsetto mimicking one of the Special Education teachers she was pretty certain had to be certifiably crazy.

"Crap! Valentine's Day is next week! Monday! Crap! What am I going to get Tommy to confess my undying love for him?" Brendon said to himself mostly.

There was another commercial break.

"I should call Jack and Billy and be all angry and ask how they could make Brendon gay!" Mr. Hollins announced after his zombie-like trance the television had on him was broken up with an ad for some erectile dysfunction drug.

"Oh no you don't, Frank!" Mrs. Hollins said firmly, although, to be fair, it probably wasn't as firm as she thought it was since the words were slightly slurred and slow to come out thanks to an excess of Merlot flowing in her bloodstream.

Brendon was still busily mentally working out what to get Tommy for Valentine's Day when Sheree asked, "Is Tommy even, you know?"

"Gay? I don't know. Kwirk thinks he is."

"C'mon Beth! It's only a prank. I was just kidding about that whole bit about the gays making more gays crap. Let me just have a little fun," Mr. Hollins said with pouty lips just like Brendon's Mrs. Hollins suddenly realized.

"I said no, and that is final," Mrs. Hollins said, standing her ground, though if she actually had to stand at that moment it would have been a fairly difficult task to accomplish. Truly it would have been a monumental feat.

"Kwirk? Does Mom know you are hanging out with him?" Sheree asked.

"No. Don't tell her, she'll freak out," Brendon said quietly.

"I told you to stay away from Kwirk Werewolf! That kid is trouble!" Mrs. Hollins shouted from the den.

Sighing heavily, Mr. Hollins told his wife, "You take away all my fun."

Smiling heartily, Mrs. Hollins told her husband, "That's what you get for saying 'I Do!'" then gave him a sloppy kiss that smeared her fuchsia lipstick halfway across her face like a French Revolution whore in a sketchy brothel and a lot of debt to work off.

Stretching her lower lip into an upside down smile as if to say EEK!, Sheree said, "I forgot that even Drunken Stupor Mom has superhuman hearing."

Rolling his eyes, Brendon shot back to his mother, "Why do you hate him so much? You don't even know him!"

Crawling over her husband's lap, Mrs. Hollins grabbed the arm of the sofa and shouted, "The boy tried to burn down the middle school! I work there! That's not okay!"

"That was an accident!" Brendon shouted back. "Besides, he didn't actually burn it down, did he? No!"

"You know, we could carry on this conversation like civilized people without shouting at each other if we were all in the same room," Sheree said, stating the obvious.

Mr. Hollins then did the unthinkable. He turned off the television.

"Oh, shit," Sheree said in disbelief at the events that were unfolding.

"That's it! Time for a family meeting!" her father announced, tossing the remote control onto the coffee table in front of him. Even it shivered.

These family meetings never ended well, at least where Brendon and Sheree were concerned. It always concluded with more chores or less allowance or a soda tax. Seriously, one time the whole meeting was about how they kids drank too much soda so their dad instilled a soda tax which they had to pay in order to drink the sugary soft drink. The Soda Tax Funds didn't last long because Sheree switched her caffeine intake to coffee-related beverages and Brendon quit cold turkey, which made him a bit shaky and crotchety for a few days afterwards before his system was able to fully adjust to living without the drug.

Both Brendon and Sheree had fake smiles on their faces as they entered the family room or den or whatever the room next to the living room was actually supposed to function as, and as they sat down, Sheree asked, "So Dad, what's up?"

"Well, Brendon had some pretty big news he shared with us tonight, and I think we should talk about this in a more respectful manner. You know, like a regular family," Mr. Hollins told everyone.

"But Dad, we aren't a regular family. I mean, how many nine-year olds can feel like they can safely come out to their parents in a nonchalant manner like I did?" Brendon asked, more pensive than usual.

Oh my gawd, I can't believe that Brendon is gay. And how does he even know the word 'nonchalant'? Sheree thought to herself, or so she thought.

Oh my gawd! Brendon's gay? Jennifer's voice said in her mind.

"Oh, Frank! We've raised such a brave and thoughtful young boy!" Mrs. Hollins cried, giving him a hug and wetting his face with her tears.

Yep. Flaming McFlamerson now. Says your boyfriend is too, Sheree thought with a bit of bitterness as she watched the boy get all the attention as usual because of his penis.

I know. Maybe I'll break up with him after the Valentine's Day Dance. I mean, we just picked out our outfits thanks to Courtney's advice, Jennifer thought, regretting the last remark, as she knew it would set Sheree off like a hog in Las Vegas during feeding time.

"We did!" Mr. Hollins pulled his son in closer for a three-way hug with his wife. "I love you so much, Brendon."

Maybe I should find out from Courtney what I should wear since I'm probably going stag anyway. Or maybe I'll make Sky come with me. She's kinda butch. People will buy the whole dyke thing and maybe leave us alone, except that she's also kinda boy-crazy and really wants your boyfriend even though he's gay and all but really, who is going to take her to the dance if I don't? I'll be doing her a favor, Sheree rambled on in her thought process, almost forgetting that the psychic connection with Jennifer was still open, and beginning to visibly turn red with anger as she watched the loving familial display play out in front of her. *I fucking hate my brother and his goddamned penis!*

No, you love your brother, penis and all, Jennifer thought but almost vomited in her mouth before adding, *But not in that creepy* Flowers in the Attic *way, just normal sister-brother love.*

"Come here, Sheree! Group hug!" Mrs. Hollins said with a face full of tears and a lipstick smear that reminded her of The Joker.

Relinquishing to the fact that if she didn't do this one thing for her family right here right now, she'd be forever branded as an asshole, she leaned in for the group hug. Her dad squeezed her tighter than she was expecting, joined by her mother's clammy hand then Brendon's plump arm, and all at once, all the anger and frustration she was building up for resenting her brother for having a penis was gone, replaced with a feeling of peace and love she hadn't fully been able to feel since before Jeff passed away.

Jennifer's voice popped into her head with, *I suppose this is as good of a time as any to tell you. Sky has a date to the dance. Harry Wood asked her out after cheerleading practice today.*

Chapter 6
Playing Games

"I still can't believe your brother is gay!" Jennifer announced the next morning as she walked up to Sheree at her locker.

"Oh my gawd, your brother is gay?" Sky said rather loudly. "Isn't he like in the fourth grade?"

Rolling her eyes and tired of hearing the word gay, Sheree turned to face her two very annoying best friends and said as calmly as she could even though she suddenly had the urge to stab them both in the throat with an ink pen, "Yes, it is true. My brother is a Friend of Dorothy."

"Who the hell is Dorothy?" Jennifer and Sky asked in unison, shocking them both since they didn't have the whole in-sync thing Jennifer and Sheree shared.

"Seriously? You've never heard that term? Whatever. Ask your faggot boyfriend, Jennifer. He'll tell you," Sheree told them coldly before she stormed off to first period.

Somewhat disturbed by Sheree saying the word 'faggot,' Jennifer fell into the lockers, shaking. This was not like Sheree. Sheree would never use that kind of language, especially with her newly identifying gay brother. She knew there was only one explanation, and it terrified her. "Sheree is slipping away."

"You've got that right. I mean I've never heard of Friend of Dorothy before, have you?" Sky asked, still trying to figure it out, starting to wheel her way down the hall with Jennifer by her side.

Smiling a half-smile down to her friend, Jennifer said, "What I mean is that Kayla is slowly taking over Sheree. That was a very Kayla thing to say."

"That's bad, isn't it?" Sky asked.

Jennifer nodded yes.

"What can we do to keep Sheree in control?" Sky asked.

Jennifer nodded no.

"Wizard of Oz!" Sky shouted like a bolt of lightning, slapping her mouth as soon as she blurted it out.

"What?!" Jennifer shouted back, throwing her free hand that wasn't carrying books up in the air.

"The Scarecrow, Tin Man, and Cowardly Lion are all friends of Dorothy in the *Wizard of Oz*, and they're also a bit gay-acting if you think about it. That's gotta be the reference," Sky said, pleased with herself for figuring it out.

"Hmmm... you might be on to something there, but I'm not quite sure. I never thought of them as representatives of the homosexual community," Jennifer told her friend.

"Says the person who is dating a gay guy!" Sky shot back.

"Ouch! Damn! You fight dirty!" Jennifer said, trying to sound truly hurt, but it came out more like she wanted to high-five Sky for her quick wit.

"Of course, even gay, I'd still totally date him if you ever broke up," Sky informed her friend, completely serious.

"Of course," Jennifer said, shrugging her shoulders as if that was completely obvious, which, of course, it was.

Sky stopped just outside her first period class and asked, "So how are we going to stop Sheree from crossing over to the dark side?"

Jennifer's eyes began to well up with tears just on the verge of bursting through as she said, "I don't know if we can," then walked away, wiping her face with the sleeve of her sweater as she quickly walked down the hall and disappeared after turning the corner they just went around to get to her class before the tardy bell rang.

In third period, Sheree seemed completely oblivious to her earlier comments when Sky asked her ever so gracefully, "What the hell was that all about this morning?"

"What?" Sheree asked, then laughed. "You guys were annoying me with all your questions about Brendon, so I decided to leave."

"Yeah, you left," Sky said. "But not until after telling Jennifer to go ask her..."—Sky looked around then leaned in closer to Sheree to whisper— "...faggot boyfriend what Friend of Dorothy means."

Sheree looked pale as a ghost as the blood drained from her face.

"I really said that?" Sheree asked.

Sky nodded yes.

"Oh my gawd. How did Jennifer take it?" Sheree asked, her face scrunched.

Sky nodded no.

Two girls walked in talking loudly about their chemistry project they were working on. Sheree recognized them as Kori and Ami. Seniors, both dating the same guy at the same time: John Upcock. It was the best thing Ravenwood could scavenge up for a scandal: a threesome.

They're probably making some new designer drug, Sheree thought as she watched them take their seats next to each other, continuing their conversation, not knowing that she was right. Her eyes began to get fiery red as she sat there, staring at them talking, making overly exaggerated hand gestures and smiling the whole time, probably both secretly wishing the other would drop out of the picture so they wouldn't have to share the finest male specimen at Ravenwood High School.

Sky noticed Sheree's rage building and quickly said something to extinguish it. "Chocolate?"

Shaking her head slightly to break the trance, Sheree turned to Sky and asked, "Seriously? I'd *kill* for some right now!"

"Well, please refrain from your homicidal tendencies and allow me to take out this magnificent Hershey Bar from my bag for your gastrointestinal gateway gratification," Sky said quite articulately as she did just that. "Here you are, my lady!"

"Oh my gawd, thank you! If I was gay, I'd kiss you on the mouth right now! Oh, screw it," Sheree told her friend before doing just what she said she wouldn't do because she's not a lesbian.

The kiss surprised Sky as she sat in her wheelchair completely frozen, eyes wide open, and watching the other students stare at them. *At least this got Kori and Ami to stop talking!* Sky thought.

"You girls know the rules against kissing on school property," their Algebra teacher said walking into the classroom, sounding more annoyed than surprised. "Break it up now."

Ending their embrace, Sheree quietly told Sky, "Thank you for the chocolate," before taking the bar out of her hand.

In the same quiet voice, Sky said, "Thank you for giving me more action than I've seen since the night your sister killed my boyfriend and crippled me!" far too enthusiastically.

"Well that's morbid," Sheree said, taking a bite of the chocolate bar and allowing her anger to fade to oblivion.

"It's the meds," Sky told her. "They've put me in a state where I feel everything and nothing all at once. It's hard to explain. It's gray."

Nodding her head, Sheree informed Sky, "I think I understand. With my psyche's emotional roller coaster and split personality complex, maybe I should also be on drugs."

Kori and Ami quickly stopped their conversation at the mention of the "D" word, looking rather paranoid someone might have overheard them and will rat them out. Sheree was just glad their chatter was over so she could focus on Algebra and chocolate as she licked her lips and suddenly started to cry as the cherry

ChapStick Sky must have used to moisten her lips from the dry Northwest winters reminded her of Jeff.

The classroom turned their gaze towards Sheree once again.

"Stop gawking, assholes. Obviously she's on her period," Sky lied to the entire class right before the bell rang.

The teacher gave Sky a free pass for cussing in class, another no-no along with kissing and passing notes and other typical teenager stuff because, quite honestly, he knew that his class was mostly filled with assholes.

❦   ❦   ❦

After Sheree and Sky had procured edibles for lunch, they went over to their usual table to sit with Jennifer who was already giggling incessantly at something Chad must have said to her when Harry Wood pulled up a chair.

"Hi, Sky," Harry said, smiling a goofy smile that seemed ill-fitted to his six-and-a half foot, two-hundred fifty pounds of muscled man-meat.

"Hi, Harry," Sky beamed back, blushing a horrifying shade of red that made her look like she had a bad case of rosacea.

Feeling left out and wanting to ruin everyone's day for having relationships while she was stuck with being possessed by the ghost of her dead twin sister for company, Sheree verbally vomited out, "Sky is an amazing kisser and she gave me chocolate. Try not to be jealous."

Harry looked hurt and turned on all at once. Typical boy. "You kissed Sheree?" he asked. "You haven't even kissed me!"

Still somewhat in shock at Sheree spilling their little Advanced Algebra smooch, even though she knew it would be all over the school by the time they saw each other again at cheerleading practice, Sky told him, "She kissed me! I swear to God, she kissed me!"

"But you gave her chocolate?" he asked. "You haven't even given me chocolate!"

"Because she's on her period!" Sky lied again, though saying it so loud it caught the attention of quite a few faculty and students nearby.

This caused Harry to burst out in uproarious laughter and Chad to spit up the bite of cherry pie that he'd just put into his mouth onto his lunch tray, which made Jennifer tell him, "Yeah, that's pretty much what it looks like, too," which caused Chad to run towards the boys bathroom to throw up.

"Oh, the wicked games we play," Sheree said before biting into previously frozen lasagna-like food product.

Harry lit up. "Speaking of games, I can't wait for Friday when we get to go up against Bay's cheerleading squad! We are so going to own them!"

Both Jennifer and Sky looked at him and tried to take in the absurdity of his statement.

"You do realize that it is a basketball game, not a cheerleading competition, right?" Jennifer asked Harry.

"Yeah, but…" Harry started, but was interrupted by Sky.

"You do know that as cheerleaders, we are like support staff. Interns. Gophers. 'You, fetch me my water' people, right?" Sky asked Harry.

Shaking his head and grinning at their ignorance, Harry informed the two new girls to the cheerleading team that, "You don't understand, do you? I may be a football player in the fall, but winter I'm all cheer. We are already set to go to Regionals, but after the recent accident, I have a feeling we won't be making it to Nationals."

This realization made him look sad.

"I didn't realize it was that big of a deal," Sky said, putting an arm around Harry to comfort him in his time of need.

"We'll totally step up our game and take out those Eagles!" Jennifer said emphatically.

"I can help break a few kneecaps if you'd like," Sheree offered in a gravelly voice that sent a chill through the air and shivers down the spines of all three of the other occupants of the table.

Jennifer and Sky shot Sheree a wide-eyed glare, and Harry piped up with, "Um, well, thanks Tonya Harding? But I don't think that it will be necessary to Nancy Kerrigan them. We'll simply have to do with destroying them with our mad cheer skills."

"C-R-O-W-S! Crows…" [*clap clap*] "…are the best!" Sheree mocked, though was actually rather impressive.

Jennifer and Sky looked at each other then looked at Sheree before saying in unison, "We're still better than you."

Looking shocked although she was anything but, Sheree shouted back, "You evil bitches!"

"You're evil bitches, Sheree! Seriously, look in the mirror and tell me which one of yourself you see!" Sky said rather matter-of-factly.

Punching Sky in the shoulder, Jennifer said, "What the hell, Sky? You can't just go around saying things like that."

Harry looked confused.

Chad sat down to find that there was a whole lot he missed out on while vomiting up the remainder of his stomach's contents into a public school toilet, just the thought of which made him queasy enough to throw up again.

"It's her damn period!" Sky lied again so the boys wouldn't get suspicious, not even surprised at how easily they came these days. "Her menstrual cycle is making her schizophrenic!"

Jennifer breathed a sigh of relief and Sheree rolled her eyes.

"Seriously, girl. You need to be on the pill to straighten out your hormones," Sky told her before taking a huge bite of cherry pie. "Speaking of hormonal, my mom said she'd take Jennifer and I home tonight after practice, so you're off the hook, Sheree."

Sheree felt a thousand bees attacking her all at once as Sky coolly told her that basically she wasn't needed. "Okay," she said quietly, looking down towards her half-eaten lunch and picking at it with her fork, suddenly no longer hungry.

It's probably for the best, Sheree, Jennifer said in Sheree's thoughts.

I know. Still, it hurts knowing that I can't control myself sometimes, Sheree said in Jennifer's thoughts.

I'm sorry. We'll figure a way out of this.

I hope so. I'm afraid that the longer she's inside me, the more powerful she gets.

Jennifer looked at Sheree solemnly and tried to conjure up a smile, but failed. *We will get through this.*

If only I had your faith.

After lunch, Jennifer was heading towards her fourth period class when she heard someone yell.

"Hey, you!" Courtney shouted as she walked towards Jennifer with a purpose. Stopping in front of her, she folded her arms across her chest and asked, "What the hell be goin' on with Sheree?"

Jennifer fumbled for words. "Sheree? Crap! What do you know? I mean, uh, nothing? Why do you ask?"

Without missing a beat, Courtney shot back, "Look, I don't know what kinda laced ganja you two be smokin' or whatevuh, but, like, that girl be messed up."

"Messed up?" Jennifer tried to play the part of the aloof friend, but even she thought she was doing a terrible job.

"Totally, girl. She be all like matchin' her denims. Sheree knows better than that! Who wears the same color jeans and denim shirt? Bitch looks like Levi Strauss took a shit all over her!" Courtney started laughing hysterically to the point her hair looked like it was laughing too before walking away. The laughs continued to echo down the hallway.

Shit, Sheree. This is bad.

What?

Please tell me you aren't wearing matching denims.

Son of a bitch.

Courtney is going to nail your ass, and not in a good way!

Crap. This is bad.

Fashion Emergency bad?

Worst. I don't even remember putting these clothes on.

Shit, that is bad.

Maybe I can go to the janitor's closet and toss a little bleach on my jeans?

That sounds like the worst idea you've ever had in your entire life.

The fourth period bell rang.

Can this day get any worse?

Shut your filthy mouth before it does!

Staring down the steep cliff just on the other side of Ravenwood forest, Sheree could barely breathe as the ghost of her dead sister held her in mid air, suspended over a stretch of rock that had split apart by a massive earthquake hundreds of years ago to form what appeared to be a near perfect circle that many assumed was a meteor impact crater upon first sight. Kayla just stared at her.

Stared with hatred.

Stared with rage.

Stared with hurt and anger and frustration.

Stared at her with those teal eyes that were identical to her own.

Then Kayla continued with her ritual. Continued saying the foreign words she couldn't understand. Words that seemed to take just a little part of her soul away with each new utterance, like plucking a daisy. Words she knew would eventually be the death of her.

Sheree looked around, trying to find a way to escape, but all she could think about was the bodies.

Her best friend.

Her brother.

Both dead.

Both twisted and mangled and tortured because they tried to help save her. The moonlight glistened off their glasslike doll eyes that were still wide open and filled with terror, and casting an eerie blue luminescence from their skin.

The stars danced in the night sky.

Kayla's gravelly voice grew louder and louder.

The moon shone brighter and brighter until it filled her entire spectrum of vision, causing the gruesome images of Jennifer and Brendon's broken bodies lying in unnatural positions to fade to nothingness but pure white light that felt so warm and inviting.

Is this heaven opening up for me?

Sheree opened her eyes to find nothing but her ceiling with the light on. It was all a nightmare. A horrible nightmare about how that night could have ended if everything hadn't gone the way it did. Feeling a presence, she turned her attention toward her bedroom door.

"Can I sleep in here with you tonight, Sheree?" Brendon asked with a shaky voice as he stood in the doorway holding the knob, praying the answer would be yes.

He looked so sad, so terrified, and so helpless at that moment. Was he having the same nightmare? It certainly wouldn't be the first time their dreams were connected.

"Of course, Bren," she told him, pulling back the covers on the right side of the bed.

He turned off the bedroom light, leaving the door open with the hall light on and hopped into the bed with his sister. "If I weren't gay, this would be a bit creepy at our ages, wouldn't it?"

"You're not even ten yet," Sheree said, tussling his brown hair. "Just allow yourself to be a kid for as long as you can."

"Thanks," Brendon responded, flashing a big toothy grin filled with big perfectly straight teeth inside his perfectly round head.

Tucking him into the bed, Sheree smiled back before saying, "Now get some sleep. We need to be awake before Mom and Dad find out we actually like each other."

"Agreed."

And they slept.

The next morning, Sheree awoke first. No more nightmares or thoughts of Kayla or hurting anyone or killing or anything bad, just peaceful slumber. She looked over to Brendon who looked like a hot mess with his hair completely tousled beyond anything a brush could work out and drool sliding down his cheek and onto his neck from his lower lip. She almost didn't have the heart to wake him up, but knew she better before…

"Good morning, you two!" Mrs. Hollins announced with an overjoyed smile on her abnormally perky pre-coffee morning face. "Frank! Grab the camera! We need to document this!"

But alas, by the time Mr. Hollins reached Sheree's bedroom with their ancient 35mm camera he'd had since a college photography class, it was too late. Brendon was out of the bed looking bewildered as to his whereabouts, eyes practically glued shut with sleep, and Sheree was putting the finishing touches on her hair and makeup for the photo shoot in case this ended up in a scrapbook or framed on the wall or worse, High School Yearbook. Disappointed at not being able to capture the moment, her parents left the room and went downstairs to make coffee and eat breakfast and watch the news before getting ready for work.

"That was close!" Sheree told Brendon with a sigh of relief.

He mumbled something nondescript before running into the closet door. Wiping the sleep from his eyes, he said, "Ugh. What the…? This is not my room! Crap. That's right. Mom and Dad didn't see us together, did they?"

Shaking her head from side to side, Sheree said with a slight smile, "I'm afraid they did, kiddo. Sorry."

"Crap."

"Hey, Brendon."

"Yeah?"

"I don't even care that they saw. I'm not sure how, but having you next to me while we sleep keeps the bad dreams away. It keeps Kayla away. Honestly, until I can figure out a way to get her out of my head, I'd really like to keep sleeping with you."

Looking a bit perplexed, he laughed, "You want to keep sleeping with your brother? Pervert."

Laughing as she realized her unfortunate choice of words, Sheree told him, "Well, it's a good thing your gay then, isn't it?"

"So does this mean we can have sleepovers and talk about boys and do each other's nails?" Brendon said, sounding far too flamboyant for a child his age.

"Brendon, you're not that gay," Sheree said.

"You're right. I'm just gay enough. And please, I'm a slob and I know it, so no fashion advice either, okay?" he pleaded.

"Crap! Fashion Committee! I've got to get going! We've got a meeting before school starts! Crap!" Sheree yelled, furiously throwing clothes out of her dresser and onto her unmade bed while Brendon took this as a cue to leave her be and possibly get away with eating her share of Lucky Charms since she'd probably have to skip breakfast to make it to her superficial committee meeting.

The Fashion Committee Meeting was a bust. It basically consisted of Courtney practically balking at the horrific dress selection at the town's only boutique and saying that they should all boycott it next dance unless they do something about what they have available for the fashion-forward female. Sheree barely got in the word "yeah" before Courtney continued her rant, which somehow melded into a ferocious hatred of the Hudson's Bay Eagles cheerleaders and how their coach is a traitor for leaving Ravenwood High a few years back and how they would dominate at Regionals even if they didn't have a chance to go to Nationals because two people died while trying to do a Wolf Wall. Sheree wished she'd stayed home and ate her Lucky Charms as she sat and watched Courtney's giant Afro bobble back and forth as she yakked and yakked and yakked like a Chatty Cathy doll pulling her own string over and over and over seemingly without taking a breath. It was mesmerizing.

"Let me in."

No.

"Earth to Sheree, wake up!" Courtney said loudly, violently shaking her shoulder.

"What?" Sheree said groggily as she lifted her head off her crossed arms over the desk she was sitting at. "Sorry, your hair rocking to and fro while you were talking must have put me into a sleeplike trance."

Not buying her excuse, even though it was probably the most valid one Sheree had ever given her, Courtney said, "Listen, girlfriend. First of all, you need to get yo' shit together if you wanna stay on this committee cuz Anna already threatenin' a vote to kick you off. And secondly, what the hell you think I should do with my hair? I swear to Lawd Geezus that it gotta mind of its own!"

At lunch, Sheree decided to tell Jennifer and Sky that Brendon was her beacon of calm, which she soon regretted with the coming onslaught of suggestions that came forth from her so-called friends.

"You should take him to the game tomorrow so you don't take out the other cheerleaders's kneecaps!" Sky suggested with such exuberance she practically floated off her wheelchair.

"I've got it! You can take Brendon to the Valentine's Dance so you don't kill anyone out of jealousy or malice or whatever reason Kayla's unfiltered rage focuses on!" Jennifer said with a squeal at her ingenious proposal that reminded Sheree of Ren off of the cartoon *The Ren & Stimpy Show* when he thinks he's come up with the best idea ever.

"I hate you both," Sheree told them before taking a bite of a hamburger that tasted more like it was boiled than fried.

However, they both had a point. Now she only had to convince her brother to be her date not only to tomorrow's basketball game but also to the Valentine's Dance. *Hmmm… maybe I should have Brendon invite Tommy to the game so they can have a pretend date even if Tommy doesn't know Brendon wants him to be his boyfriend.*

Holy crap! Brendon already has a pretend boyfriend! Jennifer's voice said, sneaking into her head.

Uh, it's a kid in his class he has a crush on who apparently has donuts for eyes and dimples big enough to swim in. I was just thinking of a way to make this whole Not-Really-Dating-Your-Nine-Year-Old-Brother thing work, Sheree's voice said in Jennifer's head.

Oh, that's so sweet! Already trying to hook your brother up with boys. You're like the best sister a gay nine-year old kid could ever ask for! Jennifer's voice said all gushy and lovey-dovey it was ridiculous.

"Seriously, bitches! We are the only ones at the table and I'm tired of being excluded. Can we use actual words so I can be involved in the conversation now?" Sky said, furious. "You're really starting to piss me off with how in-sync you are."

"But we are in-sync!" Jennifer said, beaming a toothy grin that made her eyes turn into squints like sliver moons.

"Yeah, we're totally N'Sync! I'm Justin," Sheree announced gleefully before turning to Jennifer with a look of disgust and continuing with, "you get to be Pineapple Head Chris."

"Ugh! Why do I always have to be Pineapple Head Chris?" Jennifer said in a playfully argumentative manner and looking the part of a deflated birthday balloon.

"Because I called Justin. Snooze you lose, biotch!" Sheree informed her friend.

"I don't like this game anymore," Jennifer said, pouting.

Sky giggled. "I think it's great! I'll take Lance! Oh, he's so dreamy!" She said, swooning in her wheelchair to the point she looked like she might just melt and dribble onto the mismatched vinyl-tiled cafeteria floor.

"Yeah, he'd be my second choice, but after Brendon came out I think some of his gaydar spilled over to me, and I'm pretty sure he's also a Friend of Dorothy. He just puts off that vibe," Sheree said nonchalantly while staring at what the school lunch ladies deemed an acceptable interpretation of a hamburger.

"Shut your whore mouth!" Sky screamed loudly, much to the chagrin of Mrs. O'Hurley who was walking by their table at the most inopportune time.

"Language, Sky!" she said, shaking her head and realizing that Sky's choice in friends was possibly having a very bad influence on her. Or a very good one.

Chapter 7
Emergency Family Meeting

"Knock knock," Sheree said, tapping on Brendon's open door after she got home from school.

Looking up from his *Super Samurai Slugs* comic book, Brendon asked in a gangsta rap voice, "Wazzup?" even going so far as to mimic the slight head lift that is normally associated with the greeting.

Letting out a heavy sigh, Sheree knew that if she didn't just let it all out in the open right then and there, she would never. And then she'd have to deal with either not going to the game to cheer on her cheer friends or killing the entire Hudson's Bay cheerleading squad, possibly taking out some of the basketball players in the process, which she'd already deemed was unacceptable. "I need you to be my date to the basketball game tomorrow and you should bring Tommy and it will be like a kinda-sorta date without actually having to be on a date okay?"

"That sounds awesome! Hot sweaty high school basketball boys and my number one crush, it'll be the best non-date ever!" Brendon said far more ecstatic than she was anticipating. *Super Samurai Slugs* were thrown to the floor during this grand announcement.

Another heavy sigh was released before Sheree added, "And I'll need you to be my date to the Valentine's Dance so I don't go all Carrie on the school."

Brendon didn't look as enthused at this proposition as the first, and understandably so. A potential non-date with a potential boyfriend was good, but going on an actual date with his older sister sounded as dirty as sleeping with her every night, even if it was for a noble cause to prevent their dead sister from, well, to put it lightly, kill everyone that ever mattered to them.

"I knew there would be a catch. Oh, the price we pay for love," he said before finishing with, "I accept your terms. Handshake?"

"Handshake," Sheree said, pushing out her hand into his before shaking their agreement and cementing the contract with sweaty palms that made her look at him with disgust before wiping off the moistness onto her blouse. "That's gross."

"Sorry!" Brendon said excitedly though with just a touch of sincerity. "You brought up the whole kinda-sorta date thing with Tommy and I got all nervous and heart pitter-pattery and stuff!"

Shaking her head in a yesward fashion, Sheree told him, "I get it. Or I used to get it with Jeff."

The realization that, even months after the death of her boyfriend, his sister was still having a hard time letting go hit

Brendon as his nose scrunched up and teeth clenched and lips parted in such a way that up would be a huge smile and down would be a huge frown but leaving it there in between showed empathetic pain before he quietly said, "I'm sorry."

"Don't be. Maybe I'll go have a date with Jeff at his grave before dinner tonight," Sheree told him before leaning over his bed to give him a hug that lasted longer than she originally planned, but just long enough to quiet her soul.

"I love you," Brendon said as they let go of each other.

"I love you, too," Sheree said as she heard the front door close, indicating that their mother had entered the residence.

"Whew! Perfect timing to end this!" Brendon said with a smile and relieved look on his face that they were not caught in the act of liking each other once again.

"That's for sure!" Sheree said laughingly before exiting his room and entering hers, shouting, "Hi, Mom!" first.

Nothing.

Silence.

"Mom?" Sheree called out, stepping backwards out of her room.

No response.

Just as Sheree put her foot down onto the first step of the creepy creaking staircase with its three obviously-recently-replaced balusters that magically appeared last Christmas just in time for family to celebrate the holiday even though they had been broken for nearly four months before, there was a ferocious amount of chatter coming from the kitchen. She just let that foot stay there, the other ready to run down or pull herself up to lock herself in a bedroom depending on the circumstance. Not with a real lock, mind you, despite multiple requests.

"Mom, is that you?" Sheree called out again, louder but with a hint of fear.

"I can help in case it isn't Mom."

No, you can't help.

"What are you so afraid of?"

You.

Oh my gawd, Kayla, why the hell can't you stay dead? Jennifer's voice popped in, breaking up the sibling rivalry.

It was Brendon who screamed loud enough to grab the attention of who or whatever was in the kitchen with, "MOOOOOOOOMMMMMMMMMM!!!" as he ran out of his room but was met with Sheree frozen at the top of the stairs.

"What do you want?!" Mrs. Hollins asked sternly as she put the phone to her chest and looking rather annoyed.

"I might have a possible date tomorrow and have nothing to wear, so you need to take me shopping!" he informed her as if it was the most important thing in the world.

"Oh my gawd, seriously?" Mrs. Hollins asked, though not really expecting an answer. "Mom, I'm going to have to call you back... Brendon needs me to take him shopping... Because he has a date with some boy... Yes, I know you've been telling me since he was born that he was gay... Uh huh... Okay... I'll tell him... Mom, really, your crisis is going to have to wait... Uh huh... Love you too, bye."

CLICK

"Are you freakin' kidding me?! You're gay for a day and already need to go shopping with your mother? Jesus, kid, learn not to be such a stereotype!" Mrs. Hollins said rather harshly, completely not like her.

Sheree decided that other foot needed to make a move down the stairs to find out what was going on with Grandma Lowell that caused their mother to act out of character even for someone possibly going through menopause or "the change" as some people liked to refer to it, as if saying what it really was would be some great sin against humanity or something. Once she reached the bottom, followed closely by her brother who seemed to be using her body as cover like they were entering a warzone and she was the front line soldier, she asked in the same gangsta voice her brother used only minutes earlier, "Wazzup?" head lift and all.

"It's nothing," their mother lied badly, decidedly not looking at either of her children as if that would make the lie less than what it really was.

Catholic guilt.

"It's something, otherwise you owe Brendon an apology and while you're at it, possibly his head that you chewed off at the neck and spit out onto the floor," Sheree told her mother more authoritatively than she intended. "Now seriously, what is going on that has your panties all in a bunch. Literally. I can see them all scrunched up under your skirt, Mom."

Looking at her own rear end, Mrs. Hollins said, "What? Seriously? Oh my gawd, I hope that hasn't been like that all day! I work in a damn middle school and those kids are devils! Shiiiiiiiiiiit…"

It was at that moment Sheree realized just how much like her mother she really was, even down to the final cussword stretch.

"Wardrobe note from co-chair of the Ravenwood High School Fashion Committee: Always wear a thong with slinky skirts to avoid embarrassing panty lines," Sheree said with her assertive wisdom.

"Okay, Mom, now tell us. I'm serious about needing you to take me shopping!" Brendon told his mother in a panic.

Shaking her head no, Mrs. Hollins tried to find a way out of it, but didn't seem able to do much of anything except cry as the front door flung open and their dad stood there in the open doorway wearing lilac scrubs that reminded Sheree of Easter, staring at his wife before they ran for each other; hugging; crying; mumbling nondescript sobs into each others shoulders. It was like watching a romantic movie or the end of a horror flick where the survivors feel the need to embrace.

"This is bad," Sheree piped up, wide eyed and morbidly curious.

"This is very bad," Brendon said in the same manner.

They watched as their parents held each other until it was simply unbearable to feel the cold rushing through the open door, filling the room with a chill not unlike the presence of Kayla. Sheree walked over to the door to close it with Brendon acting as her shadow still. As if in slow motion, Mr. and Mrs. Hollins allowed their arms to fall and their foreheads to connect but their eyes remained closed.

"I think we need another family meeting," Sheree said to break up the silence.

Eyes still closed, foreheads still connected, Mrs. Hollins said, "I think you're right."

Halfway between the den, their usual haunting grounds, and the formal living room, usually reserved for extended family get togethers and overflow seating during parties, they all instinctively went over to the dining room table, possibly the most uncomfortable place to have a conversation that might well last hours. Already feeling hunger pangs though it was only almost four o'clock according to the cuckoo clock that was just about to pop out four times cuckooing with each thrust to announce the time, Sheree hoped this would be quick and painless, but should've known better when her mother finally looked at both her and Brendon, smiling a half-assed smile that signaled the Oh-Shit-Hold-Onto-Your-Fucking-Hat! look.

However, nothing could've prepared Sheree for the first word to seep out of her mother's mouth.

"Kayla."

"Oh my gawd, no," Sheree said in horror, backing out of her chair and standing up. "No! No no no no NO!"

Her father put his hand out to catch her arm and pull her back down, "Please, you have to listen to what your mother has to say. Trust me, this is difficult for all of us."

Sheree hesitated. Her mother just said the name of her dead sister after frantically talking to her grandma. Nothing good was going to come out of this, nothing at all. But Sheree tried to subdue her fear and put it in the virtual bottle where her emotions used to find solace with each other before it cracked and leaked and overflowed last year. Instead of following her gut and running out of the house and out of the town of Ravenwood and out of everything that brought so much everything to her life, she calmed down and sat in her chair again and mentally prepared herself for whatever horrible news her mother was about to relay. She hated the fact that she couldn't erase the image racing through her mind of her dad as an Easter egg because of the color of his work clothes.

Brendon just stared in awe like a deer in headlights.

Like Kayla and the semi truck.

Bug.

Windshield.

Squish.

"First of all, I'm sorry for lying to you Sheree about your sister last year and calling you gullible after telling you that Kayla was a witch. Truth is, she was a very powerful witch, something my mother took great pride in since I was, well, never blessed with any Wiccan abilities. Second…"

"I know, Mom," Sheree said, trying to be sincere, but regretting the interruption.

"Please, let me finish what I have to say because if I don't say it all now, I swear to God I will open up a bottle of wine and drink myself into oblivion and try to forget about ever agreeing to tell you this," Mrs. Hollins said with clenched teeth and such restraint as if she was fighting back the urge to kill a puppy that just took a dump in her newly planted flower bed.

Nods from Sheree and Brendon indicated that the message was received: Loud and Clear.

Mrs. Hollins continued. "After... after..." Tears started flowing down her ugly cry face and Mr. Hollins grabbed her hand as if that would give her the strength to go on, which it must have because she started talking again. "After Kayla died, my mother would not let her go. She kept insisting that Kayla could defeat death. Even at her funeral, my mother simply would not believe that I could give up on my daughter so easily. Easy? Really? Her body was so broken and small! If I could have given up my life to save hers, I would have, but she was already gone! After that, I forbid all mentioning of her name, of her existence, of anything that reminded me of her because I couldn't live with the fact that I lived while she was taken away. This meant that I had to make my mother promise never to bring up her ideas that a four-year old witch could somehow cheat death. And she kept her promise... until about an hour ago when she called me at the school in such a panic I had to leave early. When I called her after getting home, she told me about her premonition that Kayla was trying to find her way back to the living world."

"Even Grandma wants this to happen, Sheree."

Shut up.

"She can't!" Brendon screamed, terrified.

Sheree put her hand on his, but decided that wasn't enough, so she pulled him closer to her; holding him like a baby; protecting him from danger; keeping him out of harms way. Or is it Harm's way? "Let Mom finish, Bren. This isn't the time."

"She says it is inevitable," their mother continued as if Brendon's outburst hadn't happened. "Kayla will return to us. It is only a matter of time."

Sheree could sense that Brendon was about to say something, so she used every bit of will power she had to conjure up a connection into his thoughts and said, *Not now! They can never know what Kayla did, do you understand?*

The confused look on his face told her that the connection was a success. She'd reached him.

How are you in my head?

Magic. Not literally. Well, maybe. It's a Kayla thing. I don't really know, quite honestly.

But, they know about her being a witch!

Yes, because practically all the girls in Mom's family are witches.

Really?

Really. Dad told me.

Holy shit! Crap! Don't tell Mom and Dad I cussed!

You cussed in your thoughts. Doesn't count.

Shit shit shit shit shit shit shit!

Don't go overboard now, Bren.

We can't tell them that she's inside your head and the only way she will live again is if you break down and let her?

Never.

I hope you know what you are doing.

I don't.

You could've lied to me.

I could never lie to the gay brother I'm dating and sleeping with.

Thanks for making me feel like a dirty whore.

Promise me you won't tell them.

I'm hesitatingly going to promise you.

Okay.

Promise me you won't do anything rash?

Crap, did Jennifer tell you about that rash? I swear it's eczema, not some awful STD!

Oh, really? You had to tell me that?

Well, I figure that since we are sleeping together, you should probably know about my past and present conditions.

I'm rethinking our planned dates and sleeping arrangements.

I'm joking. I promise I won't do anything rash.

Okay.

Okay.

The exchange lasted a mere four seconds thanks to Rapid-fire Brain-to-Brain Transmission Technology possibly made possible by the presence of magic and/or evil, which meant that they didn't have to worry about suspicious questioning from their parental units. In unison, they turned towards their parents and Brendon announced a little too enthusiastically with the fakest smile he could summon, "Group hug!"

Chapter 8
Preparing to Date Your Brother

Mr. Hollins ordered a pizza for dinner after their emergency family meeting was over, which meant that Sheree had just enough time to go to the cemetery and have a graveside date with her dead boyfriend. Her parents seemed to understand her need to visit him after the revelation that her twin sister who died twelve years ago was going to come back into their lives once again. If only they knew she was practically already back and trying to kill them all, but alas, Sheree felt the need to keep secrets even if they killed her… some literally. As she walked toward the cemetery just a few houses down at the back of Song's End, the dead end street she lived on, and appropriate use of the words 'dead end' considering the end was, after all, a cemetery filled with dead people, there were little hints in the February late afternoon that spring was just around the corner. The smell in the air had just a hint of chimney smoke, but carried with it a sweetness of cherry blossoms in the near distance.

Along the sidewalk, despite the fact that Ravenwood just had the coldest winter on record in decades, crocuses were sprouting and looked like they would burst open at any moment, their yellow stamens and purple petals only accentuating the Easter thoughts Sheree could not put out of her head over the last week, which she assumed was because Easter was filled with so much chocolate, and she really, really, really loved chocolate. Even though it was almost Valentine's Day, another chocolate-filled holiday, yes, but without a Valentine (other than her brother, of course), Sheree felt no need to buy chocolate for a day associated with love when her one true love lay six feet under the cold clay dirt of Ravenwood Cemetery.

Life was beginning to spring out of winter's death.

Jeff's grave was filled with death and decay. Rotting flowers and leaves were scattered over the gravestone to the point that, unless you knew exactly where it was, you'd miss it. Anger built up in Sheree as she stared at the unkempt plot and wondered why his parents would allow such a travesty when she suddenly realized it had been months since she, too, had last been to where his body was laid to rest.

So much rage.

So much pain.

So many emotions Sheree wasn't even surprised by her sudden maniacal outburst of tears and wailing as she fell to her knees and cried to the soggy ground. Courtney would have a tantrum and deem her unfit to continue co-chairing the Fashion Committee if she were to find her slumped into the slushy muck the recent rains brought forth; her red blouse and black skirt and grey pea coat all mingling with the brown mud and musty leaves and pathetic excuses for grass.

"Don't cry, Sheree."

"I can't help it, I miss you so much," Sheree said brokenly through hot tears that stung her cheek as the wintery winds lightly brushed against her face.

Jeff put his hand under Sheree's chin, lifting it up to look him in the eyes as he said again, "Don't cry, Sheree. I'm right here. I'll always be right here."

His blue eyes were sparkling. His brunette hair exactly as it was in life. His smile that could melt the Grinch's heart and cause it to grow three sizes too big even caused one to form on her own face.

"How long have I been dead?" Jeff asked like someone would ask the last time they saw a movie or ate a cheeseburger.

"Since October. Four months," Sheree told him, trying her best to keep any more tears from flowing, but failing miserably.

"That's all? It seems like forever."

"It feels like forever."

Jeff reached around Sheree and she leaned into him for a hug. And there they were, in the dirt, embracing for all and none to see. The silence between them spoke volumes, as words would have only ruined everything.

"The itsy bitsy spider went up the waterspout..."

Sheree tensed up, not out of fear, but from anger. *How dare you do this to me now!*

"Down came heaven's light and knocked the spider out..."

"You can ignore her, you know," Jeff said, his voice so calm and reassuring.

"If only it was that easy," Sheree told him, not daring to let go of his shoulders and back her arms were firmly wrapped around as if releasing her grip would release his very existence from her life.

"Now that Mom and Dad know, it's just a matter of time…"

She's not really here she's not really here she's not really here, Sheree thought to herself even though she knew otherwise, squeezing Jeff so hard she was amazed he didn't squish like a late September tomato.

"Before the itsy bitsy spider is released from this childish rhyme!"

Evil, vengeful, glorious laughter swept through the cemetery like morning fog: slow and covering everything in its tracks. It was deafening. So much so, Sheree didn't even realize her brother was standing right next to her.

"I know I'm intruding, but I'm scared and I need you," he said, looking so much smaller than he really was even though he was towering over her while she was sunk into the soft loam.

Jeff was gone.

Kayla's laughter was a distant ringing in her ear.

"You're not intruding," Sheree said as she relinquished her grip on the air between her and Jeff's headstone.

Brendon looked over his sister. She looked worse than the day a couple months earlier when they were out in the forest wandering aimlessly and exploring and digging through the mud for her missing locket. "I was going to ask for a hug, but you appear to be balls deep in the mud above your dead boyfriend."

A short laugh escaped Sheree's mouth. Even in all seriousness, her brother was still, well, her brother. He always had a sense of humor even when he didn't mean to. It was a personality trait that, while most of the time she despised because his humor was inordinately targeted towards her, she secretly hoped would never leave him.

"And that's saying something considering you don't even have balls," a voice from behind Brendon said, startling them both even though it was a familiar one.

"What are you doing here, Jennifer?" Sheree asked, now feeling even more humiliated that her brother and best friend had fodder for the herd of their relentless taunts by way of her completely mud-splattered dry-clean only clothing ensemble.

"The usual… Kayla. Gawd, your sister is such a bitch, she completely ruins my daytime fantasies about what I would do with Chad if he weren't, you know, gay and all. Ugh, I hate the gays sometimes. Present company partially excluded, of course," Jennifer informed them while looking at Brendon, still in her cheerleading practice outfit that looked quite at odds with the down filled parka she was wearing over it.

Brendon looked furious even though he had a smile on his face as he shouted, "YOU TOLD HER?!"

"C'mon, Bren," Sheree said back. "She's my best friend, we talk about everything."

"Then what am I?" another voice shouted from the closest walkway about a hundred feet from where they were. It was Sky.

Getting up off the ground, leaves and dead flowers scattering off her and kamikaze-ing to their figurative deaths, Sheree shouted back, "My other best friend with whom I talk about everything."

Scowling an evil scowl, Sky said, only slightly quieter but still rather impressively able to use her diaphragm for projecting her voice, "Except when you and the evil bitch monster also known as Jennifer are carrying on secret convos in your heads because that is what you evil bitch monsters do!"

Somewhat hurt and taken aback, Sheree wasn't sure if Sky was being serious or joking with them, but part of her knew there was a bit of truth to what she was saying. They did keep Sky out of the loop of a great many things. But it was for her own good, right? The less she knows the less her chances of being tagged with a bull's-eye as Kayla's next victim, right? Or so Sheree thought.

If only she knew the truth.

"Sky, you know we don't mean…" Sheree began to plead, but was interrupted by Sky.

"You totally know that I'm just joshing with you, right?" Sky revealed.

We totally walked into that one, Sheree thought.

I know, we totally did, Jennifer thought.

I can't believe I didn't see that one coming.

I know, right?

Crap! We're doing that thing we do that she accuses us of doing!

Crap! We need to stop doing this.

Why am I stuck in here with you two?! Brendon's voice cried in both Sheree and Jennifer's head.

Oh great, a threesome, Sheree thought, rolling her eyes which tipped Sky off that they were indeed carrying on a whole conversation without her even though she was right there in front of them which only irritated and depressed her even more.

I did not sign up for this when I suggested you start dating your brother, Jennifer thought, flashing Brendon a smile that made him feel dirty.

"GET OUT OF MY HEAD!!!" Brendon shouted before saying much quieter, index finger digging into his right temple, "I've got enough voices in here as it is," eluding to his insistence that he had one-hundred-ninety-two personalities all trapped inside his brain and all of whom were relentless in their efforts to come out on top. Especially Juan Benito, which is understandable considering he is the self-proclaimed Ruler of the Universe. John's a pedophile and Quabilah keeps everyone in order. Even he admits it's exhausting keeping track of everyone.

Sky couldn't help but feel hurt knowing that the only friends she had left in the entire world would be perfectly fine and probably never think twice about it if she simply disappeared and never came back. Poof! Gone. This thought terrified her. The look on her face must have given away her emotional state as Sheree and Jennifer both looked at her with sincerity while walking towards the path she was on. Brendon looked like he was having a mental argument with himself.

"I'm sorry, Sky," Sheree said first.

"Me, too," Jennifer said second.

Letting out a sigh and a tear from right eye, Sky said, "I know you don't mean it, just part of me wishes that I had that special connection you two have, you know?"

"You mean being tortured and almost killed by a maniacal ghost-witch with a fixation on spiders and nursery rhymes?" both Sheree and Jennifer said in unison, completely negating any sincerity the words might have offered since they were still N'Sync and Sheree was still Justin and Jennifer was, despite all efforts to avoid, Pineapple Head Chris.

"Goddammit, I hate you both!" Sky said as sternly as she could, but unable to hold in the laughter building up inside her as it burst out of her mouth like a plus-sized drag queen squeezed into a dress meant for someone about five sizes smaller than her right after stepping out on stage in six-inch stilettos, bursting at the seams then everything falling to pieces around her, exposing herself freely to a captive audience who didn't know whether to be aghast or cheer. Just try and get that image out of your head.

From where they all were, Sheree could see the pizza delivery guy pull up in front of her house, not giving any of them enough time to take in the exuberant laughter Sky was still belting out, though, be things as they may and breath only able to expel so much before requiring a refill, it was obviously on its descent.

"Brendon and I need to get home for dinner," Sheree said to her friends.

"What? You're not going to invite us over for dinner?" Jennifer asked, obviously offended.

"But…" Sheree started, but as usual, Sky interrupted, which really annoyed the hell out of Sheree since she had only ever known people who interrupt like that to have come from large families with a multitude of siblings and Sky was an only child.

"We came all this way and you deny us food and drink?" Sky asked, just as offended as Jennifer but looking even more so since she was wheelchair bound.

Fucking cripple.

Shut up, Kayla.

I swear to Buddha, if that bitch of a sister wasn't stuck inside your head I'd destroy her right here and now!

Make it stop, Sheree and Jennifer, please! My nine-year old brain can't handle this much input!

"I don't know if my mom would appreciate the extra company, what with the recent revelations during our emergency family meeting and all," Sheree forced herself to say out loud, trying her best to make her sister go away and stop spouting off horrible thoughts.

"Shuh, as if! Why do you think we are here?" Sky asked, as if the answer were obvious.

"We know," Jennifer said. "That whole Psychic Friends Network you and I are privy to was open during your family chat. I heard everything your brain was thinking. Like Easter."

"I've never met your parents so this will be a great excuse!" Sky announced, bubbly and cheerful, so incredibly different than she was just moments before.

"I don't know," Sheree said as Brendon walked up to where they were, finally joining them after mentally trying to rid himself of all things unpleasant. "I also don't know if it would be such a great idea to go to the game tomorrow with you, Brendon."

"What?!" he screamed, a sad rage behind his brown eyes. "You can't back out on my non-date date with my potential boyfriend! I already called Tommy and he already said yes!"

Sighing heavily, Sheree said, "It's official, I'm dating my brother."

"About time," Jennifer said, adding, "our small town hasn't had a good scandal in *years*!"

As they meandered the path back to the sidewalk on Song's End that would lead them all back to the Hollins residence, Jennifer and Sky ping-ponged a conversation as to the pros and cons of dating one's brother to sooth the violent outburst of a hell-bent spirit when Jennifer suddenly, mid-explanation of why it wouldn't technically be considered incest for also sleeping with one's brother, turned to Sky and told her, "Just so you are prepared, Mr. Hollins is hot. He's a total DILF."

"Really?" Sky asked intrigued, looking at Sheree and Brendon just steps away from their driveway as if either of them would confirm.

"Don't even make me answer that. It's bad enough what you guys are making me do with my little brother," Sheree answered.

Brendon on the other hand, despite being asked and ignoring questions and one-half of the brother-sister duo dominating the conversation, was apparently talking himself up to being brave enough to ask Tommy if he was also a boy who liked boys. "DILF? What does that even mean?" he asked, naively in between the dialogue he was carrying on inside his head.

"Oh my gawd, you two are corrupting my innocent little brother with your filthy whore mouths!" Sheree shouted as the front door opened and Mr. Hollins appeared dressed in a tight fitting T-shirt that showed off his upper body physique and soccer shorts that practically exposed his junk for the world to see thanks in no small part to the fact that polyester practically contours itself to the body and he probably wasn't even wearing underwear.

Leaning towards Jennifer, Sky whispered with her hand covering her mouth from his view, "Sweet Lord Jesus, he's a total DILF!"

Leaning back, opposite hand covering from view, "I told you."

"Company?" Mr. Hollins asked his children as they approached him.

"It would appear so," Sheree told him. "Is that okay?"

"Of course!" he said before continuing with, "Hi, Jennifer! You must be Sky?"

Blushing, Sky said back, "Are you just taking an innocent guess or is the fact that I'm the only person your daughter knows who's trapped in a wheelchair clue you in?"

Mr. Hollins seemed at a loss for words, and as he fumbled for what to say in response to that, either an apology or smartass remark or a combination of the two, Sheree said to reassure him, "She's got a wicked sense of humor, Dad. You're going to love her."

After everyone else was inside the Hollins's house, Sky sat there at the entrance and waited. She looked like José Nieto Velázquez in the famous painting *Las Meninas* by Diego Velázquez, watching the ignorant characters in the scene of either the King and Queen having their portrait painted by Diego Velázquez himself (because yes, he's that conceited) or the princess watching her ladies and a dwarf play with a dog (because dwarves and dogs are much more entertaining than parents when you are a princess) or whatever the painting is supposed to represent from the back of the room, practically unnoticed by its occupants as he is perfectly framed in the doorway.

"What are you…? Oh my gawd, I'm so sorry!" Sheree said as her and Jennifer went back for their friend and helped her cross the threshold which was a good six or seven or possibly eight inches up from the walkway leading to the door.

Without missing a beat as they lifted her up on either side, Sky started singing in her magnificent voice, which, given the recent mentioning of the Psychic Friends Network made it all the more relevant, Dionne Warwick's "That's What Friends Are For." Uproarious laughter ensued before the ritualistic consumption of delivery pizza, sans Mrs. Hollins's bottle of merlot and Mr. Hollins's bottles of porter as they apparently decided that the company would appreciate them not drinking themselves into oblivion, even though both of them felt a tinge of needing that tiny escape. Being present for their children was more important.

Once the pizza was devoured and paper towels and box tossed into the trash, Mrs. Hollins asked Brendon, "So, do you want me to take you shopping now?"

Both Jennifer and Sky lit up and said, "Shopping?!" together as if they were now in-sync.

Brendon looked nervous. "Um, yes?"

"What the hell? You practically forced me to get off the phone with my mother while we were talking about…"—she looked at Jennifer and Sky as if their faces would remind her what not to talk about—"…you know, stuff, and now you're not so sure?"

"I just don't know what to wear for a first non-date date with a boy who may or may not even like boys!" Brendon cried in desperation, letting his head fall over the back of the chair so his face looked up at the ceiling, making him even more pathetic.

Mr. Hollins chuckled. "Brendon, you are gay for a day and you already have a date? I think we need to have a conversation about the bees and the bees."

Looking at his father as if that was the most ridiculous thing he'd ever heard, Brendon told him, "I already got the gist from Uncle Billy and Uncle Jack last Christmas."

"Of course you did," Mr. Hollins said, looking partially hurt at not being able to have the one conversation most dads dread with their boys that he was secretly looking forward to, even if that boy liked other boys and he'd have to change the pronouns to adjust for gender. Then he mumbled under his breath just audible enough for Mrs. Hollins to hear, "I bet they got a frakking toaster or something for recruiting him, too."

A hard punch to his bicep told him that was probably not the appropriate response.

Mrs. Hollins looked furious as she said loudly but not overly loud as to frighten the dinner guests, "That's not funny!"

Rubbing his shoulder and realizing that Sober Beth was rather strong compared to Slightly Inebriated Beth or Drunken Beth, Mr. Hollins said, "Not even a little?"

"No, Frank!" Mrs. Hollins yelled, rolling her eyes at the absurdity.

"Well I think it is," Brendon piped up as if to announce that yes, indeed, there were other people in the dining room with his bickering parents who could hear their not-so-quiet altercation. "And they got a toaster oven, not just a toaster. Apparently the younger the…"

"Brendon! Do not indulge your father!" Mrs. Hollins shouted playfully, but was already starting to laugh.

Mr. Hollins was practically already on the floor, possibly due to the hilarity of the situation and also to use the table as a shield against any more of his wife's oncoming wrath.

Sheree simply looked at her friends and said, "Yeah, so, this is my family. Unfiltered."

Sky looked at her friends and said, "My parents barely acknowledge I'm even there most of the time, too absorbed in their own lives to care."

Jennifer looked at her friends and said, "My dad visits like once a month and even then it feels like pulling teeth just to have him stay at the house while my mother is completely oblivious or simply doesn't care what he does with his free time even if it involves sketchy foot massage places where I'm sure the foot isn't the body part being massaged as long as he gives us money to feed the Buddha and plot her revenge against you, Sheree, for not selling your hair to her so she could have it made into a wig."

The table was silent while Jennifer finished her parental rant.

"I must meet this woman," Sky announced, dead serious.

"I'd like to hear more about this foot massage place," Mr. Hollins said before running out of the room and into the den to avoid another punch in the arm from his wife.

Just as Mrs. Hollins was about to chase after her husband and give him a matching bruise on the other bicep, Brendon told her, "You know, maybe the ladies would like to help me instead."

"What, and I'm not a lady?" Mrs. Hollins asked, trying to sound hurt but not so much that he would renege and back out of his suggestion and force her to go shopping when she really just wanted to decompress after all of the day's unfolded laundry lay piled up in her emotional basket waiting to be put away.

"You're Mom. That is so much more than a lady," Brendon said, surprising even himself with that compliment.

Smiling one of those smiles that looks just on the verge of crying, Mrs. Hollins walked over to her purse, took out her wallet, pulled out a one-hundred-dollar bill and handed it to Brendon, telling him, "This should impress him."

Looking expectant, Sheree said, "If I'm taking him, I'll need money for gas."

Walking away, Mrs. Hollins turned her obviously-dyed-an-unnatural-shade-of-red-from-a-grocery-store-brand-of-hair-coloring head and said like a sassy black woman, "Then it sounds to me like you need to get a job," before cuddling up with her husband on the couch as he sat there without the television on, which was highly unusual. You could almost hear the "Mmm hmm" even though it was never uttered.

The way they were looking at each other told Sheree they'd better leave before witnessing a Very Special Episode of the Hollins

Family: How to Deal With the Fact That Your Parents Still Have Sex. "C'mon kids! To the mall!"

"Don't forget about me!" Sky called out from behind the other three as they all walked towards the front door. "Unless you want to see what a person in a wheelchair looks like when they fall over and face-plant concrete!"

"Shit, Sky, we're not that big of assholes!" Sheree said louder than she normally would have with her parents mere feet away. A quick glance told her that they were too enraptured in each other to take notice. Then they kissed. Then Sheree motioned for Sky to wheel herself out faster before she'd have to claw out her eyeballs and brick up the sockets and still probably wouldn't be able to get the image of old people making out from her mind. Sky opened her arms out as Jennifer and Sheree lifted her up as if she was about to sing again, but Sheree shouted, "Shut it! We don't have time! GO GO GO!!!"

Front door closed.

Racing to the little blue sedan.

Off they go.

Brendon broke the silence as they sped off toward the main road. "Whew! That was close!"

Sky looked back at him from the passenger seat and said, "They aren't my parents. Besides, your dad's a DILF!"

"Total DILF!" Jennifer agreed, laughing a schoolgirl laugh that made Sheree want to vomit.

"What's a DILF?!" Brendon asked again. "I don't understand why you dorks keep…"

"DON'T CALL ME A PENIS!" Jennifer shouted inches from his face, cutely furious but frightening nonetheless, like a lion or a screeching howler monkey.

"What? I didn't! Oh my gawd, I hate being nine! There are so many things I don't understand. Why can't I just be ten already?" Brendon cried so dramatically it was almost convincing.

"Next week, Brendon. Next week," Sheree told him in a mockingly reassuring way, turning onto Main Street and heading toward town to take her brother shopping for something to wear to a non-date date with a boy who is probably not even gay or know what gay is and then find him something fancy to wear so she could take him to the Valentine's Dance because, seriously, her life wasn't messed up enough. Including her clothes, which she forgot to change. "Son of a bitch!"

Shopping with Brendon pre-gay:

"You like this?"
"Sure."
Item thrown into cart.

Shopping with Brendon post-gay:

"You like this?"
"Oh my gawd! I would not be caught dead wearing something so dreadful as that horrible piece of trash! What do you think of this ascot?"
No items thrown into cart.
Cart empty after an hour and a half.
Why bother even having a cart?
Cart left in an aisle.
Yes, they were in a clothing store with aisles.

Jennifer sat in Sky's lap who, apparently never having been informed of how to act appropriate in public, proceeded to pretend like she's getting a lap dance and air-slapping Jennifer's tiny little ten-year-old boy ass while sit-dancing to the store's overhead music: "Seasons in the Sun" by Terry Jacks.

Just when Sheree thought that the night couldn't get any worse, the one person she really didn't want to run into shouted, "Hollins! Puhleeeze tell me that you not in this crappy ass store buyin' yo'self some crappy ass shit for the dance Saturday?"

It was Courtney.

"Uh, I'm helping my brother pick out some clothes?" Sheree said, but it sounded like more of a question, as if she really wasn't sure why she was there.

"How sweet," Courtney said, although the way it came out sounded anything but sincere. "They havin' a dance at the grade school or somethin'? Darryl didn't say anything about them also havin' a dance at the grade school."

To clarify, her little brother's name is Darryl. He's also in the fourth grade. He also may or may not be gay. Brendon hadn't gotten around to asking him, but he had his suspicions as he turned around to say, "Hi, Courtney! I never would have suspected you of shopping in a rundown place like the Clothes Depot Outlet Store."

Much to Sheree's disgust, they air kissed each other's cheeks like old British friends. She almost vomited. No, vomitted. With two Ts.

"So whatchoo need a new outfit fo'? Darryl didn't say nothin' 'bout no dance and he tells me everythang," Courtney said to Brendon as if she hadn't already announced it loud enough for the whole store to hear only seconds earlier.

"Two reasons. I've got a date tomorrow at the basketball game against Bay with someone, and also need to get some fancy duds for the Valentine's Dance. I'm Sheree's date," he told her.

Sheree turned red from both embarrassment and anger, especially when coupled with the fact that her outfit was completely smothered in mud. She picked off a dead carnation from her blouse and tossed it into a section of white striped polo shirts available in: Your Choice of Red, Blue, or Green for Only $4.99* [*with coupon]. The dead carnation stuck to the second button down of one, drastically improving its appeal.

Courtney looked more interested in their conversation than she'd looked interested in anything Sheree had ever seen her be. "Oh…" she feigned jealousy as her head pulled back. "Who's the lucky boy?"

"Tommy…" Brendon said dreamily.

"Seriously? Does the entire world already know you are gay, Brendon?" Sheree asked in shock.

"Not the entire world, but Darryl and Kwirk are like me two best friends. Of course they know!" Brendon said, letting a toothless grin form as he shrugged his shoulders.

"That's so sweet of you to take yo' brotha to the dance. I be takin' this piece of work," Courtney said, pointing toward her friend Nikki, a rather plain looking plump Russian girl. "She's frumpalicious. Frumpy now, yes, but given proper die-rection, girlfriend could be as deeelicious as a Russian teacake!" The way she said it made her Afro look like it was just as ecstatic about Russian teacakes, too.

"I can see that," Brendon said before adding, "And this store sucks. Next!"

"Did you really just say 'me two best friends'? American English, not English English, okay?" the Vietnamese girl said while shaking her head, still seated on Sky's lap who had, for the moment anyway, stopped air slapping her ass.

Brendon ignored her comments as they made their way out of the crappy store and into one that made his eyes light up like fireworks on the Fourth of July: Fabulous Freddy's Formalwear and Further (because it had to have an 'F', 'More' was out of the question). His excitement was short-lived as he caught sight of a price tag for a pair of socks he thought he would never be able to live without but realized it would take up his entire hundred-dollar budget to purchase. He looked crushed like an empty can of Coke about to be thrown into the recycle bin.

Courtney grabbed him by the arm and said cheerfully, "Follow me. Clearance stuff is always in the back! Like I tell my besties, just go straight fo' the rear!"

Mixed feelings were running through Sheree as she watched her sworn enemy helping her brother not only pick out clothes for his non-date date with Tommy, but also for the Valentine's Dance that she probably coordinated as well because she's an overachieving freshman who thinks she can do it all without compromising. Nobody has that much time to be able to attend meetings before school and cheerleading practice after school then take on charity work, because Nikki was definitely charity work, even if they'd been friends since the first day of kindergarten and inseparable since. When does she do her homework?

"Wouldn't it be a damn shame if that shelf accidentally fell on top of her?"

Yes it would. Go away.

"You know you want to do it."

That doesn't mean I will do it.

But before Sheree knew what was happening, her hands were already fidgeting with the bracket that anchored a heavy case of clothing, hidden behind a rack of button down shirts in a fabulous array of colors that made it look like a rainbow circle jerk. The screw was barely threaded in, making the work quick. Just as the case started to teeter, Sheree was brought back by someone shouting, "Courtney, look out!" It was Jennifer.

"That case is about to fall!" Sky shouted, grabbing Courtney's attention so she pulled Brendon out of the way before the case slid forward from the wall on one side, folded denim jeans falling to the floor, unraveling their perfect tucks into a mess of indigo.

It fell short of falling thanks to the anchor on the other side.

Sheree stood there, blankly staring.

Jennifer and Sky started towards them from the front of the store.

Courtney was asking Brendon if he was okay.

Nikki was nowhere to be found.

Blink.

Blink blink.

"Brendon, are you all right?" Sheree managed to force out once she was in control again, finally able to move her own feet to where she wanted them to move.

"I'm fine thanks to Courtney!" Brendon said with a huge smile on his face. "And look, we found two outfits for me!"

Showing off what Courtney and he managed to pull together in a matter of minutes compared to her hour and a half shopping bust they just went through made her furious. Jennifer grabbed Sheree's arm and opened her mouth and shoved a chocolate bar into it. The confusion was enough to bring her back once again as the chocolate slowly started to melt in her mouth and drool started to fall from her jowls like a Great Dane after lapping up water.

"Hey Court, what do you think of this?" Nikki asked as she walked out of the dressing room, staring down at the very girly and very unNikki-like red skintight dress she had on, straightening out the creases over her curves that were suddenly noticeable. Looking up, she saw the mess and frantic employees and her friend and other people she casually knew looking like messes themselves. "What the hell happened?"

"Denim wall came tumblin' down!" Courtney joked, laughing as if it was the funniest thing she'd ever said in her entire life. Her hair thought so, too.

"Did the prices fall with it?" Nikki joked back dryly.

Everyone started gawking at Nikki who looked absolutely ravishing.

"Girl, who you tryin' to snatch up with that thing?" Courtney asked, suspicious and showing just a tinge of jealousy and pride in her voice.

"Nobody," Nikki said back, expressionless as usual. *She's going to make a great spy someday.*

"Nobody gotta name?" Courtney tossed in her direction.

"Nobody's already taken," Nikki volleyed.

"Damn, cuz you is fine in that dress!" Courtney told her with the biggest smile her strawberry lips could make.

"She's right, you look amazing," Jennifer told her.

"I'd totally wear that, but being in a wheelchair and how short that thing is, everyone would have a prime view of my crotch!" Sky said boisterously, causing everyone except for the clerks frantically picking up the jeans off the floor and trying to figure out how the case got loose, and Sheree because she was busy having a moment with the chocolate that was shoved down her throat to avoid killing people, to laugh.

Must be Thursday.

Am I talking to Sheree? Jennifer's voice asked.

Um, I hope so, Sheree's voice answered. *How'd this chocolate get into my mouth? I mean, I'm not complaining, just somehow feel a bit violated.*

You tried to kill Courtney and Brendon.

"What?!" Sheree shouted out loud rather than in her head like she intended. *Quick, cover it up!* "You cannot be Nikki Boloski! You look stunning in that dress!" *Nice.*

"See, Nik? Even the girl who hates me and hates you by extension thinks you be lookin' hot. Buy it. Yo' daddy can afford it.

He did leave you a credit card befo' he left, right?" Courtney said, carrying on a series of questions and answering them for her friend before she had a chance to. Typical Courtney.

Looking to her right, she saw that a shelving unit had partly fallen over. A very heavy shelving unit that was right next to where she last remembered seeing Courtney and Brendon perusing a clearance rack. All color drained from her face as she thought to Jennifer, *I have no recollection of doing this. Did I really cause that to happen?*

Yes.

Shit.

What?

Every other time Kayla has gotten into my head, that's it, I know she's there but I'm still in control of my body. I'm becoming unstable. Like a degrading nuclear bomb. If I am starting to black out as Kayla takes over, I… I…

I don't understand how this is happening if Brendon is so close by.

Oh my gawd, is his presence no longer helping to subdue Kayla? I need to test a theory.

Now?

Yes now.

But there are so many people.

Exactly. Lots of people to stop me if things go wrong.

How?

Take the mannequin's arm off and hit me over the head!

Jennifer started to undo the arm.

Not now! If I lose control.

One must be prepared.

"Brendon, let me see what you picked out," Sheree said, bubbly so as to not attract too much attention, which wasn't difficult because Courtney and Sky were busy trumping up Nikki's confidence and using every dirty trick in the book to make her spill the beans as to who her taken crush might be but having no luck because, like all good spies, she could withstand torture.

Holding up an assortment of tops, bottoms, overs, and unders including a fancy pair of socks almost identical to the hundred-dollar pair but a fraction of a fraction of the price, Brendon looked so happy as he said, "Aren't these great?"

"Yes, uh huh. I need to make Kayla come out to find out if you really are my lucky charm or not so don't freak out on me okay?" Sheree said quickly, hoping to confuse him with the speed of the words evading her mouth.

"Okay. Wait, what?" Brendon said back, but it was too late.

Jennifer had her hand on the mannequin arm ready for mortal combat.

Summoning Kayla to the forefront was scarily easy for Sheree, who now had fiery red eyes where her aquamarine ones once were, and a wicked smile upon her face as she looked over to Brendon and said, "Hello, Little Brother. I didn't mean to almost take you out, it was meant for that black bitch over there smiling her fake smile and laughing her fake laugh. You would have merely been a casualty of war."

"Kayla!" Brendon said quietly but still alarmed as the clothes he was holding fell to the ground and a little pee dribbled out before he could stop it.

"Grab her hand, Brendon," Jennifer told him.

"Are you serious? She wants to kill me!"

"Grab it!" she said again, louder and more forceful, breaking the arm off the mannequin and slowly walking in their direction.

And he did.

And then Sheree was back.

"Arm not needed, but thanks Jen," Sheree said, smiling a forced smile as she realized her theory was true. "I'm sorry, Brendon, but apparently the only way to keep Kayla at bay is for you to be touching me."

Brendon deflated with realization. "So I have to hold your hand the entire time I'm on my non-date date with Tommy?"

"Well, I don't think you have to hold my hand since when we are sleeping you aren't holding my hand, but since my bed is small we inevitably are touching, so maybe just a little touching?" Sheree said, hoping not to disappoint him but knowing by the look on his face he was.

Rolling his eyes, Brendon said, "There goes my social life."

Courtney turned around and couldn't have dreamed up the scene in front of her if she tried. Sheree and Brendon holding hands while Jennifer held a mannequin arm in her hands like a sword next to three store clerks busily folding jeans and trying to fix the shelving unit with their hands. "Crazy Asian, you can't just take plastic people's arms. They need them!"

Sheree had to admit that Courtney really wasn't as much of a bitch as she made her out to be. Then again, she also had to admit that she didn't know if she could let go of Brendon for the rest of her life, which depressed her to no end, especially when her bladder signaled it needed to be emptied.

Chapter 9
My Brother, My Valentine

The basketball game was held at Hudson's Bay in Vancouver, so while Sheree drove Brendon and Tommy to the school, she had to consciously leave her arm down for Brendon to touch with some random part of his body. To avoid suspicion or gossip, Brendon chose his foot, never taking his eyes off of the boy he had an ever-growing crush on who seemed completely disinterested in whatever they were talking about and kept asking Sheree if she was a model. Just what she always hoped her Friday nights would be in high school.

The game itself was not much better.

Ravenwood High was already a good fifty points above Hudson's Bay before the second quarter was over, and between listening to her brother talk more than she'd ever heard him talk before to a boy who kept interrupting him to continue to ask Sheree if she was sure she wasn't a model because she could be if she wanted to, and watching her friends cheer better than the Eagles's cheerleading squad, Sheree was about to flip some shit. For reals, yo.

After Harry Wood casually tossed Jennifer up into the air then caught her ass in the palm of his hand, both smiling exaggerated stage smiles for the crowd to applaud, the scorned looks of Chad and Sky burned through the air between them nearly causing Harry to lose his grip which only made him squeeze harder which made Jennifer giggle as her lady regions were tickled which could have been a disaster worthy of an ambulance or coroner. The routine was soon over and Jennifer safely on the ground. Crisis averted. Sheree looked on with disinterest.

"You totally could be a model," Tommy said for the thousandth time like a broken record unable to skip over the rut in the groove.

"Yes. I am. I've just been lying to everyone trying to live a normal life as a sixteen-year-old high school girl to avoid the pressures of model life," Sheree said with such monotony that all the syllables sounded the same and were practically indistinguishable from one another.

"I knew it!" Tommy said, his excitement noticeable.

"I know, right?" Brendon asked, completely thrilled Tommy responded to something he said, clueless he hadn't.

Sheree rolled her eyes.

Tommy jiggled in his seat trying to make him just a little closer to Sheree, "I was talking to your sister, Brandon."

"Brendon," Brendon corrected.

"Whatever, so, like, when did you start modeling? What magazines are you in? Do you know Gisele Bündchen and Tyra Banks?" Tommy started, his questions rapid-fire like an automatic weapon and just as relentless.

"I was joking. Why don't you talk to Brendon? I mean, I'm just a chaperone for you two," Sheree said, rather annoyed and fighting the urge to move her foot away and break the link that kept Kayla from taking over her body so the evil twin could destroy the pesky little twerp.

"I don't even know Brandon that well. I only said yes because he said you'd be taking us," Tommy revealed.

"Brendon," Brendon said quietly and visibly beginning to tremble.

Asshole!

Moving her foot ever so slightly away from Brendon, he caught on, grabbed Sheree by the arm, put on a fake smile even though it was obvious tears were beginning to form, and said with counterfeit enthusiasm, "We should go get some fries!"

"Best idea yet!" Tommy said, not taking his eyes off Sheree like the preteen stalker he was.

Catching on to what Brendon was really asking, Sheree told Tommy with sugar in front of the spice behind her voice, "Why don't you hold our seats so we don't lose them, okay?"

Fortunately he agreed.

Getting up was easy. Walking through the barricade of people in the bleachers was not so much. Once they reached an aisle, they quickly made their way out of the gym and towards the concessions where Brendon broke down crying. He was crushed that his crush did not crush on him back. Instead of trying to ruin everything with words, Sheree just let him cry on her. Fortunately he hadn't yet decided to become one of those gays who wore mascara, because then her dry cleaning bill would have to come out of his allowance money and that would never happen and Sheree would be out a shirt. She'd never seen him this emotional and knew that it was only a small sign of things to come in the looming yet not-so-distant future. Middle school was going to toss this boy around like a shuttlecock; back and forth, back and forth, back and forth until he falls to the ground or gets stuck in a racket.

"French fries," Brendon said through muffled sobs. "I don't want Tommy to miss his model non-girlfriend too much."

Ruffling his soft brown hair, Sheree said back, "Want me to 'accidentally' mix Tabasco into his ketchup?"

"Thanks, but it probably won't matter if you do because he wouldn't notice as he'd be too absorbed in ogling over you and your tits," Brendon said before his bloodshot eyes widened to the size of saucers, "Don't tell Mom and Dad I said tits!"

They shared a laugh and it felt good, even though they'd have to face the obsessed stalker slash horrible friend once again soon. It was no coincidence they kept allowing people to take cuts in front of them as they stood in line to order their fries, deliberately wasting as much time as possible pretending to not know what they wanted to order before reentering the gym. They figured they'd waited just long enough when someone ordered what looked like the last of the French fries, meaning they'd have to make more, which would take more time.

A minute remained in the third quarter when they returned to their seats, Tommy beaming with excitement as Sheree scooted him down so there was nothing between the two of them in order to make the transition easier for Brendon who was trying his damnedest not to break down again in tears. She also felt the need to treat Tommy like a toddler so as to ruin his mental image of her.

"Does widdle Tommy-Wommy want a fwench fwy?" Sheree teased, giving her best performance to crush the little shit and pretending like the fry was an airplane heading towards his mouth. "Rrrrruhmm Rrrrruuhhmmm!"

Tommy's face was red as ketchup.

"Oh no, Tommy-Wommy's embowassed!" Brendon chimed in to alleviate the hurt.

The game was close, with Hudson's Bay apparently deciding to actually play the fourth quarter, but was not enough to win. Their cheerleaders looked as sad as the players, exhausted from trying to out-cheer the Ravenwood team who still were cheering hard despite the fact that the game was over and people were filing out of the gymnasium to celebrate their victory or sulk in their defeat. The look on Courtney's face was priceless as she yelled, "That's what you get when you don't bring it!"

Way to rub it in, Courtney.

Sheree, Brendon, and a visibly upset Tommy were heading down to the gym floor when Courtney, Jennifer, Chad, Harry and Sky all gathered to meet them. Chad and Harry were high-fiving each other, Jennifer and Sky were all giggles as they rode their emotional high, and Courtney looked Brendon straight in the eye and asked, "So is this that boy you like? Cuz if it is, honey, you could do so much better!" before her laughter ricocheted off the walls.

"What do you mean, 'like'?" Tommy asked, arms folded and still as red as a ripe tomato from his rejection.

"I mean," Brendon said with as much sass as he could muster, "that I liked you and thought you'd be a great boyfriend. But don't worry, honey, that ship has sailed."

"Huh? I don't get it," Tommy said, completely clueless.

"And you never will. Shotgun!" Brendon yelled, using the universal word to indicate that he got the front seat, leaving Tommy to the backseat by himself.

Tommy did not look amused.

The ride home was silent from the back, as Sheree and Brendon decided to listen to a Matchbox Twenty CD and sing along despite not knowing all the words. Except for the line on the second track "but no one else would take this shit from me" as they knew that one rather well, singing it to each other with enamored expressions. The song was eerily relevant to her life at that moment, she realized, as the words sunk in. She even went so far as to think that if her life were a movie or television show, this song would have to be on the soundtrack. Tommy still did not look amused at Brendon and Sheree's car karaoke rendition of "Long Day" or any other song on the CD, and didn't even say "goodbye" or "thank you" for the ride or anything as he got out of the car and stormed up to his house. Brendon couldn't help but feel bad for him, even if he did behave like an ass on their non-date date. Sheree put a hand on his shoulder and flashed him an award-winning smile. Seriously. She even had the seventh grade certificate framed and hanging in her bedroom to prove it. A small smile crept onto his face before she backed out of Tommy's driveway and they headed home.

Later that night as Sheree and Brendon lay in bed together, calf-to-calf, neither of them could sleep. Too much had gone on that day. Too many things did not go according to plan. Too often will this happen in life.

"This morning, I was so sure how much I liked Tommy, and now I want nothing more than to punch him in the gut," Brendon said to his big sister.

"That will pass," Sheree said to her little brother.

"Yeah."

"When you told me you were gay, you said you'd never change being a slob."

"Yeah."

"Then you practically begged Mom to take you shopping."

"Yeah."

"You wore fancy clothes for a boy who didn't even notice you were there."

"Okay, so I was wrong, all right? You win!" Brendon said loudly then slapped his hand over his mouth.

"That's not where I was going with this."

Brendon released the hand. "Oh."

"I was going to tell you that you should never have to change yourself for someone else. If you aren't genuinely you, you'll never be happy."

"But I really liked him and thought he might like me too."

"And if you aren't genuine, how can you expect anyone you like to be genuine too?"

"For a blond girl, you make a lot of sense."

Sheree smiled. "Like your absolute inability to give a compliment that isn't backhanded. That just wouldn't be you to tell me 'thank you, Sister. You make an excellent point'," though thinking about it, he had been rather nice lately and hadn't given a backhanded compliment in a while. Perhaps the fact that a psychotic monster was trapped inside her body and just about anything could set her off had something to do with it.

"But…"

"Brendon, what I'm trying to tell you is never change, especially for a boy. If they don't like you for you, they are not worth your time or effort."

"Thanks. I love you," Brendon told her, actually sincere.

"I love you, too. Now I just need to figure out what we're going to tell Mom and Dad when they find out we've been sleeping together," Sheree told him matter-of-factly.

"I wish you'd stop saying that, it makes me feel dirty," Brendon told her squeamishly.

The next morning, Sheree discovered that she was alone in her bed and that she was still herself despite all fears to the contrary. Having been separated the day before with school, Sheree knew there was another way to keep Kayla at bay: Chocolate. Jennifer's Chocolate Distraction Theory had its merits. It worked when Sky gave her a chocolate bar earlier that week during a rather unfortunate math meltdown, and it worked when Jennifer shoved one down her throat at the store. It worked throughout the school day, surprising Sheree just how long a Tootsie Roll could last if you just leave it in your mouth like a hunk of chew. Of course, Jennifer was prepared to knock her out with a heavy dose of injectable anesthesia she stole from the nurse's office, not even knowing under what circumstances that would be needed. However, she was still Sheree and lacking in either Brendon or chocolate, and she was utterly confused. Well, confused until she opened her mouth to let out a morning yawn and a Hershey Kiss dropped down and she started choking on it. Leaning over the side of her bed, still trying to cough up the Kiss, she found Brendon had apparently fallen off and landed on the hardwood floor of her bedroom, face first. The Kiss dislodged and hit Brendon in the eye. He did not appear to notice.

"What the hell, Brendon?" Sheree screamed, quickly reaching for a body part of his to latch on to. Pinky toe won.

Groggily coming to, Brendon found himself on the floor and completely disoriented as to how he could have managed to end up in that position. "What? Why am I… where's my five-dollar?"

Seeing that he was clutching a five-dollar bill, Sheree decided to play along. "It's in your hand."

"Oh. I'm too tired to sleep," he said, head dropping back down onto the floor with a loud *THUD!*

Rolling her eyes and still holding onto his small toe, Sheree said, "Obviously. How'd I end up with a Kiss on my lips last night?"

Brendon's eyes shot open like a bullet train. "I didn't kiss you last night! Did I? Oh my gawd, this will totally ruin my reputation! Oh, the scandal!" he wailed before asking, "Why is there a five-dollar bill in my hand and what is all over my eye? Is it poop?"

"I have no idea about the money, and I spit out the Hershey Kiss that was resting on my lips and almost choked on when I opened my mouth. It landed in your eye when I managed to cough it back up," Sheree informed him while looking at her nails and wondering if her brother would be opposed to getting a manicure with her before the dance. Hers were in desperate need of one. His still had ketchup from last night's fries.

"Whew!" Brendon said, full of relief. "I had to pee real bad last night and didn't want to wake you up so I tried to put a little piece of chocolate in your mouth but you sleep with such pursed lips it was impossible to pry them open so I had to take my chances and leave it on top of your lips so I didn't wet your bed. Really, you should be thanking me."

"Thank you." It was anything but sincere, especially when she realized that he used his bare hands to place said Kiss on her lips, and obviously didn't wash them after using the bathroom. "Good thing Jennifer's theory works, huh?"

"Yeah."

"Too bad I can't just eat chocolate all day long and not gain weight or get diabetes so you don't have to be my talisman, huh?"

"Yeah."

"I need to poop."

Brendon deflated. "Yeah, I was afraid of that."

The Valentine's Dance had Courtney's name written all over it. This pissed Sheree off more than she was expecting it to. For one thing, she and Courtney had actually been on good terms since Thursday night, so much so that Friday morning Courtney sought her out for advice on some last minute changes that needed to be made for the dance. It made her sick… and jealous. If Courtney weren't around, Sheree definitely would have filled the role of the most popular freshman that everyone loved and hated and feared. Then again, word spread pretty quickly about her spider hallucinations and threatening to kill the entire cheerleading squad during tryouts, so perhaps they were on equal ground, only with her popularity being in the Loony Bin category rather than the Sit With Us At Lunch At The Cool Table category.

Courtney caught her glare and rushed over before Sheree could make an exit. "Gurrrrrlll! You look dressed to *kill*!"

"Uh, thanks," Sheree mumbled. "You look amazing as usual. I love what you've done with your hair."

"You do?" Courtney said, scrunching up her nose. "I almost didn't do it cuz I thought you'd hate it and then we'd be all hatey and shit and Valentine's is for love!" before she hugged Sheree and made Brendon feel awkward while he stood there waiting for it all to end, staring at the origami roses stashed in small clusters throughout her Afro and wondering if she folded them all herself or had one of her minions do it.

Staring at Courtney made Sheree think of chocolate, probably because her skin tone was of the milk chocolate variety and just as silky smooth. Her mouth continued to move up and down with her red tongue swishing back and forth conjured up a chocolate covered cherry. Her eyes sparkled like lacquered truffles laced with gold flakes she'd seen in a magazine for rich and famous people who had so much money they could eat gold and make their poop shimmer in their rose petal laced toilets. Her delicate fingers might be Tootsie Rolls she could suck on before nibbling and chewing them, taking in all their delicious juices. "Chocolate!" she cried out loud uncontrollably.

"Buttercup, you gonna have to start puttin' out if you wanna start callin' me pet names!" Courtney said, bursting out into uproarious laughter that caused a couple paper roses to fall to her feet. She casually kicked them aside with her six-inch open-toed blood red stilettos.

There was a look of absolute horror upon Sheree's face as she realized what she had said and done. The color drained from her face so quickly she looked white as a ghost as Courtney stared back at her. Brendon stared at the origami roses on the ground, hoping nobody stepped on them before he could pick them up.

"Damn, girl, you know I just teasin' you! We gotta whole table of chocolate delights to indulge in over by the punch, so you just have yo'self a few and tell me all about it later, 'kay?" Courtney said with a smile that three days ago Sheree would have thought to be fake but now found to be genuine before she disappeared into the crowd to meet and greet and pretend like she was the hostess to this fabulous party even though she was only one of the architects for a high school dance.

Bel Biv Devoe's "Poison" hung in the air as Sheree and Brendon spotted Jennifer and Chad wearing adorably matchy-matchy outfits just walking into the magically transformed school gym, and Harry Wood walking alongside Sky wheeling away from the backdrop where a photographer was busily snatching up pictures of happy couples.

"This song is so retro!" Sky squealed upon approaching her friends.

"Totally retro!" Jennifer agreed, squeezing Chad so tight he looked like he might just burst out of his white tux with red cummerbund and bowtie that practically mirrored the white dress with red sash around Jennifer's waist and a smaller version of a bowtie around her bare neck.

The cuteness was enough to make Sheree puke. Fortunately she didn't. Instead, she said, "I love Bel Biv Devoe! We should dance!"

"Yeah!" Jennifer shouted far too enthusiastically like maybe she had been drinking before coming to the dance, which would have been completely not like her.

Maybe her dad's in town.

"Sounds great to me!" Chad said, sweeping Jennifer onto the dance floor and probably about to perform something he saw in a musical, though given the beat of the song, Sheree couldn't figure out which one.

Brendon looked less than thrilled, but decided to indulge his sister anyway so she didn't make any rash decisions that would cause his other sister who hated everything to crash the party and destroy the entire universe or something drastic like that. "You ready?" he asked, decidedly not smiling a fake smile as a reminder of only being genuine from here on out.

"Yeah, you coming, Sky?" Sheree asked her friend who seemed a little awkward in her wheelchair next to a guy that was easily three times her size.

"Uh… um… er…" Sky fumbled for words.

Harry Wood knelt down beside Sky and asked in a gentle voice one would not expect to come out of a person his size, "Please don't take this the wrong way, but if you want, I can sit on your lap and we can sit dance together which might crush you and break your wheelchair and then I'd have to explain that to your parents, or I can pick you up and hold you so we can dance."

"You mean so you carry me like a baby?" Sky said in her usual deadpan that made it difficult to tell whether she was joking or not.

"Or I could put Baby in a corner and dance with someone else," Harry Wood said back in the same deadpan manner.

Not being one to let a moment pass that she couldn't use a line from a movie, Sky said back dramatically, "Nobody puts Baby in a corner!" before holding out her arms for Harry Wood to pick her up and awkwardly dance to a song that was decidedly difficult to dance to in the first place, especially for a bunch of white folk and an Asian.

Giving his sister a stern look, Brendon said, "Do not get any ideas."

"You weigh too much," Sheree told him.

"That hurt. It's not my fault I'm chubby."

"You're right, it's pizza's fault."

"Yeah, pizza."

"I'm sorry, Bren. Let's go crazy on the dance floor. I'll even let you lead."

Prince's "Let's Go Crazy" started playing immediately after Sheree said the words.

"That was creepy, but also a sign! C'mon!" Brendon shouted as he pulled his older sister out to the middle of the dance floor, pocketful of chocolate to pop into her mouth every time he decided to let go to get his groove on, especially for the guitar solo. One must have two hands free to perform this after all.

But for all the love in the air when the evening started, sadly much waned before the evening was fully over. Sky was having a heated argument in one corner with Harry Wood who looked like he was about to explode. Jennifer was yelling at Chad for something he may or may not have even done and he was crying profusely like a sprinkler system or Liza Minnelli. Brendon and Sheree were too busy indulging in the chocolates to take notice of their surroundings until they heard Harry Wood shout, "Go to hell, Sky!" and Jennifer shout, "Gawd, Chad, you are such an asshole!" at the same time before they both stormed out of the gym.

"That ain't no way to end a Valentine's Dance," Courtney stated from behind them, causing Sheree to drop her punch cup, which fortunately was almost empty.

From where Sheree stood, she could see Sky was crying on her left while Chad was crying on her right and was suddenly conflicted as to whom she should go over to comfort. Sky was her friend, but Jennifer was so cruel to Chad she almost felt responsible for getting them together in the first place. Suddenly her answer came in the form of a once frumpy girl he never even took notice of before despite their years of friendship.

"Oh, snap! I did not see that comin'!" Courtney said with actual shock in her voice. "Russian Teacake's crush is Chadwick Walker? Lawd have mercy on his soul!" before walking off to use the ladies room.

Giving his sister a look of utter repulsion, Brendon said, "Chad still doesn't know he's gay, does he?"

"Apparently not. And apparently Nikki moves fast, they're already making out!" Sheree said, astonished at the speed of which Jennifer broke his heart and Nikki snatched it up and repaired it. The whole scenario was a matter of seconds. High school.

"Go check on Sky, and don't forget to take some chocolates with you. I'll be right here, okay?" Brendon said, acting more mature than Sheree was used to.

Sheree smiled.

Before Sheree had even reached her friend, Sky started talking through angry tears. "What the hell is wrong with me? A guy shows a tiny amount of interest in me and I make him feel like shit for wanting to date a fucking invalid!"

"You're a piece of work, Sky," Sheree said, deciding to use sarcasm rather than consolation for this round.

"I know I am."

"Seriously, Harry Wood is hot! I mean, how many six-and-a-half-foot guys with a body and face like that do you think exist in the greater realm of the high school experience?" Sheree asked without expecting an answer before adding, "That stud could be a porn star if the rest of him was as well furnished."

A laugh escaped Sky's mouth.

Mission: Accomplished.

They both caught sight of Nikki and Chad in obvious need of a room.

"And it appears my chances with Chad are also out. Strike two for the night," Sky said with a sad smile and laugh to match as she wiped the tears from her face with a tissue.

"I'm sorry, Sky. I'm a bad friend," Sheree said with truffle-laced words.

"No you're not," Sky told her, taking her hand

"Yes, I am. Apparently I never informed you of what mascara to use, especially when there is a possibility of the night ending in a full on cry session," Sheree said, dead serious.

Horrified, Sky asked, "Oh my gawd, is it that bad?" but she didn't need an answer from Sheree to tell her, the look on Brendon's face was enough. "Shit."

"Indeed. Let's go find Jennifer," Sheree suggested forcefully. "She's probably in the nearest toilet stall crying and cussing up a storm in a flurry of English and Vietnamese."

And she was right. Walking into the nearest girl's restroom revealed Courtney trying to calm down a thoroughly inconsolable Jennifer through a closed door. "I can see right through the crack, Girlfriend," Courtney told her as if this would be news. "Stop ignorin' me."

The next few words Jennifer shouted could not be made out as nobody in the bathroom spoke Vietnamese, however, they didn't sound like words that would be part of a friendly conversation.

Finally an English word snuck in that they all recognized: "FUCKER!"

"I thought you said he's not a fucker and that's why you were going to break up with him. Something about being a chronic masturbator?" Sheree reminded her friend, hoping the same sarcastic non-consolation would work with Jennifer as it did with Sky.

It didn't.

If anything it made her more enraged.

"GODDAMNEDMOTHERFUCKINGCOCK-SUCKINGSONOFABITCH!!!" Jennifer shouted at the top of her lungs.

"What the hell, Jennifer?" Sheree asked.

Her sobs quieted down a bit before she answered, "He didn't notice my shoes."

Sky laughed. Sheree stood there, shocked that this was what her best friend's idea of break-up worthy behavior consisted of. And Courtney put her hand on the stall and said, shaking her head no, "Chad is my best and closest friend, but that rat bastard needs to die and go to hell my sweet little Banh Bo Nuong."

The fact that Courtney of all people knew not only a Vietnamese dessert, but also Jennifer's favorite cake of all time and called her it was enough to break her anger for just a moment and allow a short chuckle to surface. "Thanks, Court. He doesn't need to die, he just needs to get a clue."

"Mmm hmm, you got that right," Courtney agreed.

Sheree and Sky were silent.

The door burst open, revealing a distraught Brendon announcing, "I think I need a therapist after watching Chad make out with Nikki! They're licking each other's faces like lollipops!"

Silence.

An origami rose fell out of Courtney's hair onto the bathroom floor. The sound was deafening.

The stall door opened and Jennifer walked out and said without any readable expression on her face, "Seriously?"

In unison, all four of them said with hesitation in their voices, "Yes?"

"Why is he kissing another girl if he's gay? Oh Buddha, what have I done?!" before the wailing continued, sans curse words.

Looking around at all the single ladies in the restroom and her brother by her side, Sheree said with a tinge of repulsion, "I never would have guessed that of all the couples that came to the dance tonight, by the end it would only be you and I. My brother, my Valentine."

"Ugh, don't remind me. I was totally rooting for Harry and Sky to make it out on top, but alas, that hunk of man-meat was gone faster than Mom can down a bottle of wine!" Brendon said with so much sassiness it reminded Courtney of herself; his gayness shining brighter and brighter with each passing minute like the sun through a rainbow flag. At this rate, he'd be a flaming queen by Monday.

"Reign it in, Brendon. You're not that gay," Sheree reminded her brother

"How am I supposed to find out unless I try?" he asked.

"You are too young to be that expressive."

"But I have to explore!"

"You have to be a kid."

"I will not be oppressed!"

"I'm not oppressing you!"

"This is who I am!"

"No it's not!"

The room was silent once again. Even the sobs of Jennifer were quieted for the time being.

Awkward.

"You're right. I'm a chubby gay with a passion for greasy pizza and no fashion sense. I'm doomed."

The four girls in the girl's school bathroom all leaned into Brendon and hugged him and said, "You're not doomed!" "You have me!" "We'll teach you how to dress to impress!" "Now I want pizza." That last one came from Sky.

"Oh, that sounds goooooood. You don't s'pose Ravenwood Bar & Grill is still open, do ya'?" Courtney asked, rubbing her stomach as the universal symbol of hunger.

"It's Saturday night and it's a bar, of course it's still open," Jennifer told her.

"Then what are we waiting for! To my car, now!" Sheree shouted, opening the restroom door to let everyone out.

Stopping after Jennifer was out of earshot, Courtney asked Sheree, "What about Nikki and Chad? I don't feel right leaving them here alone?"

Sheree found it amusing how her ghetto talk could switch so quickly back to proper English. Then again, Courtney was an enigma.

"They can walk home. I mean, they both live on the same street and only a couple houses down from each other. They'll be fine," Sheree told her, but quickly added as the concern on Courtney's face grew. "We should check on them before we head out just in case, though, okay?"

"Okay!" Courtney said, bubbly.

As predicted, Chad and Nikki were still making out without any adult supervision or intervention. For a moment it looked like Chad was making a move for Nikki's left boob, but then his hand reached up for her hair instead, entangling his fingers within it.

"See, they're fine," Sheree stated.

"Oh, my lil' baby's all grown up!" Courtney mock-cried, wiping away a tear that was never there. "Two days ago was the first time I got her to wear a dress since kindergarten and now she's all stealin' boys and suckin' face. I fear my work is done."

"You know he's gay, right?" Sheree asked with caution.

"Obviously. Known since the third grade when we became besties. I don't want no straight boy defilin' my Nikki!" Courtney said as if the question were completely absurd.

"Sadly, that was the same logic I used to get him and Jennifer together. I fear we are more alike than I'd like to admit," Sheree confessed, putting another chocolate candy into her mouth since her brother was nowhere to be found and probably waiting for her at the car.

"Ebony and Ivory!" Courtney started singing.

"Please stop," Sheree implored.

"Hehehe… girl, I misjudged you!" Courtney told her, grabbing her by the arm and skipping through the halls in a way no person in six-inch stilettos should be able to do. "Ravenwood Tavern, here we come!"

Chapter 10
Barely Holding On

Sunday consisted of sleeping in. Normally this would be a good thing, but given the opportunity, Mr. and Mrs. Hollins took advantage of the situation and got that picture they missed out on the other day.

Monday, being Valentine's Day, was the easiest for Sheree to get away with eating chocolate all day and avoid suspicion. Jennifer and Sky ordered Candy Grams to be delivered every ten minutes throughout the day to Sheree, each inscribed with a note as if from a secret lover. By lunch, the whole school was talking about it and trying to guess who the boy or boys might be. By the end of the day, every girl in school was jealous and every guy hated her guts.

Tuesday, Sheree appeared to be flaunting the fact that she got so many Candy Grams that even if she were to eat everything at a steady constant rate, she'd still have leftovers by the weekend.

Jennifer and Sky may have gone overboard. Now she just looked like a jackass.

Wednesday, having been Kayla-free for the sixth day in a row, Sheree decided to allow a little more time between chocolate fixes. She even went so far as to tell her brother that maybe he could sleep in his own room that night. He reluctantly agreed, only because he was exhausted from having to consciously keep contact even while unconscious. While her daytime was rather unremarkable, her dreams without her brother around to protect her were intolerable.

As she lay in bed alone, just beginning to fall asleep, pleasant images gathered... at first. It didn't take long for those happy bunnies and kittens to turn into rabid animals with sharp, blood-tinged fangs before morphing into creepy, crawly, large, hairy spiders.

"Again with the spiders?" Sheree said in her dream that was quickly becoming a nightmare.

One of the spiders, about the same size as her, walked up with its eight hairy legs and thousands of eyes all staring directly at her, and said, "Of course, Sheree. What other form would you prefer I take?"

It was obviously Kayla.

"I'd prefer you didn't take form at all," Sheree told the spider slash sister.

Managing a frown, the spider responded with, "Why would you say such an awful thing like that?"

"Because you are a murderer and a sadistic bitch," Sheree said in her dream as she suddenly watched herself in the third person while knowing what third-person Sheree was thinking. Dreams are weird like that sometimes.

The moonlight hit the spider fur and made it all shimmer teal. "Oh, Sister, you don't really feel like that, do you?"

"Yes, Sister, I do."

Sheree had to admit that it felt more real than not, but at the same time knew that she was dreaming even if the conversation was actually happening between her dead twin sister and herself. Crazier things have happened, so she decided to go with it. After all, Kayla wasn't trying to kill anyone… yet.

The spider morphed into a morbidly beautiful combination of its former self and Kayla, as if Kayla wasn't sure she completely wanted to reveal herself. Perhaps she just felt more comfortable as her chosen symbol of horror. Or maybe it was the fact that she wasn't as powerful as she once was, either by the constant presence of Brendon or Sheree's unsustainable amount of chocolate consumption keeping her from fully being able to represent her true self. Either way, Sheree felt oddly more at ease with Spiderwoman Kayla than Spider Kayla or Evil Ghost Witch Kayla, as if the combination negated each other's terror factors.

A smile crept onto Spiderwoman Kayla's glowing teal face. Sheree had to admit that the image was hard to stop staring at, after all, being twins, it was like looking into a mirror or what could have been her had circumstances been reversed. Of course, she would have had to be a witch, which she wasn't, and she would have also had to be evil, which she only pretended to be.

"My dear sweet Sheree, my evolution is inevitable! Why don't you just give in?" Spiderwoman Kayla asked with such sweet bitterness it made Sheree shudder as her truths struck a chord.

It was true that Kayla would have to return to the real world. It was true that Sheree was beginning to wear down, barely holding on to her life anymore. It was also true that she was going to do everything in her power to stop all of this from happening, even if it meant suicide.

Suicide.

Suddenly the idea was there and she couldn't get it out.

Spiderwoman Kayla sensed this as well. The fear in her eyes was real. Obviously she never predicted that Sheree would even think such a thing was possible, but there it was, out in the open and difficult to ignore.

Sheree stared at her sister, thinking she may finally have a way to rid herself and everyone she loved from the wrath of this evil monster once and for all. The only thing it required was for her to give up her life. To cease to exist. In essence, die. And she had to do it alone. Nobody else could bear responsibility for making the world a safer place. Too many lives had already been lost, most senselessly and without reason.

Spiderwoman Kayla was shivering, and as she shivered, the spider fur and extra legs fell off like tissue paper as it floated to the ground revealing a four-year-old girl. It was the Kayla that Sheree remembered. The one who used to knock over her stuffed animals during tea parties and cuddle with at night to keep the bad dreams away. It was the innocent child begging for her life as it was snatched away so cruelly.

In the background, though sounding as if right in front of her, Sheree could hear the screeching brakes of the semi-truck that crushed Kayla that fateful day twelve years ago, along with the sound of breaking bones and horrified screams.

So long ago.

So present.

Looking at the little girl in front of her, Sheree told her, "I wish it didn't have to come to this."

The child began to cry. "What can I do to make you change your mind? I'm not ready to die yet?"

She looked so small and helpless and it reminded her of Brendon. "You are already dead, Kayla. This is true whether you accept it or not."

The child's tears were streaming and her face becoming visibly red from fear. "This isn't fair."

"Life's not fair."

"Neither is death."

"That's not my fault."

"What makes you think your fate will be any different than mine?"

The question caused Sheree to pause. What did she mean by that? "Are you saying that I will end up like you, stuck in limbo?"

"I didn't ask to be like this."

"Yes you did! You put a spell on me and shoved your spirit into my head! You not only asked for it, you made it happen!"

The child paused, contemplating what she'd just been told as if it was news to her. "This is true, but now that we are so intertwined, me being a part of you and you of me, who's to say we won't end up in limbo forever glued together?"

This thought didn't sit well with Sheree. Suicide was supposed to release her from this hell, not prolong it for eternity. Was Kayla only saying this to survive the measly existence she'd granted herself after death, or did her threats have merit?

And so they stood there in a nondescript field that was too green with a sky that was too blue in a setting she didn't recognize where everything had an eerie glow to it like the place was radioactive, and stared at each other, waiting for the other to make a move. One proposed death would end them both while the other proposed that death would only lead to conjoined purgatory. Neither option was particularly appealing.

"I'm willing to call your bluff and end this once and for all," Sheree said decisively, even though the thought terrified her.

The child stared at her with unblinking eyes for what seemed like hours.

Checkmate.

"I'm willing to stay away for a while if and only if you promise not to kill yourself, Sheree," the child informed her.

"Are you serious?" Sheree asked, unsure if she could trust Kayla, knowing she shouldn't; wanting to find a way to live and keep on living; needing to be normal again, whatever that means.

"I don't want you to die, Sister. I just want to live. Perhaps some time will help me figure out a way to make that happen without destroying us both," the child said as she morphed into a sixteen-year-old version that looked like a mirror to Sheree.

Sheree couldn't believe what she was being offered, even if that time was limited. It was a chance to be normal for a short while before making a decision that would alter so many lives around her. It was a chance to be free from the fear of accidentally killing off people because they pissed her off. It was a chance she was willing to take on one condition. "I need you to promise me that you will keep your end of the bargain."

"Is my word not good enough for you?" Kayla's gravelly voice asked with a tinge of vengeance masked by a cloak of trepidation.

Pulling from behind her back a doll, Sheree said again, "I need you to promise me."

Kayla's eyes saw the doll and immediately recognized it. Casey. Her beloved doll; the one she tried to save from getting run over in the road; the one that ultimately was the death of her. Her eyes began to well up with tears. "I promise."

Half expecting the doll to make her sister go back to the four-year-old, Sheree stood there with the bald plastic baby doll in her hands. "I know this won't make you go away completely, and I know that this is really just a temporary truce, but if I give her to you, I also need to make sure you understand that if you go back on your word I will have no choice but to kill myself, even if there is only a slim chance of taking you with me."

The tears from Kayla's unblinking eyes staring at her precious baby doll were sparkling with radiance from a light source Sheree could not locate. Their teal color so surreal, even in this dream, they looked like two small rivers carving their way through cheeks and jawline and neck before disappearing into the abyss.

"I understand," Kayla managed.

As Sheree passed Casey, the ugly baby doll her sister loved more than anything in the world over to Kayla, she couldn't help but feel like this was a mistake trusting her. However, she didn't have much time to contemplate matters as the sight of Kayla faded out of view so quickly after the hand-off that it made her quite nauseous, suddenly waking up to the sight of Brendon holding her hand in her bedroom with the light of dawn just beginning to break through her window. He didn't look so small anymore.

"I tried to get here faster," he told her, squeezing her hand tight.

Sheree smiled. "I'm glad you didn't."

"Don't believe her. Don't trust her," Brendon said.

"You practically stole that line from Captain Kirk, you know that, right?" Sheree said, laughing just enough to break the tension.

"Of course I do. It doesn't make it any less true," he said, so convinced of what he was trying to tell her.

"I realize that, but you also have to realize that if I didn't make a compromise, I'd lose myself completely. I couldn't justify living if it meant Kayla would be the one calling the shots. You understand, don't you?" she pleaded for his support, his acceptance that she did not have any other choice.

He stood over her, holding her hand, staring at her, trying to figure out what to say next. What came out of his mouth was not expected. "I guess Mariah Carey sang it best..." and then started singing "Without You" even though she was only one of like a dozen people or groups to sing that song, that version of it was the one they knew best because their parents had the CD.

This song must also be on the soundtrack of her life, she decided.

"Happy birthday, Brendon," Sheree told him, squeezing his hand just a little tighter.

A smile formed on his chubby face as the realization hit him. "Oh my gawd, I'm finally TEN!!!"

"Just because you are ten, doesn't mean that life will be all rainbows and puppies," Sheree told her brother, hoping to extinguish his happiness.

"Of course it won't be!" Brendon said gleefully, "But at least I won't be a single digit age anymore! I'm practically a preteenager! My newfound homosexuality will be totally legit! People will have to take me serious now that I have two numbers in my age!"

His logic was astounding.

Chapter 11
Freedom

It had been so long since Sheree felt normal that she almost forgot what it was like. What it felt like, she decided, was amazing. Her fears of eating so much chocolate that she would feel the urge to give it up for the rest of her life were a thing of the past. Sleeping with her brother was also (thank God) a thing of the past. Even getting shit from Courtney for whatever random thing she was doing wrong was a thing of the past as they quickly became good friends, though decidedly not as close of friends as she was with Jennifer and Sky, who at this very moment were discussing boys and how freeing being single was during lunch.

"I still can't believe how quickly Chad rebounded. I mean, that has got to be a record or something," Jennifer said nonchalantly as if she wasn't talking about her own ex-boyfriend but some other girl's.

"Right? It's just so weird, because I thought for sure he'd realize that without you by his side that he'd look at his dick and get turned on and realize he was gay. But no! Nikki Boloski slapped her ass on his lap and they started swishing their tongues around like someone paid her to do it!" Sky responded, her expression like mock shock. "You don't think someone paid her, do you?"

Sheree listened to the two of them go back and forth for a while before deciding to join the conversation. "Honestly I thought that Nikki and Courtney were lesbians. I had no idea that Nikki even liked boys until she was macking on Chad."

"Me too!" Jennifer shouted louder than she intended to, hoping that nobody noticed her outburst because this is high school and things like being noticed when you don't want to be noticed are bad but not being noticed when you want to be noticed is really bad.

"Seriously, look at them?" Sky said, pointing in the direction Chad and Nikki were seated in the cafeteria, unable to keep their hands off each other, before shouting loud enough for them to hear, "Get a room!"

Chad ignored the suggestion. Nikki flipped her off. Courtney and her hair laughed and laughed and laughed.

"Ugh. I hate how happy he looks. Doesn't he look happy? I don't think he was ever that happy with me. Shit, I ruin everything," Jennifer said, mostly to herself as she watched her ex-boyfriend and his new girlfriend explore each other's mouths with their tongues in ways that made her nostalgic for the days they used to do the same.

"What?!" Sky screamed, throwing her hands up into the air. "I call bullshit on that. I screwed up majorly with Harry Wood."

"As hairy wood can do. I mean, c'mon guys! Trim the bush to make the tree look bigger!" Jennifer said, laughing.

"It's such a basic concept!" Sky said back, making scissor motions with her fingers while holding an imaginary penis.

Harry Wood entered the cafeteria and immediately saw Sky. He put his head down, and walked to the other end before disappearing into the crowd.

"Awkward…" Sheree said, her eyes wide open and slowly turning to face the opposite direction.

"Totally awkward, especially since we're still on the cheerleading squad. He hasn't said a single word to me since Saturday," Sky told her friends.

"Well, you are kind of responsible for that, you know," Sheree told Sky, shaking her head yes with a smirk on her face.

"Yeah. I mean, he's totally fuckable, but he's a horrible dancer," Sky said rather matter-of-factly as she popped a grape into her mouth.

"Says the girl in a wheelchair," Jennifer said before taking a drink of chocolate milk in a paper carton.

"Well, I haven't even thought of dating again since my boyfriend was killed by my evil twin sister's ghost," Sheree said, shoving half a slice of School Lunch Board Approved Pizza down her throat.

"Depressing much!" Sky said, pushing her head back to the point it made her look like she had five chins.

"Sweet Buddha, never do that again!" Jennifer told Sky.

"Agreed, it makes you look like Jabba the Hut," Sheree concurred.

"Really?" Jennifer asked Sheree. "I was thinking an uncircumcised penis."

Sheree and Sky both looked like they were going to vomit.

"And where would you have seen an uncircumcised penis?" Sheree asked, cloyingly curious.

"My dad," Jennifer told them as both took a drink.

Chocolate milk and Sprite mingled together in mid air before landing on all of them in some form or another. Whoever invented the Egg Cream never intended lemon-lime flavoring to be a welcome addition for good reason.

"Why the hell did I ask?!" Sheree shouted, patting her shirt with a napkin.

"I don't know, Sheree, but I will never forgive you!" Sky said, crying as she tried to do the same.

"Are you telling me you've never seen your parents naked?" Jennifer asked quite seriously. "I've seen mine naked so many times I lost count!"

"Never," Sky said, still blotting. "And I thank God every day for that!"

"Once, and I've tried to forget it since!" Sheree said, spitting on the napkin to get out a rather stubborn chocolate stain, but knowing that she'd be doomed for the rest of the day with it in the center of her shirt for the whole school to see and make fun of her.

"Really?" Jennifer and Sky said in unison with genuine enthusiasm.

"Your dad is totally hung, isn't he?" Jennifer asked, all smiles.

"Seriously, he's got a pretty big dick, doesn't he?" Sky asked, also all smiles.

"Jesus Christ, people! I'm not going to tell you how big my dad's penis is!" Sheree shouted. A few heads turned from nearby tables. She turned red with embarrassment. *Oh my gawd, please turn invisible right now.* Alas, her prayers were not answered.

"You're right, we don't need you to tell us," Jennifer told Sheree, reaching her hand across the table to pat her shoulder.

"Yeah, I mean, we pretty much already know the answer thanks to those shorts he was wearing last week, don't we Jennifer?" Sky said, nudging Jennifer with her elbow and winking.

"Mmm hmm. Praise be to Buddha for soccer shorts!" Jennifer said, allocating some of her lunch as if she was going to take it home and place it upon his alter.

"He's such a DILF!" Sky said back as if in ecstasy.

"You guys are disgusting," Sheree told them, giving up on the stain and surrendering to the fact that it was just going to have to stay and be the bulls-eye fate had in store for her that day.

Then, as if to make matters worse, Jennifer and Sky started pounding the table and shouting, "DILF! DILF! DILF!" over and over and over again.

I'm regretting not killing myself this morning.

Chapter 12
Rainbows and Puppies

After school was over, Sheree said goodbye to her friends as they headed off to the gym for cheerleading practice. As much as she'd have loved to stay and watch The Battle of the Exes, it was her brother's birthday and she wanted to get home to decorate for his party.

Due to Brendon's recent announcement that he was gay, Mr. Hollins decided all the décor should be rainbows. Mrs. Hollins thought something a little subtler would be better. Mr. Hollins doubled the amount of rainbow decorations he'd already purchased. Mrs. Hollins agreed that rainbows would be perfect.

By the time Sheree pulled up to the house, she realized it was too late. Someone beat her to the decorating. As she walked over a yellow brick patterned carpet and through the archway of balloons resembling a rainbow to get to the front door, she knew that her Uncle Billy and Uncle Jack were already inside. Of course, the fact that their car was parked on the street in front of the house was also a dead giveaway. Taking a deep breath to prepare herself for what lie in front of her, she opened the door.

"Sheree!" came shouts from the living room and dining room.

"Oh. My. Gawd. Dad, you've totally gone overboard," Sheree told her father, knowing that this was definitely all his idea as this was too gay even for the gays.

"He may have a little bit," Uncle Billy said, giving her a hug.

"I don't know, it's beginning to grow on me," Uncle Jack said, hugging her on the other side so that she was now the Oreo filling between the two cookies.

"Where should I hang the 'Pin the Hag on the Fag' game?" her dad asked.

"Please tell me you're joking?" Sheree begged, but the stern wide-eyed looks from Uncle Billy and Uncle Jack told her he was not. "How about somewhere out of the way. Don't want Mom to freak out because kids are pinning hags to her drapes now do we?"

"Excellent point. Front window it is. I hate these curtains. Maybe we should put the cake over here too in case the kids decide they want to use these nasty things for napkins!" her dad said, overly excited and showing no signs of remorse for hoping his wife's beloved musty faded family heirlooms get destroyed by fourth grade terrors.

"Mom is totally going to kill you," Sheree told her father.

With a completely serious look on his face, he responded with, "She'll have to crush her only son's dreams of having a fabulous birthday party in the process. I win."

The penis always wins.

While she helped her dad place the game next to the front window as close to the drapes as possible, Uncle Billy and Uncle Jack rearranged the living room to make it more conducive to a party. The antique side table her mother never allowed any food to be on housed the cake, which was centered in the bay window to show off the magnificent glory of edible art Uncle Jack managed to whip up the night before. He's got mad culinary skills. The coffee table that probably never had a cup of coffee laid upon its top during its entire existence was covered in a colorful array of candies, trinkets, and toys. Six throw pillows—red, orange, yellow, green, blue, and purple—were arranged on the living room sofa, practically begging kids to jump onto it and attack each other with them.

Looking at the living room and dining room where the party supplies were concentrated, Sheree couldn't help but think the Great and Powerful Wizard of Oz took a rainbow shit all over her house. She also wouldn't be surprised if her mother came in, saw all of the obvious disrespect towards her furniture, left, came back with divorce papers to sign, packed up her bags, and moved to Maui with some fancy cabana boy named Ricardo who kept the wine flowing while fanning her menopausal heat away.

When the door opened, Sheree half expected it to be her mother and was about to sit back and watch the shit-show commence, but it was just her brother who upon opening the door shouted, "No. You. Didn't! This is FABULOUUUUUUUUS!!!" And yes, his FABULOUS was worthy of three exclamation points. Brendon immediately ran up to their dad and hugged him tightly. "Thank you so much, Dad!" he said, before turning to Uncle Billy and Uncle Jack and thanking them as well with hugs. Then he turned to Sheree and thanked her with a hug, too. "How are you doing today?" he asked quietly while they embraced.

"Surprisingly well, considering my friends want to bone Dad," she said back just as quietly.

"Good," he said decisively then added to clarify, "I mean that you are doing well, not in your friends's taste in male companionship."

The hug was lasting longer than either of them intended, so they both let go to avoid any further suspicion. However the damage may have already been done.

"Ever since Brendon came out, they've been so close!" Mr. Hollins said, tears about to fall out of his eyeballs.

Uncle Billy and Uncle Jack held him as he cried his happy cry, which made the scene perfectly set for Mrs. Hollins to walk in and find the house completely rainbowfied, three grown men crying, her children casually talking, and her fancy furniture strewn with party paraphernalia. "Frank! The house looks FABULOUUUUUUUUS!!!" she shouted. And yes, her FABULOUS also deserved three exclamation points.

Sheree thought it was eerie how much her brother and mother were alike in their word choices and phonetic diction. Then she thought it was eerier how similar she was to her father. And then out of morbid curiosity, she wondered whom Kayla would have taken after… had she lived. And further still, she wondered how their family was going to be able to adjust to having Kayla back in their lives. Maybe after that she'd have her answer to the parental influence question. The thought terrified her to no end, but was quickly shelved as the first of the party guests started to arrive.

Much to Mrs. Hollins's dismay, the first person was Kwirk Werewolf (who isn't really a werewolf, but has a brother named Wayne who is a werewolf, but that is a different story for a different time.) Sheree had never actually met Kwirk, but found him hard to describe. Except for his bangs, as they were so jacked up to Jesus she couldn't understand how gravity was failing to keep that flaming red hair of his from falling down. The thing looked like a reverse mullet with a couple cowlicks for good measure. Sheree could freely admit that there were a lot of mysteries she didn't understand when it came to hair.

Before the door closed, another red headed child ran through it. Sheree was pretty sure this one was a girl, but couldn't be certain until Brendon shouted, "Anni!"

Anni. Girl's name.

Then, as Sheree was trying to remember why her mother hated Kwirk so much, she followed her gaze directed towards his vivacious red hair with its subtle hints of blond and burgundy and how her own flat red hair with no subtle hints whatsoever was from a grocery store boxed dye kit and it hit her: her mother wasn't upset about him trying to burn down the middle school, she was totally jealous of his naturally redder-than-red hair.

The fire that raged in her mother's eyes at the sight of his perfect hair color that he didn't have to put any effort into, also gave her the answer to her previous thought about Kayla. She definitely took after her mom.

"Doesn't the house look great?" Sheree asked with faux enthusiasm to break her mother's wrathful rage toward an innocent nine-year-old child.

"It does! Billy, Jack, obviously you helped out with this, right?" Mrs. Hollins asked, putting on a fake smile and wishing the punch was sangria, and thinking she might just have to make her own sangria with it while nobody was looking.

Billy spoke first with, "I tried to get him to tone it down a bit!"

Jack spoke second with, "This might be too gay even for the gays!"

Brendon spoke third with, "I love it so much! I have the best family ever!"

He looked genuinely happy, happier than Sheree could ever remember seeing him. Maybe turning ten was really going to be a turning point in his life. Or maybe this was just the calm before the storm.

More friends continued to arrive, including Johnny who has two dads and lives in a round house, and Andy who has two moms and lives next door. It soon became obvious to Sheree that Anni was her brother's hag as she could not leave his side and kept whispering things into his ears and making him giggle. Kwirk pretended to look like he was in the loop but mostly looked aloof. The only person she didn't see was his friend Darryl, Courtney's little brother.

The doorbell rang.

Brendon opened the door.

There stood Darryl and Courtney who smiled a big goofy smile and shouted, "Let's get this party started!"

Brendon looked ecstatic as they air-kissed each other's cheeks like old British friends.

Sheree looked like the blood had drained from her face as she realized she didn't have her best friends nearby for backup in case Courtney was too Courtney for her to deal with. However, just as she was reaching for the phone, Jennifer and Sky were at the doorway, with Courtney lending a hand to lift Sky over the threshold as she sang in her beautiful voice "Somewhere Over the Rainbow" almost as good as Judy Garland. Almost.

"Thank God you are here!" she said to her friends and Courtney by extension whom she was on good terms with but still uncertain about. "I was about to crawl into a hole and beg for death to take me swiftly away from all these fourth graders!"

Looking at her like she was a freak for even thinking something like that, Courtney said, "Girl, that's just crazy talk! My momma picked us up from practice and we all said we wanted to come here for Brendon's B-day. Ooh, cake! Yuck, those are some nasty-ass curtains. Oh my gawd, Pin the Hag on the Fag! Ha! Love it! Looks like lil' red androgi-girl's already pinned herself. Ha HA! Damn, who decorated all this?"

She talked so fast it was dizzying.

"Uh, my dad?" Sheree answered, hoping that was the correct answer but not really sure because she was still trying to take in all the words that overflowed from Courtney's mouth so quickly like a sink someone plugged up to do the dishes but forgot to turn the faucet off when they went to answer the telephone.

"Point him out to me," Courtney demanded, using her own pointer finger to try to get a fix on which of the three grown men in the house it could be.

"The one in the middle," Sheree said quietly, hoping the next words out of Courtney's mouth weren't what she was thinking.

"Damn! That is one fiiiiiiiine specimen!" Courtney said before looking at Jennifer and Sky and adding in barely above a whisper, "That man is a total DILF, you know what I'm sayin'?"

Son of a bitch.

Sheree looked deflated as her suspicions came to life.

This can't get any worse.

"What's a DILF?" Mrs. Hollins asked the girls.

Me and my stupid brain.

"Honey, yo' man is a Dad I'd Like to…" Courtney started, but Sheree's hands quickly covered it up, smiling a big fake smile and hoping that her mother wouldn't catch on.

It was too late.

"Is that like MILF?" she asked before the realization of what the D in DILF stood for struck her. She looked like a deer in headlights before managing to pull herself together and proudly walked over to her husband, gave him an extended kiss on the mouth, turned around and told the hornier than thou girls, "Sorry ladies, but he's all mine."

Crisis averted. Dad may even win the new curtains argument.

BARK! BARK BARK!!

Maybe I thought too soon.

The room became silent at the sound of a dog barking.

Sheree's thoughts raced back to divorce papers and Maui and Ricardo.

"Did you really get him that stray from the park you found and took to the vet?" Mrs. Hollins asked her husband, her expression unreadable.

All her father could do was smile. Then he went over to the downstairs bathroom, opened the door, and out came this black and white Boxer-Boston Terrier mix (with maybe some Pit Bull?) with a crazy eye who went straight up to Brendon and started licking his face profusely like it was a lollipop.

Nothing could prepare Sheree for her mother's reaction.

"Oh, Frank, it is! I just love that little guy!" Mrs. Hollins said, crying happy tears, which made Sheree realize her family cries a lot.

"Thanks Mom and Dad! Does he have a name?" Brendon asked between licks.

"Nope. That honor is all yours," Mr. Hollins told his son, his wife hugging him tightly, both of their smiles incomprehensibly huge.

Looking the mutt over, Brendon said, "Well, does he look more like a Rex or a Deschutes kind of guy?"

The smiles quickly faded from Mr. and Mrs. Hollins's faces as they recognized the names from their wine and beer respectively.

While Brendon was trying to decide with the help of his friends each weighing in on the Name Game, Mrs. Hollins whispered, "Do we want to set a precedent of naming our pets after alcohol?"

Mr. Hollins whispered back, "Every family pet I had growing up was named after alcohol."

Uncle Billy shook his head in the affirmative towards Mrs. Hollins.

"Rex it is!" Brendon shouted, causing Mrs. Hollins to cringe and look pleased all at the same time while Mr. Hollins looked sad and pleased all at the same time. Emotions are weird.

Another set of barks rang out from the bathroom.

Oh my gawd, please no.

Out came another black and white dog that looked almost identical to the first, but was slightly larger even though it was obvious he was still rather young. They were practically twins, and Brendon was instantly doubly excited.

"Deschutes!" he cried as the second dog bounced on top of him.

Mrs. Hollins looked at her husband with wide eyes. "Where did that one come from?"

"Someone else brought him to the vet clinic that the other went to. They were pretty sure they are brothers. I couldn't take one without the other!" Mr. Hollins told his wife. "Besides, he already named him, so, you know, it's a done deal now."

Opening her mouth as if she was getting ready to speak, Mrs. Hollins instead let it form into a smile as she saw how happy they made her son. Sheree on the other hand, looked annoyed, as she knew that, although these were technically her brother's dogs, she'd probably have to split pooper-scooper duties.

Goddamned penises.

Walking over to her brother who was surrounded by gawking children and slimy dog tongues ferociously licking his face, Sheree bent down to her brother and said, "Okay, so apparently I was wrong. Being ten *is* all rainbows and puppies."

"I know, right?" Brendon said giggling.

He looked so happy, so incomprehensibly happy. Sheree tried to feel the same happiness, but instead was knocked over by a rambunctious dog and fell flat on her ass before the mutt began licking her face too, smothering it in puppy kisses. It was in that moment she finally felt it.

Dogs can do that.

Chapter 13
Normal

That Saturday, the family went shopping for new drapes.

The drapes managed to outlast half a dozen children, cake with an obscene amount of food dye in the frosting and cake itself, and a horde of hags haphazardly pinned to them. They could not, however, handle puppies.

Rex and Deschutes were quickly finding new ways to destroy things. Being that they were youngish (the vet said maybe seven or eight months tops), it was natural for them to want to chew on, well, anything they could chew on. They were nondiscriminatory over their choices of chewables. Chair legs: yes; throw pillows: yes; heirloom drapes that have been in Mrs. Hollins's family for generations: YES! YES!! YES!!!

Mrs. Hollins was not well pleased with the new additions. Mr. Hollins loved their knack for destroying everything he hated while leaving his beloved den sofa perfectly intact.

So now they were shopping for curtains and having no luck agreeing on which direction to go with the pattern or style. Mr. and Mrs. Hollins kept pleading their cases to each other. Brendon tried to find compromises to appease them both. Sheree found the whole ordeal to be terribly boring.

If this is what being normal is like, I'm not sure I want any part of it, Sheree thought to herself as she noncommittally looked through a section of jacquards in various colors to help pass the time; wishing her friends were there with her so they could entertain her; realizing that she was acting like a whiny little bitch; part of her hoping Kayla had a plan in place so her head wouldn't feel so lonely.

She quickly flushed that last thought down the toilet of her brain in hopes that it never returned, but it was too late. There was a clog and it kept resurfacing. A sick and twisted part of her wanted Kayla to come back and she knew it. The only question was how she was going to pretend that she was fine when in reality she was the clogged toilet bowl.

"Sweet Lord Jesus, guys! Just pick out some fucking curtains already!" Sheree shouted in the crowded department store, much to the surprise of her family as it was to her.

"Language, young lady!" Mrs. Hollins shouted back.

"If you want this to go by faster, then find something you think your mother will like and I won't hate!" Mr. Hollins shouted back.

"Make them get these!" Brendon shouted, pushing a muted floral print that was surprisingly masculine at the same time in her face.

Sheree had to admit being gay had indeed changed her brother. She hoped it was a phase. Not the being gay part, just the being fabulous part. "Seriously, Mom and Dad. Brendon found the perfect drapes."

It was hard to argue. They were the perfect compromise. Not too feminine and not too masculine. Her parents agreed. They bought the curtains and left the mall to drive a half an hour home and hang them.

And it was all terribly boring to Sheree.

The next week was also terribly boring.

The week after was even more boring.

The weeks passed by without incident, and it was all still terribly boring to Sheree, and still she secretly wanted her psychotic ghost-witch sister back in her life so she could feel like she was living again and not just floating in the air like a dust mote.

Finally, a few weeks before Easter, something happened. Jennifer and Sky got into a huge fight in one of the school hallways after cheerleading practice.

Excellent.

"What the hell, Sky?! Why are you being such a bitch?" Jennifer asked her so-called-friend.

"Me?! I'm being a bitch? What about you?" Sky asked, red-faced and on the verge of angry tears.

Sheree decided not to intervene, but merely watched to see how this played out. After so much normal, whatever that means, this fight over something she hadn't determined yet was welcome.

"He's my ex-boyfriend, I have every right to give him shit!" Jennifer shouted, looking as ferocious as ever.

Sky wheeled to within inches of Jennifer and shouted back, "We are still on the cheerleading team together, you don't have to make it impossible to…"

"What?! Be aggressive?" Jennifer yelled, spit flying through the air and landing on Sky who took it like a champ. She didn't even bothering to wipe it off her face. "I thought we were supposed to be aggressive, be be aggressive!"

"Oh my gawd, you are being ridiculous! Why don't you treat Chad like I treat Harry? It'd make it a hell of a lot easier to deal with them if you would stop calling Chad an asshole every time he cheers," Sky said, trying her best to calm down, but failing miserably.

Sheree wished she had popcorn.

"Why, because it throws off his groove?" Jennifer mocked, making Sky even more furious.

"Because one of these throws, he might just decide to not catch you, that's why. Then you'd be hurt. Or worse, dead," Sky told her.

The truth comes out.

"You're pissed at me because you care about me?" Jennifer asked, her anger quieting.

"Yes. Fucker," Sky told her, arms folded across her chest and looking to the side at nothing in particular. "And because I know you and Sheree do a lot without me."

"What?" Sheree asked after hearing her name.

Looking confused, Jennifer looked like she was thinking for a moment before saying, "We hung out like once without you."

"Uh huh," Sky pouted, still not making eye contact.

"Seriously? That's what's got your panties all in a bunch? The fact that I went over to Sheree's unannounced and I didn't ask you to tag along?" Jennifer asked, uncertain how to take this revelation. Be flattered? Be totally creeped out by the stalker vibe she was getting?

"She's right, we didn't plan anything without you. She just showed up to talk about her parents, that's all," Sheree said, hoping that would alleviate the tension in the room.

"Then why couldn't you invite me to be a part of that conversation?" Sky asked, crying torrents of tears that matted the hair around her face.

Suddenly Ella Fitzgerald's "Cry Me A River" flooded Sheree's brain and she laughed out loud before she could stop herself.

Jennifer and Sky looked at her in amazement.

"Oh Good Lawd! Cry me a river, girl! What up with you?" Courtney asked before stopping right in front of them and continuing with, "You keep pullin' that shit with Chad and you gonna get yourself kicked off the squad, mmmkay Banh Bo Nuong?"

Jennifer refused to look at or even acknowledge her even though she suddenly had a craving for the dessert Courtney had nicknamed her.

"She's got a point. It's the same one I've been trying to make," Sky said to her, bitterness in her tongue.

"Hold up, Wheels!" Courtney told Sky, her hand out in the STOP position while moving her head in a circle like the sassy black woman she was. "You's best be keepin' yo' fancy trap shut durin' practice too!"

"What?!" Sky shouted, uncrossing her arms and throwing her hands up in the air.

"You heard me, girlfriend," Courtney said. "You may have the right intentions, but you just as disruptive durin' routines as her 'asshole' remarks."

"Son of a bitch," Sky said, arms falling down to her lap as she deflated.

"Court, you don't need to be so mean to them," Sheree told her frenemy, putting a hand on her shoulder.

Courtney was not amused. "Listen, I'm just trying to look out for my besties, okay? Anna's gotta lotta clout, and you both be givin' her angry eyes. We need you two on the squad, but we also need Chad and Harry, got it?"

Staring at the scene in front of her—crying Jennifer and crying Sky and snarky Courtney—Sheree decided that perhaps a study date was in order. The three of them. Together. Maybe even the four of them if Courtney was in for it, although she couldn't think of a single class they had in common which seemed odd considering how small of a school they were in. Then she remembered it was Biology and she hated Biology because it was a soul-sucking waste of time. And first period, which, that in and of itself was probably the real culprit.

Sky was the first to apologize. "I'm sorry, Jen. The doctor has had me on some experimental antidepressant and I think it's messing with my logic. I need to talk to her about that."

Giving Sky a hug, Jennifer said back, "I'm sorry for being such a bitch and calling Chad an asshole even though he totally is one and for almost getting you kicked off the cheerleading squad because you were trying to look out for me."

To the shock of everyone, Courtney started crying. "I'm sorry," she said through muffled sobs, fingers lifting off tears from her sockets to prevent needing to touch up her makeup. "Ever since Nikki stole Chad away from you, it's been so lonely. Nikki and I been best friends since kindergarten, and Chad and I since the third grade, and they both only seem to have time for each other now, leaving me to be all by my..."

Great, Sheree thought, rolling her eyes discreetly as Courtney continued pouring out her heart. *Now this is going to turn into a Courtney Love session. Screw the popcorn, what I need is some chocolate.*

Sure enough, it did. Sheree decided the study session would be just for the three of them. After all, there was only so much Courtney one could deal with.

Chapter 14
Hey Pretty

Soapy bubbles danced around plates and between the tines of forks as Sheree washed the after dinner dishes. In almost a mindless trance she scrubbed the remnants of chicken enchiladas from practically every piece it came in contact with. The plates, silverware, even the glasses. How the hell baked on Tillamook Pepper Jack cheese got encrusted on the glasses was beyond her. Okay, so with her family and the way they use their hands as extra utensils to shovel food into their oral portals, it definitely was not outside the realm of possibilities that the cheese would indeed find its way onto three of the four glasses, the exception, of course, being hers, which looked remarkably clean and probably didn't even need rinsing except that it bared an impeccable lip gloss mark close to the rim.

Damn.

Droning over the rinsing and clinging of dishes as they landed in the dish drain as if by magic, it wasn't long before she came to the knife. This wasn't just any knife; it was The Knife. For years, it was the only one she could remember her mother or father using for practically every cutting need imaginable. The Knife was a nine-and-a-quarter-inch beauty made of high-carbon steel and a thermo-resin handle that fit so comfortably into your hand you'd swear it was custom made just for you. Sheree stared at its long, mirror-finish blade and tried feverishly to scrape the bits of garlic and cheese allowed to harden onto this magnificent work of art. Once every bit, every speck of foreign material was removed and The Knife was properly cleaned, rinsed and carefully dried with a freshly laundered microfiber towel, she continued to stare at the blade's sexy lines and watch as her reflection waxed and waned as she inspected it. Staring straight down the line of the cutting edge, she could see a minor imperfection and quickly grabbed the honing rod from the wooden knife block and began counting down as she honed the blade back into shape—five, five, four, four, three, three…—alternating sides to ensure an even outcome. Another inspection once the process was complete passed her rigorous standards, but still, she could not let The Knife go from her grasp.

Staring.

So sharp.

I bet it could crack a skull open like a melon.

With a swift jolt, The Knife was firmly planted between her eyes and into her skull and nose. Blood gushed profusely, getting all over the dishes she had just spent so much time cleaning, all over the counters and floor and her brand new blouse that brought out the aquamarine in her eyes like no other blouse had ever done before. However, now her eyes were hidden in a sea of red.

"Now look what you've gone and done, Sheree!" her mother screamed with a harshness she hadn't heard in years. "You'll have to rewash all those dishes! Such a waste of perfectly good soap and water, too."

Brendon was indifferent as he casually looked up from a men's underwear catalog he was perusing not for the underwear, but the young men modeling said underwear.

Her father shouted that he was trying to watch the news and needed complete silence.

"Well, young lady? What do you have to say for yourself?" her mother asked, giving a scornful look only a redhead could offer, even if the red hair was fake.

But with The Knife so deep, her lips were also victims of its wrath and she had to force every muscle in her face to pry away from the blade, which sounded like ripping a raw chicken breast apart with your bare hands after merely slicing the end, in order for her to say, "I was just experimenting."

With a roll of her eyes that slightly tossed her bangs to the left, suddenly making her look ten years younger and exponentially more attractive, her mother asked with a fervent plea, "Why can't you just do drugs or have risqué sex like any other normal teenager when you feel the urge to experiment?"

Staring.

The sharpness of the blade was impressive indeed, and now it had been faithfully restored. Sheree carefully placed The Knife into its proper slot in the knife block, along with the honing rod and cursed her vivid imagination for scaring the shit out of her. Pulling the plug from the sink drain, she caught a glimpse of her reflection in the swirl of murky water and soap bubbles, and as if the reflection was its own person said to her, *"You know you want to do it, to know what it feels like to experience the thrill of death,"* in a gravelly voice followed by a small child singing, *"C'mon, Sheree! It'll be fun to die! Hehehehe!!!"*

"Kayla!" Sheree said loudly, though with the commotion of the television being turned up so loud so her father could watch the news, the only person within any distance that could hear her was Brendon, whose ears perked with a morbid and chilling curiosity.

In a shaky voice, he slowly lowered the men's underwear catalog down as he asked with one hand in his pocket as if he was reaching for something, "Why did you say her name?"

"I'm sorry, I…" Sheree started to say, but found herself too choked, too frightened to finish her sentence when the phone rang, causing her to jump.

Glad The Knife wasn't in my hand! Shit! Calm yourself down!

The sharp sound was deafening, even amidst the local evening news anchors blaring out of the television set, piercing the air with bravado. After the fourth ring, Mrs. Hollins looked at her two children and said, "Seriously? I have to get the phone even though you two are right next to it? Sheesh! Hello? Of course she is, though I might have to knock the phone over her head to break her out of whatever trance she appears to be in." Handing the phone to Sheree, her mother said, "It's Jennifer."

With a sigh of relief, Sheree grabbed the phone from her mother and said into the receiver, "Hi, Jen, you are not going to believe what is going through my head right now. Or maybe you will since, you know, stuff."

Sheree was trying to be coy since her mother was still in earshot.

"It's not Jennifer," the voice on the other end said coldly.

Confused, Sheree asked, "Wait, huh? Then who is this?"

"Not Jennifer."

"Okay, enough with the cryptic. Oh, sorry. Hi, Sky. I swear, you think my mom would know the difference between a white girl and an Asian's voice by now. What's up?" Sheree asked, bouncy and completely absent of all the fear she felt mere seconds ago.

"I thought you were coming over tonight to study for that history test we've got tomorrow. You know, the one you are terrified you are going to fail unless you study for. Unless, of course, you've got some grand plans to brush off the exams and go shopping," Sky said cunningly, knowing full well Sheree probably did have those plans running through her head.

That was her grand plan, to get the three of them together to study. She wasn't terrified of failing. In fact, she didn't even think she needed to study for the test since she probably knew the topic rather well thanks to her father's infatuation with war documentaries. However, she also wasn't going to screw up the chance to bring back the trio that had slowly fallen apart since the Valentine's Dance.

"I'm on my way now! Just finished with dinner and dishes. Want me to grab something for dessert on the way there?" Sheree asked, knowing full well what the answer would be.

"Just get here pronto! There is only so much pacing one can do in a wheelchair and I'm afraid the carpet can't take much more… and bring something chocolate!" Sky demanded.

"Way ahead of you. See you in a minute!" Sheree told her.

After hanging up the phone, Sheree grabbed the chocolate cream pie she bought earlier from the fridge, her jacket, car keys, and headed towards the door.

"You might need these, too," her mother said, pointing towards the pile of schoolbooks and notepads.

"Thanks, Mom. What would this poor little blond girl do without you?" Sheree said, putting the pie on top of the book and notepad she "needed", throwing a pen into her coat pocket for good measure, and walked out the front door before her mother could answer.

Mr. Hollins peeked his head out of the den, Rex and Deschutes on either side of him on the sofa like throw pillows. "Is she gone?"

Mrs. Hollins responded, "Yep."

Brendon squealed, throwing his men's underwear catalog into the air, "Yay! We can finally have dessert without fear of Sheree eating it all!"

The dogs seemed just as thrilled and bounced off the couch and into the kitchen as if they would also be receiving dessert. They even did a little dance with their front legs off the ground and paws in the air, twirling. Brendon decided to teach them some simple choreography for some musical he was plotting. Apparently their cuteness won them dessert as Mrs. Hollins scooped up a couple spoonful's of vanilla ice cream into their dishes, making them sit before allowing them to swallow it all in one bite then demand to be let outside to pee because when they got excited they had to pee. Silly puppies.

A few minutes later, Sheree arrived at Sky's house and, carefully so as to not drop the pie and then have to risk the possibility of getting caught eating the remains off the recently rained on ground, she balanced it on top of her books and walked to the front door. Sky opened it before Sheree even had a chance to ring the doorbell.

"I didn't want you to drop the pie. I'm in desperate need of chocolate and it isn't even that time of the month! I've got a doctor's appointment tomorrow to figure this out," Sky told her matter-of-factly. "Of course, ever since I became wheelchair bound, it seems like no amount of chocolate can satiate my cravings."

"Tell me about it!" a voice from the next room shouted. Sheree recognized it immediately as the unmistakable voice of Jennifer, who bounced into view, took the pie out of Sheree's hand, and continued, "I'll cut it into thirds!"

As Jennifer walked out of the room, Sheree flashed Sky a nervous look. "Are you two okay now?"

Shaking her head, Sky confessed, "I don't hate her, I just hate her relationship with you. Your mom didn't help when she automatically assumed I was Jennifer. Ugh. You guys are just so incredibly close and I've never had a friend like that before. Besides, I think I've got a bit of a crush on her. It might be the meds. Shit, I don't even know what I'm saying. Did I tell you I've got a doctor's appointment tomorrow to hopefully figure this all out?"

"Well, take it from me, threesomes are way better than twosomes!" Sheree said and then felt the blood drain from her face. "Oh my gawd, I really just said that, didn't I?"

"Yep." Sky shook her head in agreement.

"Hmm… I beg to differ," Jennifer piped up. "Take this pie for instance. If there were only two of us, we'd each get more pie. However, since there are three of us, we'll each have to settle for a little less of the action."

"Pffft!" Sheree uttered, rolling her eyes. "That is just insane troll logic. Everyone knows you buy two pies and share one that way you've got an extra waiting for you when you get home. Now plate me up, Woman!"

Laughs were followed by a ritualistic consumption of chocolate cream pie, which were then followed by studying for the history exam. Remembering dates, names and places were not Sheree's strong suit, but she found that if she made a rhyme, even a bad rhyme, she could recall a majority of it. However, one thing that always bugged her about rhyming was a particular one about pollution she learned in grade school in a throwback to the Reagan Era, and got in trouble for questioning its validity. "The Solution to Pollution is Dilution!" her teacher sang gleefully one day, which caused Sheree to raise her hand and ask, "So instead of not poisoning our water supply, you are saying we should feel okay about drinking just a little bit of poison because it won't be as bad?" The teacher was not amused, especially when Sheree continued with, "Or maybe what you're saying is that we need to make more air to dilute the poisons we are breathing in every day. Let me put this in another way that might make more sense. Johnny has two glasses in front of him. One is a smaller glass with poison, and the other is a larger glass with the same amount of poison but also filled with water. If Johnny drinks the smaller glass, he will die. However, if Johnny drinks the larger glass, he still dies because it still has the same amount of poison in it. How does that solve the problem? I mean, unless you don't like Johnny."

"Earth to Sheree…" Sky said, snapping her fingers in front of her face. "Did we lose you?"

"Sorry, I was apparently thinking about poisoning some kid named Johnny when I was in the fifth grade," Sheree told her friends, blinking a few times to get herself out of her daydream.

"That's nice. Can we get back to World War Two so we can pass this class?" Sky asked seriously before adding, "Please tell me you have more chocolate somewhere. My mother refuses to stock such necessities in the house for fear I'll get fat especially after the whole sausage fiasco back in January. Hello! I've got a serious lack of lower body mobility here, I've already resigned myself to a bit of weight gain!"

"I wasn't going to say anything, but I've got a bag of Easter candy in my trunk," Sheree informed her friends, but made it sound like she was giving up the secrets to Fort Knox under torture.

Jennifer gave her The Look, the one that only Jennifer could give Sheree that made her realize she'd been caught in a lie.

"Okay, fine! I've got about a dozen bags of Easter candy, bitch!" she shot at Jennifer, who shot a wide-toothed grin back at her.

"As long as it's chocolate, I'm good," Sky told her.

"This is me we're talking about. I wouldn't be hoarding jelly beans in my trunk," Sheree said rather matter-of-factly, one eyebrow cocked as if she was offended. "You'll have to trade it in for this Sausage Fiasco story. It sounds interesting."

"Just get the damn candy already! We've got studying to do," Sky demanded, pointing toward the front door and trying her best to imitate Jennifer's The Look but was unable to capture it and looked more like Elmer Fudd after he thought he killed the rabbit. It was sad.

Sheree relinquished her fight and brought in a few of the bags of chocolate-like-food-products popular at Easter time. She left the good stuff in the car to sneak into her room when she got home so her parents and brother wouldn't snatch it away like they were probably doing with the second chocolate cream pie she left at the house. Jennifer gave her a mini The Look, but after unwrapping and popping one of the waxy chocolate egg shaped candies into her mouth, didn't feel like fighting the truths she knew to be true in her heart: that Sheree had brought in the crappy candy and saved the best for herself.

"If Buddhists had a comparable holiday to Easter, we'd have better candy," Jennifer informed everyone before unwrapping another egg shaped chocolate concoction into her awaiting and salivating mouth.

"Okay, back to work girls. We've got a test to pass," Sky said, demandingly before doing a quick, random oral pop-quiz to find out where they were. The results didn't look promising.

"We're doomed," Sheree told them. "But at least we have chocolate to make us feel okay about it!"

Chapter 15
Math and Zombies

Sitting on the couch, minding her own business and reading her favorite girly teen magazine, Brendon walked in, seating himself next to Sheree and giving her that look like he was about to ask something that would probably annoy the hell out of her. "Go away," Sheree replied. "I'm busy."

Taking the hint, Brendon did the unexpected thing and left Sheree alone.

Huh, I'll have to remember that.

Noticing that his mom was sitting at the breakfast bar, he took the stool next to her and asked, "Can you help me with this problem?"

"Sure Bren, what is it?" Mrs. Hollins asked, setting her coffee cup down on the counter.

Rex and Deschutes were at her feet as if expecting something to miraculously fall to the ground so they could do their duty and destroy all evidence. They were like vacuum cleaners, those cute little dogs with their cute little under bites. So much so, that they stopped vacuuming so frequently as the dogs roamed the house shoveling anything and everything that might be edible into them.

Strays.

"It's for math," Brendon told her.

"Okay," Mrs. Hollins said, shifting her foot that Rex decided was quite lickable.

"Here it is. You are the driver of a bus. When you start your shift, the bus is empty. When you go to the first stop, four people get on the bus."

"Okay," Mrs. Hollins said, counting with her fingers.

"When you get to the second stop, three people get on and nobody gets off."

"Okay," Mrs. Hollins said, still counting with her fingers.

"The third stop is an intersection and four people get off and three people get on," Brendon continued.

"Okay," Mrs. Hollins said, still keeping track with her fingers but finding the task almost more than she could bear with barely a half a cup of coffee in her system on a Saturday morning and two dogs who found her feet delectable.

"At the fourth stop, everyone gets off the bus. How old is the bus driver?" he asked, concluding the problem.

"What?!" Mrs. Hollins yelled, throwing her hands in the air and losing her finger count and accidentally kicking Rex and Deschutes who seemed to have not even noticed their faces were assaulted. "What kind of question is that?"

Laughing, Brendon said, "Let me read it to you again."

"No! It's stupid. It's a stupid question. That's like asking, if Bob has two apples and Larry has three apples, how many apples does Mary have?" Mrs. Hollins said, flabbergasted by the ridiculousness of the riddle her son just relayed.

"Seriously Mom, let me read it to you again. You are the driver of a bus…" Brendon started, but his mother interrupted.

"No, I don't want to hear it. It's a stupid question and I'll write your teacher a note about this one, because there is no way any logical mind would allow this sort of question to be in a text book!" a very heated Mrs. Hollins told her son.

The dogs decided they had enough of whatever was on Mrs. Hollins's feet and chased each other into the living room to wrestle.

"You don't get it," Brendon told her, laughing and shaking his head. "*YOU* are the driver of a bus. Mom, you're the bus driver, how old are *YOU*?"

Realizing now what the question was asking, she responded by saying, "I am not, nor have I ever been, a bus driver! That question is ludicrous!" she yelled.

"You're just pissed because you didn't figure it out."

"Am not, I just don't see the point. It's a stupid question."

"Yeah, you're pissed all right."

"Will you stop saying that?"

"It's not my fault you didn't figure it out! Apparently I was the only one in class who knew the answer."

"Good for you, but it's still dumb. I thought when you read the question, 'YOU' was like the all encompassing everybody

'YOU' not *me*, okay? If it's going to be a hypothetical question, it should start out by saying 'hypothetically'."

"Don't get all worked up about it. Oh, and the answer to the Bob Larry Mary Apple Dilemma is the sum of the remaining apples left in the crate," Brendon said smugly.

"THERE IS NO CRATE!" his mother yelled, her face a shade of red he hadn't seen since the time he told her to shove her head up her ass.

"Yes there is, you left that part out. It should have been at the beginning."

"Go to your room!"

"Why, because you didn't get a stupid question right? That hardly seems fair."

"How did you become such a smart ass?"

"You, all right! I learned it by watching you!" Brendon shouted dramatically, mimicking a Don't Do Drugs commercial they'd seen on some Remember the 80s television program recently.

"Parents who are smart asses, have children who are smart asses. Any questions?" Sheree said from the family room, not even looking up from her magazine article about putting up with your parents.

Alas, that day would be filled with more math than Sheree was prepared to deal with. This is not what Saturdays were supposed to be. Saturdays were for goofing off and watching cartoons and shopping and staying up late, not math. But, as she prepared herself for Mortal Mathematical Melee, she realized the days of carefree

Saturdays might just be a thing of the past. Something she'd look back upon with nostalgia. Growing up sucks balls.

Jennifer's house was as immaculate and gaudy as ever, the blacks, reds, and golds popping against the white walls. Buddha had a bowl of freshly sliced oranges. He looked pretty happy about it.

Sky on the other hand looked like shit.

"Sorry if I'm a zombie lately. Doctor upped my meds. Apparently when they ask you 'how are you feeling' you're not supposed to respond 'I don't want to be alive anymore. Not that I want to kill myself or anything, I just want to cease to exist.'" Sky told Sheree and Jennifer while they were studying. Sheree thought the coincidence of her words were odd, but decided she must have heard the phrase somewhere on television or a movie or a book.

Without missing a beat, Jennifer remarked, "Well, that's depressing."

"Tell me about it? Why do you think I'm on these antidepressants?!" Sky laughed, but it didn't really sound like Sky's laugh, more like a mockery of the once exuberant laugh her friends were used to.

Sheree knew that she should have felt more sympathy towards her friend, but she was having trouble focusing. Feeling overwhelmed by the pressures to perform at such a high level of academic dexterity, Sheree finally had to admit defeat. Math was not her strong suit. Sure, she understood numbers, but when you start adding letters and pretend theories into the mix and those supposed theories are given just as much importance and credence as reality, well that just boggled her brain. Give her a good language conundrum and she'd figure it out no problem. Ask how many cookies Johnny has left after deciphering the value of X divided by batches in recipes to the third power of the Inner Circle of Fault and multiply that again by X, and she'd still be thinking about cookies.

Mmm... cookies.

"Sheree, are you still with us?" Jennifer asked, holding up her Advanced Algebra book as if her next step was to smack her friend over the head with it.

"Sorry, I was thinking about cookies," she responded, still a bit dazed.

"I gathered that from the drool forming in the corner of your mouth," Sky said dryly.

The comment may have been innocent, but Sky's tone was anything but sincere. It seemed harsh. Cold. Honest.

"That was a hint to wipe your mouth of said drool, Sheree!" Jennifer shouted with a shocked grimace, reaching over and wiping her friend's mouth with her sleeve.

"Uh, thanks," Sheree managed to offer up, wiping her mouth in the same spot Jennifer just did as if to be sure to have gotten all of the drool. "My blood sugar must be low or something. I'm completely out of it right now."

Giving her friends the sympathetic look they so desperately looked like they needed at that moment in their lives, Jennifer concurred. Math was not going to happen that night. Why she decided that the first real full day of Spring Break needed to include a Marathon Math Meeting was beyond her. "I understand."

"No you don't, Jen!" Sheree said quite loudly. "You're Asian! Math is in your blood, your DNA!"

"Stereotype much! I mean, it's true, but offensive!" said Jennifer.

Sky was staring at a small tree that appeared to be made of real gold on a side table that also housed a lamp with painted bamboo, as if she was completely unaware of the events unfolding in front of her. Maybe the doctor upped her meds a bit too much.

"Later, bitch. I'm outta here," Sheree responded nonchalantly, and with a wave of her hand she was walking out the front door of her best friend's house and heading towards her car.

"What the hell? Are you just going to bail on the final too?" Jennifer asked a bit overdramatically, at once both upset and concerned and trying to figure out why Sky was being so silent.

But Sheree didn't even dignify the question with a response, especially given the final wouldn't be for another couple months, and instead started up her car and drove off. Not home, but towards Portland. She decided she didn't want to be around her family or friends or anyone she knew, but at the same time didn't want to be alone.

Dancing.

That's what she'd do.

Go dancing.

Drive to Portland, find a club, and dance.

As she drove along the highway, leaving the town of Ravenwood behind her, she felt as if she was losing control of her life. Nothing she did seemed important anymore, not since Christmas. It was as if she was succumbing to autopilot. She felt like she was experiencing life through someone else's eyes. She also felt like letting that presence take over, do whatever it wanted to do, be whatever it wanted to be.

Zombie.

No, not zombie… possessed. Not like be a demon or anything, just by another spirit, another soul itching to regain physical form again. It was that moment that Sheree realized that Kayla must have indeed conjured up a plan that she felt would be a good compromise. Sheree could feel Kayla inside her, screaming to be let out, begging to take over. And what scared her the most was that she was thinking about allowing her to do so. The last few months had been so exhausting. The sleepless nights, the horrible daydreams, even the normalcy her life had taken on since Kayla's recent hiatus; they were taking their toll. She wanted respite from it all. And here, her sister was offering a solution.

"C'mon, Sis. Take a backseat for a while."

But what if something bad happens?

"You can trust me."

Can I? You tried to kill me!

"That was months ago."

The awkward conversation going on in her head was making her nervous. *Could it really be Kayla trying to break free? What if I'm just losing my mind? Am I even driving or am I still at Jennifer's house daydreaming? Can Jennifer hear what's going on?*

"The itsy bitsy spider went up the waterspout.

Down came Sheree and wiped the spider out.

Next came a plan to dry up all the rain,

And the itsy bitsy spider was free to live again!"

Nothing prepared her for what happened next.

Chapter 16
More Revelations

His moist lips passionately embraced hers. Her hands wrapped tightly around his back. Their bodies pressed against each other, glistening in the dancing light of the flickering candles spread across her bedroom. As soon as he entered her, she felt as if she was alive for the first time with her eyes wide open to take in everything. It was as if she could taste the colors, see the sounds, and hear the emotions they both were feeling. She'd never felt so connected to another person in her entire life as she did at that moment.

"I'm not hurting you, am I?" Jeff said quietly, looking into her eyes.

"No, Jeff," Sheree whispered back.

The rhythm of their bodies continuously changed pace; fast, slow, fast, fast, slow. Just when she thought it wasn't possible for her to feel so much ecstasy, another wave would crash, causing her to grab the sheets to ground her, keep her from floating away.

As Jeff continued thrusting, his eyes looked intense as if he was solely concentrating on satisfying Sheree. He picked up his tempo again, this time fierce and even.

He must be close, Sheree thought, taking hold of the back of his neck and head. "I don't ever want this to stop," she whispered into his ear before kissing it and biting it gently.

"It doesn't have to. We can do this forever if you want," Jeff told her without missing a beat.

"How?" Sheree asked, curious.

His eyes looked hesitant, but only momentarily before he responded, "Let Kayla take your place."

"What?!" Sheree screamed loudly, not even caring if it woke her parents or brother up, causing them to walk into her room to catch her and Jeff making love. "You can't be serious?"

"Of course I am," Jeff said, his hips still swaying up and down.

Sheree couldn't believe her ears. All she wanted to do was stop, get out, and leave her room. But it was as if she was powerless as his body was on top of her, continuing to pound away. "Get off of me!"

"I can't," he said.

It sounded so pathetic and honest.

Balling her hands into fists, she tried to lift them up to punch him and try to beat him off of her, but they were so heavy she couldn't move them. "Stop! Please!"

But he didn't stop.

He just kept going.

The ecstasy she felt mere minutes ago was replaced with shame as her body was violated against her will. Tears began streaming down her face as she suddenly flashed back to last year when she was gang raped by her then boyfriend and three of his buddies, each taking turns holding her down and violently abusing her virgin body. She never told anyone about it, not even her parents who seemed so concerned when she came home late that night, disheveled and crying. All she wanted to do was forget it ever happened. Make it disappear. Pretend like it was just a nightmare because that was what it felt like.

A horrible. Vicious. Nightmare.

"I'm sorry," Jeff said.

Sheree ignored his voice, keeping her eyes closed and tried to conjure up any thought she possibly could to take her mind off of what was happening to her.

"I said I'm sorry, Sheree!"

The voice wasn't Jeff's, but sounded eerily like her own, only angrier, harsher, and gravelly. Her eyes shot open as she realized who it was.

Kayla.

Sheree stared at a mirror image of herself. Kayla was not the teal colored ghost she encountered last Christmas or the eerie spider-woman from a few weeks ago in a dream, but now flesh and blood and on top of her, holding her down, and continuing to rape her. She didn't know how it was possible, but it was happening. And she was unable to stop it.

"Please, Kayla, stop," Sheree pleaded, the tears continuing to flow down her cheeks.

An evil smile formed over Kayla's face. "You want me to stop?"

"Yes."

"You know what I want in return."

"I can't let you have it."

"Then this nightmare will continue. I've got eternity."

Sheree was not willing to allow her sister to take her place, essentially killing her in the process. However, she also didn't know how long she could endure being tortured. Then another sudden realization hit; she was dreaming. She had to be. It was the only explanation for everything that was happening to her.

"Silly girl, you really think this is only a dream?" Kayla said, laughing one of her evil, contorted laughs filled with menace and rage and glee all at once.

"It has to be," Sheree said quietly.

Kayla turned her head to face what Sheree thought was her bedroom window as she said, "She thinks this is only a dream!"

Uproarious laughter sprang up, not from Kayla, but from hundreds of different voices. Sheree turned her head to the direction of Kayla's gaze to find her school's auditorium filled with her classmates, teachers, faculty, and parents. All laughing at her as she was on the stage, taking pleasure in the fact that she was helpless, and watching with excitement as her dead twin sister continued to rape her while reciting what sounded like a monologue from some morbid play.

As Sheree looked out on the sea of faces, one stood out. He was not laughing, but seemed both sad and horrified by what his eyes were witnessing. "I'm sorry," she mouthed, unable to get any sound to come out as she was so overcome with grief. There was nothing she could do as her brother was forced to watch her body's onstage desecration.

"I'm sorry, Sheree," Brendon said back, trying everything he could to lift his hands from the armrests of the auditorium seats, but failing.

Kayla stopped her monologue when she realized that Brendon was able to speak. "Shut up, boy! You know you'd rather have her dead so you can be an only child and have our parents dote solely on you!"

"I would never!" Brendon shouted, suddenly at his feet. Realizing that he was standing, he looked right into Kayla's eyes as he ran towards the stage and straight for her. "Now get off my sister, you bitch!" he said, pushing Kayla off the bed and into the wall.

"How?" Kayla said, flustered, her eyes filled with hurt and confusion, her voice small and weak. "How could you do that? To me?! I'm a powerful witch and you are nothing but a fat faggot!"

Brendon got on top of Kayla as she sat on the floor against the wall in shock. "You better leave now! Leave this house, leave our heads, leave and never come back!"

Shock melted away to amusement as Kayla began laughing hysterically. "Do you really expect me to leave when I have so much to gain?"

"I do," Brendon said as he pulled out a small blue butterfly from his shirt pocket.

Kayla stared at the features on the wings, one side torn and broken, then looked right into its eyes and immediately recognized it. "But how can this be?"

Brendon smiled, then shoved the butterfly down Kayla's throat, causing her to start thrashing about violently. She floated up into the air, getting smaller and smaller as the audience disappeared, replaced with the familiar bay window. Sheree watched with Brendon as Kayla vanished before their eyes and they were alone in her bedroom. He ran over to his sister and hugged her, not wanting to let her go as she hugged him back, tears streaming down both their faces.

"How did you do that?" Sheree asked, finally regaining her voice.

Slowly, Brendon let his hands slide down and gently grab hold of hers as he told her quietly, "You're not going to like the answer."

Looking like a cow in a milk factory for the first time, Sheree asked, "What do you mean? You made Kayla go away! I don't care what the answer is!" Sheree didn't know how, but her body felt as if a great burden was lifted. She felt normal and like her old self again, like she did before moving to Ravenwood. This normal was so much more freeing than the normal she'd been experiencing the last few weeks where everything seemed muted, mundane, and monotonous, like walking through a familiar street in fog. But now she needed an answer.

Taking a deep breath, Brendon said, "Kayla told me."

"WHAT?!" Sheree screamed louder than she intended, knowing that it probably woke their parents up. "But you just made her go away! She's gone! We saw!"

Shaking his head, he told her, "I only released the part of Kayla that was trapped inside you. Don't you understand? I've unleashed that monster on the world! Who knows what she will do outside the confines of your body! Do you get it? The most evil part of Kayla is free!"

Grabbing her brother by his shoulders, she shook him as she realized what he had done. "Why? Why did you do it?"

Fresh tears started forming in his brown eyes as he told her in barely a whisper, "To save you."

Pulling Brendon in closer to her, she hugged him tightly again and said, "That was so stupid. Thank you."

Just then, Sheree's bedroom door opened and Mr. Hollins walked in shirtless with a pair of red plaid flannel pajama bottoms that were haphazardly thrown on, looking disoriented. "Are you serious?" he said loudly, rubbing his eyes to make sure the sight of his children hugging each other wasn't just a figment of his imagination. "It's three-thirty in the frakking morning. Go back to sleep," he said as he walked back to his bedroom where they overheard him say, "You will not believe the shit I just saw our children doing. They were hugging!"

"What?!" they heard their mother's voice say. "Did you take a picture, Frank?" Then their bedroom door shut and the conversation that continued was muffled.

Giving Brendon a smile, she told him, "We'll figure something out. I promise."

"I know," he said back, yawning. "I also know that I don't have to sleep with you anymore, but…"

"Of course," Sheree said, pulling back the covers to let her brother into her bed. Rex and Deschutes ran from Brendon's bedroom and onto Sheree's bed, too, as if the invitation was automatically extended to them as well. "Well, this is going to be a bit cozy, isn't it?"

"Yes," Brendon said with a goofy smile on his face before saying authoritatively, "Lay down, boys."

To Sheree's amazement, they did. "Ugh, my bed has too many penises in it."

Giggling like a schoolgirl, Brendon said, "You say that like it's a bad thing!"

Sheree didn't have the heart to tell him that when you aren't prepared, when those penises are used as weapons, that yes, too many is a very bad thing. It was just a joke he made. Nothing serious. Nothing he could know really happened to her. She knew that she would have to tell her parents what happened that night last year when she was violently raped, and soon before her brain tells her to bottle it up again.

Tomorrow, She thought. *Tomorrow.*

❦   ❦   ❦

The funny thing about tomorrow is that there always seems to be an abundance of them.

Sunday morning—that might as well be considered afternoon by the time Sheree finally woke up—consisted of damage control. As much as Sheree was curious to find out how Brendon managed to exorcise Kayla from her mind, she needed to tell her friends how sorry she was for how she acted the night before. Sky was easy and said she didn't even recall anything out of the ordinary and started talking about some gold tree at Jennifer's house and how mesmerizing it was. Jennifer on the other hand was a little more difficult to apologize to.

"The phone isn't really doing this apology any good, I need to see you. Face to face," Sheree told Jennifer, hoping her day was free to make good with her best friend.

"Aren't you even at all worried about Sky?" Jennifer asked, anger behind her words.

"What? Why?" Sheree asked back in response. "I want to apologize to you for last night. I already told Sky I'm sorry."

"Shit, Sheree! There is something seriously wrong with Sky right now. She's not herself," Jennifer yelled into the phone.

"Didn't she say the doctor increased her meds? She's probably just adjusting to it."

"It seems like more than that."

"Really?"

"Yes."

"She seemed fine when I just talked to her a few minutes ago. A bit loopy, but fine."

"I'm serious. I think she is broken."

"Broken? Nonsense. She's just having a bad week."

Jennifer let out a very loud sigh. "Get over here now. I need to knock some sense into you."

"Finally. Shall I bring coffee?"

"I won't stop you."

Sheree was fashionably dressed in baggy sweatpants and one of her father's Wazzu sweatshirts, but she didn't care. She had to see Jennifer. Opening the coat closet, she found a baseball cap and threw it on as well, along with the first pair of shoes she could find. If she was going to go out dressed like White Trash, she was going to go all out.

If only Courtney could see me now!

Opening the door to leave, she jumped back at the presence of someone staring back at her on the other side of the doorway. It was Courtney.

"Listen, Court, about my outfit, I can explain," Sheree started to say, but was immediately hushed by Courtney's hand practically pushing itself in front of her mouth just millimeters from her lips. Then they pressed. Her finger smelled like pancake syrup. Golden Griddle.

"No, you listen. It's Spring Break in the P-N-W and you ain't out in the real public representin'. You wear whatever the *hell* you want!" Courtney told her, smiling one of her huge smiles that you couldn't tell was fake or real or just simply Courtney.

Looking over Courtney's outfit made her feel a whole lot better. They were practically twins except that Courtney didn't have on a baseball cap because her hair was so big she probably couldn't fit one on. Well, it could rest on top probably, but not over her skull.

"Thanks, Court. I gotta go," Sheree told Courtney, smiling back, though decidedly not as large of a smile as Courtney was able to manage.

She looked a little hurt, but in typical Courtney fashion she quickly recovered with, "That's okay. I just brought my lil' brother Darryl over to play with Brendon and the puppies. I'll just hang with them. Isn't it great havin' a gay lil' brother? Part of me hopes my lil' Darryl is gay. Oh! This big sistuh would be so proud! Oh my gawd, could you imagine if yo' gay Brendon and my maybe-gay Darryl became boyfriend and boyfriend and then grow up and get all gay-married and shit? We'd practically be sisters! Ha HA!!!"

All Sheree could do was stare in horror.

"I'm just givin' you shit, girl. Get outta here!" Courtney said, pulling her arm to push her out the door as Darryl rushed in much to Brendon's delight.

Don't look back. Run.

After picking up iced coffee based drinks from the Starbucks in the corner of the grocery store parking lot ("We've been infiltrated," Sheree told her friends when it opened last month), Sheree headed towards Jennifer's house. The day looked like a typical Ravenwood spring day, full of dark gray clouds threatening rain if you look at them wrong. Sheree must have looked at them wrong, as it began pouring ferociously just as she put the car in PARK in the Hoang driveway.

Rushing to the front door of Jennifer's house, she rang the doorbell with her elbow, as her hands were busy carrying their coffees. *Overhangs are a beautiful thing. Why doesn't anyone in the Northwest have one?*

Jennifer opened the door, looking as angry as ever, and said, "I see you brought the rain."

"And coffee. Let me in," Sheree said, pushing her way through the door and into the entryway of the Hoang residence. She handed her friend her triple shot caramel mocha iced beverage and continued with, "Jennifer, I am so sorry for last night. Let me explain."

"No," Jennifer told her, still angry but a little less harsh after taking a drink of her sugary coffee.

"Yes," Sheree told her back. "Kayla came back in my head."

"That's not possible, I would have known," Jennifer said, suspecting a lie.

"I don't know how to explain it, but the other day she was in my daydream and I managed to shove her away for a little bit, but then I couldn't concentrate on math…"

"Because you're not Asian."

"Shut up."

"You can't make me."

Shaking her head, Sheree continued her explanation. "I was so angry for no reason last night and Kayla was there to keep me company, filling my head with so many thoughts I almost felt like giving up and letting her take over my body. But what I didn't figure on was Brendon."

"Brendon?" Jennifer asked, the confusion plainly obvious.

"Brendon. He made her go away. Permanently. Not just for a few weeks like the deal I made with her last time, but forever. She's gone. Well, not really gone, but out of my head anyway," Sheree finished.

Jennifer looked like she was trying to take it all in. "So she's gone? That's it? No more ghost, no more witch, no more possession? She's out of our lives for real this time?"

Hesitant, Sheree told her, "I don't think so. She's out of my head, which means that any control I may have had over keeping her at bay are gone. I fear she is much more powerful without me, even more so than last Christmas."

"Buddhamas."

"Whatever."

"How did Brendon do it?"

"A blue butterfly."

"I don't get it."

"Neither do I."

"You didn't ask?"

Sip.

"I didn't have a chance."

Sip.

"So now what?"

Sheree paused. "I have no idea."

Jennifer paused. "What are we going to do about Sky?"

"I have no idea."

"We should go over there."

"In the pouring rain?"

"Yes."

"I was afraid you were going to say that."

And so, with their coffee drinks diminished, they walked over to Sky's house three doors down, in the pouring rain, rang her doorbell, and waited for someone to answer. It was Mrs. Hawkins. "Sky isn't having a very good day. I don't think it would be wise to see her like this."

"What is going on? Is it her antidepressants or something else?" Jennifer asked bluntly.

Mrs. Hawkins seemed taken aback, apparently unaware that they even knew her daughter was on medication for her depression. "Probably," she finally managed when the shock wore off. "I will have her call you when she's awake. She sleeps a lot lately, which is maybe for the best. She needs rest right now, okay?"

Her expression was sad and numb all at once.

"But…" Sheree started to say, but was interrupted by Mrs. Hawkins.

"I'm not waking her up. Go home. She'll call you later. Goodbye."

The door closed and they were left on the front ramp in the rain without any answers as to why their friend was not right in the head. Footsteps could be heard on the other side of the door, along with some hushed words being exchanged. Jennifer and Sheree decided they couldn't stay there any longer and started walking toward the sidewalk. They both watched as Sky peered out her bedroom window, staring blankly at them as they stared back at her.

Jennifer waved.

Sky just stared.

It was all incredibly eerie to watch, like she was Boo Radley and they were Jem and Scout.

They walked back to Jennifer's house, stopping at Sheree's trunk to pull out a bag of Easter candy—the good stuff this time—before going back inside the house to eat away the afternoon with chocolate concoctions in the shapes of eggs and bunnies until they got so sick they thought they were going to throw up. When she couldn't take anymore, Sheree said her goodbyes and drove home in the relentless rain. It stopped as soon as she walked inside the front door.

Figures.

She needed answers and was hoping that Courtney and Darryl were gone so she could get them. Much to her surprise, not only were they gone, but her parents had just left to go grocery shopping, leaving Brendon home alone with the dogs reading a Men's Health magazine for the pictures of half naked men. Between that and the underwear catalog, it was the closest he could get to porn.

"We need to talk," Sheree told him, sitting down next to him on the sofa in the family room.

He looked up from the magazine, pointed to a picture and said, "You're right. I need to look like this if I want to find a man."

"So now you are pedophile bait?" Sheree joked, hoping he was joking too.

"I mean in like five or six years I need to look like this. Help," he pleaded with seriousness.

He was still a child but wanted so desperately to grow up. If only he knew how short childhood really was. If only he allowed himself to stay a kid for just a few more years. If only he wasn't so boy-crazy at the age of ten.

"Dad said he was a pudgy kid, and now look at him," Sheree told her brother, hoping that would help her brother's confidence.

It did.

His face lit up as he said excitedly, "Even if I'm only half as hot as Dad, the boys will be lining up to lick my lollipop!"

Horrified, Sheree replied, "You did not just refer to your penis as a lollipop, did you?"

"Penis? I was talking about my tongue!" Brendon shouted innocently.

Whew.

"Well, now that we've gotten that conversation out of the way, I need to know something," Sheree told her brother, her tone obviously different than before.

Putting down the magazine, Brendon answered, "I think I know what you want. You're wondering how I made Kayla go away, aren't you?"

"Well, yes. I've gone over every scenario I could possibly imagine, and for the life of me can't figure it out," Sheree said.

"I'm a witch," he confessed.

"Okay, so that possibility did not enter into my scenarios," she confessed.

He sat up. "Part of me has always known on some level that I am a witch. Maybe that is why my presence prevented Kayla from taking over your body when we touched. Do you think Mom and Dad are ready for another coming out from me?"

Sheree laughed. "I think if you are ready to tell them that you are witch, you should tell them."

"Okay."

"So, you are a witch, huh?"

"Yep."

"I still don't understand how you made Kayla leave my head for good."

"I told you, I had help from Kayla."

Sheree played the stereotypical blond, and asked again, "But how?"

Taking in a deep breath, Brendon said, "It's like this, okay. Kayla is like the facts of life where you take the good and you take the bad and you take them both and there you have the facts of life. There is Kayla the Good and Kayla the Bad, and Kayla the Good told me how to get rid of Kayla the Bad, but only from your head. Now she is in some temporary hold until the shock of being yanked from your psyche resolves itself. It's all really confusing, I know, but really rather simple, too."

Sheree just took it all in, letting each word her brother told her mingle in her thoughts until she could fully comprehend what he was telling her. *Good Kayla? Bad Kayla? She's split?* Once it sunk in, she responded with, "So you've been in contact with Kayla the Good?"

Shifting in his seat, Brendon said in a small voice, "Yes, for a while now."

"What do you mean 'for a while now'?" she asked.

"Since Valentine's Day."

Sheree had never really thought of what kind of a burden she had put on her brother, but now hearing his confession that he was in communication with the good part of their dead sister to save her from the bad part of their dead sister was almost more than she could handle.

What kind of monster am I?

As if Brendon could read her mind, he told her, "I know what you are thinking and stop it right now. I did this because I love you. Simple as that."

"One thing I don't understand still is the blue butterfly?" she asked.

There was a brief silence between them as Brendon appeared to be compiling the words he was going to say next. "That wasn't just *a* blue butterfly, that was *the* blue butterfly that Kayla was chasing when she was killed."

"But how?"

"I had to conjure up some pretty dark magic, but Kayla guided me through it. Of course, it took a while for me to trust that her intentions were good because we all know how manipulative she can be. I also had to wait until she decided to return before I could do this. When you were doing the dishes the other night after dinner, I thought it was time and quickly tried to pull the butterfly out of my pocket, but then it was just a false alarm."

"But the blue butterfly? I still don't understand how that would make her leave."

Letting out a huge sigh, tears forming in his eyes, he told her, "That butterfly was supposed to carry her soul to heaven, but it never made it. The truck that crushed Kayla also injured the butterfly and she was unable to fulfill her mission before her winged body fell to the ground and released Kayla's spirit to roam restlessly. I can't even imagine what that must have been like for her!"

His sobs were overwhelming.

"So that means she's finally crossed over then, right?" Sheree asked, hopeful for an affirmative answer even though every fiber of her being told her otherwise.

He shook his head no.

"Then what does it mean?" she asked, tears welling up in her eyes.

"It means she is bound to this world, but only to herself," he said. "It means that Grandma's prophecy about Kayla's return is my fault. I made this happen. It means that now I am responsible for anyone else she kills or hurts!"

Sheree grabbed hold of her brother and hugged him as tight as she could, both of them crying as she told him, "You are not responsible for her actions! Don't ever believe that coming forward and helping is wrong, okay? Do you hear me? This is not your fault!"

"Yes it is!"

"No, Brendon. You saved me!"

"At what cost?"

Sheree tried to think of words to comfort him. Tried to think of something to say to alleviate the pain and guilt he felt inside. Tried and tried, but failed. Nothing she could say or do would ever be able to make him understand just how important his actions were until he could see it for himself. And who knows how long that could take.

Letting go of Sheree, Brendon said, "The worst part is that when Kayla comes back, what do we tell Mom and Dad about her? Do we let them know all of the horrible things she's done?"

"I wish I had an answer, but I don't."

"I know. I've gotten to know Good Kayla so well that part of me hopes that it is her that comes back and only her, but it won't be. It can't be. It has to be all of her, not just part of her. She has to be whole, and her whole is scary," he told Sheree.

That realization hadn't occurred to Sheree. If both parts of Kayla, the good and the bad, are combined again, which part will prevail? Will they cancel each other out? Will Good conquer Evil?

They were left to ponder the question for another day as their parents walked through the door with bags of groceries to be put away, looking as blissfully ignorant as ever.

Chapter 17
Spring Break

Monday of Spring Break, Brendon decided it was time to come out to his parents as a witch. Mrs. Hollins was surprised and annoyed all at once, possibly because she wasn't a witch and only girls in their family were witches and now she had a ten-year-old son who was a witch, or at least claimed to be. Mr. Hollins was gleefully excited that not only did he have a gay son, but that gay son was also a witch. Mrs. Hollins had to stop him from having a party to celebrate. Mr. Hollins accused his wife of stifling their son's expressions of who he is. Mrs. Hollins accused her husband of flaunting their son as a token minority. Mr. Hollins shut up.

Sheree was hoping to hang out with her friends, but alas, it was not meant to be. Jennifer and her family were in Vietnam for a reunion of sorts. Sky's mother was still hiding her away from the world as if she was a freakish monster she didn't want anyone to see. Courtney, however, apparently had loads of free time to spend with her, and spent every minute of it bitching about how her two best friends were too busy for her now that they were dating each other. It was going to be a long week.

"And then, girl you is not goin' to believe this, but Nikki said she'd rather hang out at Chad's house than with me! Bitch! We should both go over there right now and knock that ho and her wigger boy over the head with a baseball bat!" Courtney said, partly serious and rummaging through the Hollins's coat closet to see if they had a baseball bat.

"Are you sure? I mean, I'm all for it if you are, but won't that put a damper on your relationship with them?" Sheree asked, wondering if she'd ever get a chance to read the book she bought yesterday after leaving Jennifer's house.

"My relationship? They only got time fo' each other! How in the fuck they don't get sick of each other, I don't know. It just don't make no sense. I mean I ain't never seen them have no conversation, they just make out. A lot. I mean, after a while yo' tongue wears out, don't it? Shit. Maybe I'm just jealous 'cuz I really like Nikki," Courtney said.

"I know, you've been friends forever. And seriously, after two months you'd think they'd like just a little time apart from kissing, but..." Sheree started, but was interrupted.

"I don't think you fully understand what I'm tellin' you, Sheree. I like Nikki. Not like a friend, but, like, I want to be the one makin' out with her," Courtney confessed.

Shaking her head, Sheree responded with, "Well, I can't say I'm surprised, but I am surprised you told me."

"Who else'm I gonna tell?" Courtney asked. "My best friends are busy kissin' each other, Sky's all housebound like Boo Radley, and Jennifer's off gallivantin' with the fam in some jungle village tryin' to get to some relative's house for phở."

"Have you told your parents yet?" Sheree asked.

"Fool! My mom'd go all Southern Baptist on my ass! Within an hour she'd have the whole congregation at the house to help pray the gay away. Fuck that shit. She ain't learnin' nothin' till I move out, not her or that white devil she shacked up with after Daddy..." Courtney said, revealing more about herself in the last few minutes than she had in the last few months. "That way bitch can stew over my soul in her own damn misery without my bein' witness. Too bad Darryl'll have to be Mom's sob buddy. Meghan might do, too. Cunt." Meghan was Courtney's twelve-year-old sister she rarely mentioned because she hated her for being her stepdad's favorite. If only she knew the truth.

"Got it. Do you need a hug?" Sheree asked, realizing just how good she had it in terms of parental units. "I mean, I come from a pretty liberal family, so I can be confident in hugging a lesbian without thinking you want to go down on me."

Courtney laughed. Her hair followed. "Thanks for bein' there, even if I kinda threw that on you like upchucked cheesecake," she said before going in for a hug.

"Any time," Sheree said back, wrapping her arms around her friend she could now confidently call a friend, Courtney's hair tickling her cheek like pubes. "I'm just glad you are a fashionable lesbian! Let's go check out my closet to see what else needs to come out!"

And thus was Spring Break; cleaning out Sheree's closet of half its possessions, Sky's parents refusing to allow their daughter to have anything to do with the real world, and Jennifer off in a third world country visiting relatives and eating phở. Sheree had a passing thought as to how they excreted, but then tried to erase the image of Jennifer digging a hole, squatting, wiping her ass with banana leaves, and burying it. The image, however, had other plans that haunted her for days. It was moments like that she missed their psychic connection that was now lost forever.

Chapter 18
Terrible Thoughts

It was Monday, the morning after the end of Spring Break, and while Sheree was certainly not feeling up to going to school, she decided she had to check up on Sky. After all, the previous week her parents refused to allow any form of contact, but surely they wouldn't keep her out of school as well, would they? And so while she lay in bed waiting for the alarm clock to go off, she decided she would pray that she might see a glimmer of her friend's personality shine through the medication that drowned her out. She never figured herself a prayer kind of girl, but after Jeff died, she found herself doing an awful lot of the practice when outside the vicinity of prying eyes.

Looking over at her alarm clock, wondering if it was ever going to alarm her, she saw it was ten minutes past her normal wakeup time. "Crap! I must've forgot to set it again!" she said, throwing the covers off herself and jumping to her feet faster than a menstruating woman devouring a chocolate bar. After her recent possession, she was pretty sure she could imagine that scenario taking place.

Heading towards the shared bathroom to unload the night's processed bodily waste, she found the door locked and could hear the fan on and Rex and Deschutes sitting and staring at the doorknob. That meant only one thing: her brother was pooping. So she carefully trekked down the stairs to the half bathroom to do her business, but was caught off-guard by her mother offering her coffee while her father asked how she slept. "Pour me a cup, fine until three, I gotta pee!"

After relieving herself, she joined the rest of the family at the table, including Brendon who had obviously not checked to make sure he didn't have toilet paper hanging from his ass because, well, he did.

"You forgot something there, bro," she said, pointing out the dozen or so tissue squares trailing from the back of the chair to the floor.

"Oh! I was wondering where that went!" he said back, pulling it from his pajama bottoms and blowing his nose with it, tossing the snot-filled butt wipe onto the table and just barely missing Sheree's coffee cup.

"Ugh, you're disgusting, you know that?" Sheree told her brother, staring at his horrifying bed head, with his brown hair going in every direction, his eyes lined with dried rheum, and the right side of his face bearing the creases from his pillowcase.

"Like you're one to talk! Do you really think that bathroom is soundproof? We overheard everything!" he exclaimed loudly before putting a hand on her shoulder and continuing, "You might want to talk to your doctor about Irritable Bowel Syndrome."

Goddamned television commercials.

Her ears were red with embarrassment and rage as she responded with, "I'll show you irritable bowels!" before preparing to punch him in the stomach.

"It's true. Perhaps you're becoming lactose intolerant?" Mrs. Hollins implied. "We did have a heavily dairy fortified dinner last night, what with the Fettuccine Alfredo, cheese bread, that glass of milk you had, and let us not forget the half gallon of ice cream you consumed all on your own."

Sheree's hand was still balled up into a fist and lingering in midair awaiting the end of the bombardment of possible causes to her digestive upset that her family was flinging at her. "What's your take on it, Dad?"

Mr. Hollins looked deep in thought before looking his daughter square in the eyes and telling her, "I think your mother is right."

"What!" Sheree yelled, standing up and causing her chair to nearly topple over. "You never take Mom's side! How could you? I thought I was your favorite? I thought you loved me?"

"I thought so too, but Honey, I really wish we had recorded those sounds because, damn, that was just plain nasty!" he said, trying his hardest to keep a smile from forming, but failing miserably.

Allowing herself to deflate back into her chair, she conceded. "Fine, I'll try not to *consume* so much dairy in one sitting again."

"I thank you, your mother thanks you, your brother thanks you, and I'm sure the people working at the waste management facility thank you too," he said with a twinkle in his eye and a slight smile on his young-looking face as he took a sip of his coffee, trying not to think of why it was looks like that made her friends want to have sexual relations with the man.

Pouring herself a bowl of Lucky Charms, her favorite marshmallow-laden oat cereal, she realized she was about to go back on that whole cutting down on dairy bit as she filled the bowl to the rim with milk, leaning down to take a loud slurp before spooning the first bite into her mouth.

Lucky Charms, why are you so magically delicious?

* * *

"Hey Jennifer!" Sheree said, hugging her friend she hadn't seen in a week. "You haven't seen Sky anywhere, have you?"

Giving Sheree a somewhat offended look, Jennifer shrugged with, "What, am I not good enough for you?"

"Cut the crap, you know what I mean," Sheree said, looking around Sky's usual hangouts, but realizing her usual hangouts were with the two of them and she was nowhere to be found.

They decided to walk around the corner from the main entrance and there she was in a corner by the girl's restroom talking with Ami and Kori. The mean girls. This could not be good. As they walked closer, Sky shoved something in her pocket in a way that she thought was discreet but decidedly was not so much, as she noticed both Sheree and Jennifer caught sight of the act. Kori and

Ami on the other hand, looked suspicious and guilty, but of what they had yet to determine.

"Whatcha doin'? Dealing drugs?" Jennifer asked with a big goofy smile on her face.

"Uhhhh…" Kori managed with a dumbfound look on her face.

"No! What the hell? C'mon, Kor. Let's go so we're not late for class," Ami said, grabbing Kori by the arm and walking off before adding as she looked in Sky's direction, "Later, Cheyenne."

When they were out of view, Sheree said, "Bitches don't even know yo' name! What you hangin' wit' dem fo'?"

"Let me guess, you've been hanging out with Courtney all week, haven't you?" Sky asked rather monotonously.

"Shit. Yes. Sorry. She brings out the Ebonics in me," Sheree informed her friends, the embarrassment shading her cheeks and ears rosy.

"Say my name, say my name!" Courtney sang upon hearing her name as she dance-walked and cuddled up close to Sheree. "Okay, Sky. Spill the damned pintos why yo' mama been keepin' you away from me all week."

"Wow, you just cut to the chase, don't you?" Jennifer asked, somewhat shocked though at the same time somewhat not since it was Courtney and that was a very Courtney thing to do.

"This whole medication adjustment thing has made me feel so fucking numb that I didn't want to see the world for a while," Sky told them, her voice barely breaking an even tone. Flat lined. "My mom was just being a little overprotective, probably because I told her about not wanting to live anymore or whatever."

"It's true," Sheree said, nodding her head. "Suicidal thoughts do tend to make mothers worry, especially after being vocalized. But you seem better now? I mean, you're definitely not the spunky Sky I'm used to, but you are better than the last time I saw you."

Sky sat silently in her wheelchair like a stalled car during rush hour traffic.

The first bell rang, signaling five minutes until classes start for the day.

"Don't think this gets you off the hook, girlfriend. Lunch. We talkin' 'bout this," Courtney said with a stern look that let Sky know she was dead serious before turning around and continuing to sing the Destiny's Child song she started only moments ago while walking to her first period class that Sheree would soon be joining.

"I need to go," Sky said, her voice as small as she looked yet lacking any real emotion.

"I need to know that you're okay," Sheree said.

"I'm functioning within acceptable parameters," Sky told them, conjuring up a half-smile that looked painfully forced.

"Liar," Jennifer said bluntly.

Sky looked at her lap and wondered why her friends still hadn't asked what she shoved into her pocket, but decided to brush it off. "Maybe coming to school today wasn't such a great idea after all. I should call my mom."

"I have a car," Sheree reminded her.

"It's true, we could all skip today and study for that math quiz we have tomorrow," Jennifer added.

"Good God, woman! Enough with your obsession with math!" Sheree said loudly.

Sky somehow managed to laugh, shocking her friends. "I'm in. Now while we still have a chance."

Rounding the corner towards the student parking lot, Sheree caught sight of someone she wasn't expecting to see, and tried to backtrack but it was too late. She saw them. And worst, Sky saw her.

Mrs. Hawkins, looking as frazzled as ever, walked towards them hurriedly. "Sky, we're going home. Now."

"Mom, this is the first day back to school in over a week. What possible excuse could you have now?" Sky asked, but in a muted and mundane and nonthreatening way that was quite different from the fiery spirit she had just a few weeks ago.

Mrs. Hawkins looked visibly upset. "It was a mistake."

"What's a mistake?" Sky asked.

"Letting you come back. You should be home where I can keep an eye on you," she said, holding back tears.

"So instead of me taking my life you are going to take it away from me?" Sky accused, her voice still lacking passion or real feeling behind the words.

The tardy bell rang.

"Let's go. Now," Mrs. Hawkins demanded. "Don't make me have to take your handles and wheel you to the car myself."

"That's the only way I'm going," Sky told her, folding her arms across her chest.

So Mrs. Hawkins walked behind her daughter, grabbed the handles, and started pushing Sky away while Sheree and Jennifer stood there, helplessly watching their friend being forced out of their lives.

Sky turned around and told them, "This is why you should never be honest with your parents."

Then Sky was gone.

"Say my name, say my name!" Sheree sang as she walked through the front door of her house.

"Sheree."

"Jesus Christ!" Sheree yelled after her skin jumped off for a brief second until she realized who had responded to her singing. "What are you doing home early?"

"Slow day," Mr. Hollins said with a beer in one hand, remote in the other with a finger on the MUTE button waiting to unmute the volume on the television. Considering his job as a morgue attendant—assistant medical examiner to be exact—slow was a good thing.

"Got it. We need to talk."

"I'm not an alcoholic."

"I didn't say you were."

"I just assumed that was your intended conversation what with me nursing a beer in the early afternoon and all while watching television in my underwear."

Sheree saw his attire and looked perplexed.

"I'm just kidding. I don't wear underwear!"

"Ew, and it wasn't."

"Then what do we need to talk about."

"Kayla."

Her father looked a bit stunned. His finger moved from the MUTE button to the POWER button and pressed. "Then let's talk."

"Let's."

There was a long stretch of silence as father and daughter stared at each other, waiting for the conversation to begin.

"Do you need a beer?" Mr. Hollins asked, motioning as though he was ready to get up and retrieve one from the fridge.

Sheree chuckled. "No. Not yet."

"Okay, then please, let's talk about this. I won't hold anything back if you don't," he told her reassuringly.

That was just what she needed to hear. Her dad always knew the right thing to say at the right time. Sheree made herself promise she would never forget just how lucky she was to have him as a father as she said, "When Kayla comes back, where is she going to sleep?"

The drink Mr. Hollins had just taken was quickly spat back into the bottle as he responded with, "You're big conundrum is wondering where your sister might sleep assuming she hypothetically comes back from the dead?!"

"It's one of the things that has crossed my mind lately," Sheree told him.

"Of all the things…"

"Seriously, Dad. I'm a pretty selfish person. You know that. I know that. The world is well accustomed to my selfishness. I hope you don't expect us to bunk together in my room. It's too small," she said with her arms folded across her chest, pouty lips and fiery eyes.

"Don't worry, your mother has been turning the craft slash office slash catchall room into another bedroom, even if it is small and lacks a closet. I smell a trip to Ikea soon," he said with a slight smile on his face and winking before taking another sip of thick brown beer from the bottle in his hands.

Sheree laughed at the sound of hearing her dad singsong the last few words he spoke. "I hope she doesn't mind being crammed into what was obviously originally conceived as a nursery."

"Considering she's been dead for nearly thirteen years, I have a feeling she won't mind at all," he said, taking another swig. "Are you sure that was all that was on your mind?"

Sheree paused. What did he mean by that? Does he know she has a million other questions about her sister that need answers? Was he just making small talk? How would he know?

"That was the most pressing one," Sheree lied, deciding safety was a better option than truth.

Mr. Hollins sensed her lie. "Something tells me you're not wanting to ask a burning question."

"What?"

"You haven't asked how she's coming back. You haven't asked why she's coming back. You haven't asked why we as your parents would even allow her to come back after she tried to kill you. So yes, I think you are holding back on me." His demeanor was both cool and alarming at once.

Sheree was shocked. What did her father know? Was he aware of the circumstances last Christmas that nearly ended her life? Did he know about why all those terrible "accidents" happened? Did Brendon tell him?

"How could you know that?" Sheree asked with a voice so small one could mistake it for a mouse.

Clearing his throat, Mr. Hollins said, "When you were four, I had to pry Kayla off of you. She was strangling you with her hands pressing so tight against your throat and screaming about how it wasn't fair that she had to die and that it should be you instead. Your mother and I assumed that she was just being dramatic because she was often dramatic. That or she saw a scary movie and was reenacting a scene, either of which was a possibility considering what fine parents your mother and I are, obviously missing the chapter in the parental guidance handbook where it says *Nightmare on Elm Street* is not a family movie night kind of show for toddlers. A week later she was dead and part of me wonders if Jessica warned her."

"Jessica?"

"Kayla used to tell us about her all the time. She'd visit her in her dreams or while she was playing by herself. Sometimes she would blame her actions on Jessica thinking that it would avoid getting her in trouble." He spoke so nonchalantly it was frightening.

"Did it work?" Sheree asked, bracing herself.

"Never."

Letting it all sink in, Sheree wondered if he was still holding back anything when he started talking again.

"I have to admit she definitely had your mother and I fooled last Christmas."

"Oh fuck." The blood drained from her face, both from her response and his admission.

"Sure you don't need that beer?" His smile was unnerving.

Just then, Sheree's mother walked in the door with Brendon in tow. "Family meeting. Now," Sheree ordered.

"Frank, what did you tell her?" Mrs. Hollins asked her husband. "Is this about the spare room? I can explain…"

"Mom, please, sit down. I know you know about Kayla and some of the bad things she has done, but I don't think you know all of them," Sheree said matter-of-factly.

Tears started welling up in Mrs. Hollins's eyes. "I know more than I've let on."

Brendon shooed away Rex and Deschutes who were thrilled to see him, but he had more pressing matters at hand. His dead sister's secret evil plan wasn't so secret after all, and he had to make absolutely clear that his parents understood just how evil the bad part of Kayla was. "She tried to kill me! Twice!"

"We know," Mr. Hollins told his son, crying solid tears that surprised everyone in the room.

"I'm not finished!" Brendon shouted, tears falling down his cheeks threatening to form canyons on his face. "She tried, but couldn't. I know why I was born now."

"But how?" Mrs. Hollins asked, her face a hot mess.

Composing himself, turning off the waterworks, and gathering his strength, he said, "To stop her."

"Brendon? Who told you that?" Sheree asked, her face just as wet and ugly-cry-like as the rest of her family.

"Kayla told me. Good Kayla. The one I trust," Brendon revealed to his family. "She told me that I am her kryptonite."

Shaking her head, Mrs. Hollins said, "I thought I was protecting you from her by keeping my mouth shut, by erasing all evidence of her, but obviously that was pointless. I don't know why I thought ignoring the problem would make it go away."

"Ignoring problems only makes them worse," Sheree said, head in her lap as she knew that it was now or never for what she had to say next. "I was raped last year."

"Oh no…" her mother let out.

Her father looked furious, clenching his fist so tight his fingernails started drawing blood from his palm, face getting redder and redder as the rage he felt inside surfaced. "Who?"

"Craig."

"I'm going to kill him," he said through gritted teeth.

"And Tyler. And Joe. And Jordan."

Her father's anger melted into a puddle of sorrow. Her mother just sat with her hand over her mouth unable to make a sound. Her brother held her tightly.

Now. Let it out.

"They held me down and took turns. I was a virgin! They stole that from me! But I know what I have to do. I have to make them pay. I can't let them get away with this any longer!" Sheree yelled much louder than she anticipated through angry tears.

"I'm going to kill them," her father said, his sudden calmness unsettling.

"Dad, I need to take care of this. It's been a year, and unless they feel like confessing, there's no proof. Not anymore."

"Why didn't you tell us? We could have helped you through it!" her mother said after finding her voice again, although now it was fragile and breaking.

Mr. Hollins got up from the couch and started walking towards the front door.

"Dad! Where are you going?" Sheree asked.

"To kill those bastards."

"You might need your keys since they live three hours away."

"I can walk."

"What are you going to kill them with?"

"My bare hands if I have to."

"Please, Dad. Let me take care of this."

"You shouldn't have to. I'm your father. It's my job to take care of you."

"And you have. You've been the best dad! I'm sorry I didn't tell you and Mom when this happened but I was so ashamed and thought it was my fault and just wanted to forget about it."

"Promise me no more secrets, okay?" Mr. Hollins said, his pain evident. "Not this big anyway."

"Promise."

Chapter 19
Good Friday

The week flew by, despite the fact that Sky was still being held hostage by her parents and Sheree's family had come clean about practically all their dirty secrets, both big and small. Courtney and Jennifer were busy every day after school with cheerleading practice for the upcoming national competition, leaving Sheree alone most nights to gather up her courage to confront her rapists. It was all very surreal.

Getting in her car after school let out on Friday, Sheree started singing, "Say my name, say my name! Oh my gawd, I hate that song! Why is it stuck in my head?!" This, despite all efforts to eradicate it from her brain, would undoubtedly make it onto the soundtrack of her life by sheer force rather than by choice.

Driving home, she sang the catchy line again, but nearly crashed into a ditch when a voice answered with her name.

"What the hell?" Sheree said, correcting course.

"Sorry Sister, but you were asking for it!" Kayla said in her gravelly voice from the passenger's seat. "Besides, we have business to discuss."

"Business?"

"Yes, business."

"What are you talking about?"

"I think you know."

"I hope it's not about talking to Mom and Dad about everything that you did."

"Partially."

"You can't…"

"We need to make those bastards who raped you pay."

Suddenly it became clear what Kayla's intentions were. And suddenly Sheree realized she was going to let whatever her sister had in mind happen as she drove past Song's End and kept going north on the main road until it met with another highway that connected with Interstate 5. "Hey Pretty" by Poe started playing on the radio as they drove onto the freeway Seattle bound, eerily capturing the moment with its cryptic lyrics and sound as Kayla divulged her plan.

Exiting onto SW Admiral Way from the West Seattle Bridge, Sheree decided to give in to Kayla's request to drive by their old house. It had been a little less than nine months since they moved out, but for Sheree it felt like a lifetime ago as she looked at the tiny place she used to call home from the vantage point of her parked car. The pole-lined street strung with power lines breaking up the sky like stained glass windows, was so busy with traffic that it struck her how odd it was they used to play in the front yard unsupervised. The cars whirring past them well above the speed limit shattered any sense of nostalgia that might have been felt.

Kayla stared at the spot where she died. Any emotions she was feeling were concealed as far as Sheree could tell, as she just stared like she was waiting for something to happen. Nothing did.

"We need to go to Schmitz Park," Kayla said.

Schmitz Park.

The site of Sheree's sexual assault.

The place Sheree swore she would never go again.

Ever.

Without hesitation, Sheree drove away from their old house without looking back, and headed west towards the park, passing up the opportunity to take the route that would go by her old elementary and middle schools. Kayla did not protest. There were so many questions Sheree had for Kayla, but felt it wasn't the right time to ask. However, after parking by the entrance to a trail that went through the heart of the park, there was one question that was burning inside her. "Are you really here?"

A wicked smile formed on Kayla's face before she responded with, "I'm as real as you want me to be."

"You mean you are only in my head?" Sheree asked, staring at the girl who looked so physically real next to her.

"No, not exactly. Let's just say I haven't fully taken corporeal form yet. Had to make a deal with the devil so to speak to finish this last task."

"You mean…?"

"Yes."

"And they will all be here?"

"All four of them. Shall we do this?"

Fear struck Sheree like a bitch slap.

Cold sweat dripped down her forehead.

Hands clammed up as they refused to let go of the steering wheel.

Kayla opened the driver's side door from the outside and offered up her hand for comfort. Some comfort. This hand was responsible for so much death. So much pain and grief and fear that Sheree didn't think she'd ever be able to take it. But she did, and hand-in-hand the sisters went into the woods to go hunting. Sheree caught herself giggling as the image of Elmer Fudd whispering, "Shhh! I'm hunting rapists!" entered her thoughts. Kayla's snickering at the same time revealed her thoughts were not hidden, that perhaps the two of them were connected once again. Reunited. The thought was both comforting and terrifying. Of course, what they were planning on doing was also.

What would she say when she confronted them? What would she do? What could possibly make all the shame and guilt and anger and rage that she kept bottled up inside for far too long go away? What made her think that the anniversary of her gang rape was a good day to do it all, and at the very place it all happened?

Sheree knew that this was going to be difficult, but the further they went into the forest, the harder it was for her to do what had to be done. They had to pay. She had to exact her revenge. Looking next to her and seeing her twin sister beside her and not feeling fear but calmness made her question her own sanity.

"You know I'm not just a part of your imagination, right?"

"Do I?"

"Dear Sister," Kayla said with her usual villainess tone. "Trust me when I say that I am right here beside you. Trust me when I say that I will never abandon you again. Trust me when I say that what we are about to do will set us both free from the hell we've been living."

Trust was a difficult thing for Sheree given her history.

Laughter echoed off the trees.

They were close.

Soon it will be time to do what she had to do.

Soon it will be time to act.

Soon.

Sooner than she thought, they were right in front of them. Sheree turned to Kayla but she was gone. Fear entered. Was she really ever there? Was Kayla just a vice her imagination conjured up to force her to do what had to be done?

The four boys turned around and their smiles and laughter disappeared.

Sheree was alone.

Four against one.

Again.

Craig was the first to speak. "Hi, Sheree. Haven't seen you in a while." His voice made Sheree want to vomit.

What the fuck was I thinking?

The four boys began walking in her direction.

Sheree couldn't move. Her feet felt like they were glued to the paved trail. She contemplated taking off her shoes, but couldn't even reach down to untie the laces.

The four boys were getting closer.

Closer.

Closer until a little girl started singing an eerily familiar nursery rhyme that caused them to stop.

"The itsy bitsy spider went up the waterspout."

The four boys looked around trying to figure out where the voice was coming from.

"Down came the rape and knocked the spider out."

Sheree had to look down to her own mouth to make sure it wasn't her singing.

"Up came the sister to wipe out all the pain.

The four boys looked confused and horrified as the words reverberated off the trees.

"And the itsy bitsy spider was allowed to kill again!"

The familiar tune was finished with a familiar evil laugh that engulfed the four boys. Sheree, however, was finally able to move again and started walking towards the four boys. As she got closer, she saw that one had pissed his pants, which made her laugh.

"You're pathetic, Tyler," Sheree said, shaking her head. "I can't believe I was ever afraid of you for what you did to me. I can't believe you were even able to get it up when you can't even control pissing all over yourself!"

She laughed and didn't even care that it sounded so much more like Kayla's than her own. She felt powerful. She felt strong. She felt invincible.

"What do you want?" Craig asked, his voice cracked.

"What do I want?" Sheree asked back. "I want to know why me?"

"What?" Jordan managed to say.

"Why did the four of you decide to rape me?"

"We didn't rape you!" Joe screamed, his voice high like a ten-year-old boy.

Three of the four boys seemed to have lost their fear, leaving Tyler and his soaked crotch to crumble to the ground as they approached her. "As I recall, you begged us to have sex with you. All of us. Said it was a fantasy to lose your virginity in a public place with a bunch of hot guys."

Lies.

"Is that what you've been telling yourself this past year, Craig? That I wanted it?"

A creepy smile formed on his smooth face. "I cannot tell a lie."

"And yet you manage to live with at least one that I know."

"So what's your plan? Tell the cops? Nobody will believe you."

"Really?"

"My dad's the D.A. so yeah, nobody is going to believe you." Craig's smugness was unnerving. "Besides, it's four against one."

His words struck a chord.

"Make that two against four!" Sheree said as Kayla pushed her way out of her body in a fiery blaze of teal and light that made the four boys fall backwards.

Kayla turned towards Sheree and asked in her gravelly voice, "Are you sure you don't want to stay and watch? I promise it will be a performance to remember!"

"I'm sure. I've said all I need to say. Now you can do what you want to do," she told her sister who looked slightly disappointed, but only slightly.

Sheree turned around and walked back towards her car. She didn't care to witness what was about to happen to the four boys who attacked her in this very spot on this very day one year ago. She didn't want to even know what her sister had planned for them. She didn't want to know that her sister would make puppets of them. Make them do things with each other. Touch each other. Make them cut off each other's dicks and stab each other's asses and continue to mutilate each other without mercy long after they begged for death.

No, Sheree didn't want to be witness to any of that.

Sheree arrived home late that night, though how she got there was a blur. She remembered getting in her car, but the drive was missing from her memory. When she opened the front door, she saw her mother and Jennifer in the living room, both crying. The television was off. Her father was nowhere in sight.

"Mom, where's Dad?" Sheree asked.

Her mother looked like she was trying to answer but only sobs managed to escape.

"Mom, where is Dad?" She asked again, forcefully.

Jennifer walked over and wrapped her arms around her. Her mother seemed unable to move from the couch. In the shadows, she could see Brendon on the floor, holding his knees.

"No. No no no no no no no!" Sheree yelled, trying to hold back tears, wanting to know what was going on before surrendering herself to grief. "Mommy?"

"She's gone," Jennifer whispered into her ear through muffled tears.

She? Who is she? Where is my dad?

"Sky is dead. She took her life this afternoon," her mother finally managed.

Shock.

"But where is Dad?" Sheree asked again, confused.

"Sheree," her mother said, "he had to help the medical examiner."

Of course. Dad works in the morgue. He'd be at the hospital helping with the autopsy.

"So Dad's okay!" Sheree said excitedly as if she wasn't just told her friend committed suicide.

Confused, her mother said, "Of course your dad is okay. But Sky..."

"Sheree, Sky is dead!" Jennifer shouted, spit flying through the air. "Don't you understand? She killed herself! She took too many pills and died!"

Sheree still couldn't fully understand what her friend was trying to tell her until Jennifer's hands took hold of hers and the shock wore off and reality hit her like a semi truck and she fell to the ground and cried until the tears couldn't flow any longer.

Good Friday was turning out to be anything but.

Later that night after Jennifer had left, Sheree told her dad, "I could use that drink now."

"Only if you promise me that you won't use alcohol as a crutch to escape your problems," her father responded.

Thinking about how ridiculous that sounded, especially since that was the whole reason for asking for a drink was to escape all the problems in her life for a short time, she decided to be honest. "I need a drink because I've had a shitty day. I confronted Craig and his friends about raping me and it took every fiber of my being not to kill them myself, one of my best friends committed suicide, and any time now my twin sister is going to come back from the dead for real, not just as a ghost. No, I can't promise not to use this as a coping mechanism."

"Very well. Have a drink of this," he said, handing her a bottle of the thick dark beer he coveted so much.

Sheree took a drink and quickly spit it out. "What the hell, Dad? That's disgusting! How do you drink that stuff?"

"Because it's delicious, but it's also an acquired taste for some people." He took a swig, letting it roll around on his tongue before swallowing.

Mrs. Hollins walked into the kitchen with her glass of red wine. Mr. Hollins was about to defend his reasoning when she suddenly said, "Here, try this instead."

Sheree took a drink and quickly spit it out too. "What the hell, Mom? Is this what all alcohol tastes like, or just the crap you deem acceptable for budgetary reasons?"

In unison, her parents responded with, "Yes."

"Ugh."

"It tastes better after you're twenty-one," her mother said.

Chapter 20
She's Arisen

Easter morning would find candy hidden everywhere in the house rather than outside because this is the Northwest and things like that pesky constant drizzle have a way of putting a damper on the Easter Bunny hiding candy outside to get wet and sticky and decidedly inedible. Much to the delight of Brendon, Rex and Deschutes surprisingly hadn't gotten it all before he awoke to the treasure trove of chocolate bounty before him. Filling his basket as he wandered the house, Sheree found herself sneaking a few handfuls here and there with her free hand, other wrapped around a coffee mug. Their parents watched on from the breakfast bar. It was rather Norman Rockwellian… for now.

Any minute Kayla would be back in their lives for good. For real. No more hauntings. No more nightmares. No more body snatching. No more mind games. No more death. That last part was part of the deal, right? That she wouldn't kill anyone else? Her quota was full and anything over her limit would result in the contract being null and void and she'd have to leave this plane of existence forever, right? There were so many unanswered questions. Would Sheree ever have the courage to ask them?

As the Easter morning rituals began to fade into cranky arguments over what to have for breakfast and emptying the dishwasher, Mr. Hollins quietly stepped out of the conversation and took a seat in his favorite spot on the den sofa and turned the television on. The news was all bad. The announcer started with a story on teen suicide that began with Sky, and transitioned to two more Ravenwood High School kids who had apparently killed themselves over the weekend. They were names Sheree recognized: John Upcock and Kori Myer.

"Oh my gawd," Sheree said quietly.

"Yeah, so that's how I spent my Saturday night. Did you know them?" her father asked.

"Only in passing. I mean Sky and I had a class with Kori. Oh my gawd. And you're sure it was a suicide?" Sheree asked her dad, knowing that he couldn't divulge into too many details.

He paused.

"Let me just say that the news isn't telling the whole story," he managed to scramble together on short notice, both revealing and not revealing what he really wanted to tell his daughter. "About all three of their deaths."

Sheree's eyes widened. "Are you saying they were murdered? Was it Kayla?"

"You know I can't tell you everything about my job or I could lose it. And no, I don't think Kayla had anything to do with their deaths." He looked like he was struggling with the ethics and morality of the position he was in before adding, "The only thing I will say for now is that they all, at least from what my examination and findings and my boss's findings conclude, are all related."

"Fucking drugs," Sheree said, shaking her head and taking a sip of coffee.

"Fucking drugs," her father said, shaking his head and taking a sip of coffee.

Then the news story turned to four more apparent suicides. Four. In West Seattle's Alki neighborhood.

"The bodies of four teenage boys were found late last night. They were reported missing Friday evening by their parents. A local girl found the bodies when she went off trail in Schmitz Park. Authorities reported to us that it appears to be a murder suicide."

Then the interviews started. Sheree tried not to roll her eyes. Her father looked perplexed at her reaction, but refrained from asking the burning question: Who were the four boys in question?

"I've never seen anything like this before," a police officer said to someone just to the right of the camera. "They were so well liked by the community. It's just a tragedy. A tragedy."

"I can't believe they won't ever be in school again!" a girl cried, her mascara running down her overly painted cheeks, striping her face like a shittily painted Easter egg.

Then the name-dropping started and her father's question was answered.

"Craig was so popular, I don't know why he would kill himself," a jock-type Sheree recognized said. "So were Joe and

Jordan. I guess you could call Tyler popular, but he was the quietest of the group."

Then the view changed to a reporter who was live from the scene as it was unfolding. He stopped momentarily when his producer pointed out three girls watching the bodies being wheeled on patient trolleys towards ambulances. Three girls who didn't appear to be sad, but that same angry happiness Sheree felt after confronting the four boys who brutally took away her innocence. Three girls who were side-by-side and staring as the bodies were transported out of the park, covered in bloodstained sheets on stretchers. Three girls who had gone for an early morning walk at just the right time to find a scene they would never forget. Three girls, who all at once flipped off the decaying carcasses.

"Rot in hell, assholes!" one of them yelled before the reporter got the camera back on him and apologized for live television feeds and the inability to filter out offensive language.

The television audience could hear the producer tell the reporter to go talk to the three girls and he grudgingly obliged.

"You don't appear to be sad about the alleged suicides of these four boys. Did you know them?" he asked before shoving a microphone so close to one girl's mouth like he was threatening to make her give it a blowjob.

The girl, after pushing the microphone away a few inches, said, "Those bastards raped me, and they raped her, and they raped her, and who knows how many other girls have been raped by those monsters."

"They got what they deserved!" the one to her right yelled.

Then Mr. Hollins turned to Sheree, gave her a long hug, and said, "Yes, they got what they deserved." But then realization hit. "You didn't kill them, did you?"

"Really? You think I could've killed them? I told you I wanted to after confronting them in Schmitz Park Friday night, but didn't. And now this is awkward because they went missing Friday night and are all dead."

By this time, Mrs. Hollins had walked into the room with Brendon by her side, face covered in a chocolate mess that made him look like he had a goatee. "Who else is dead?"

"The news is having an Easter Morning Special on Teenage Suicide. Apparently Sky was one of seven this weekend… so far," Sheree told her mother matter-of-factly.

"Oh, how dreadful," Mrs. Hollins said.

"Well, Easter is all about death. Makes sense," Brendon's chocolate-coated mouth said.

"Brendon!" Mr. and Mrs. Hollins shouted.

"It's about overcoming death and being reborn," a voice said from behind them all.

Kayla.

Nobody could figure out just how to react.

There she was.

Real.

Not a teal ghost.

Not a small child.

Not a figment of imagination or singing deadly rhymes or whispering bad thoughts or possessing another body. She was a real live girl.

"She's arisen!" Brendon squealed to break the tension. "What? You're all thinking it."

"Are you really here?" Mrs. Hollins asked, somewhat frightened at the thought of having Kayla in the family's life once again, but also suddenly feeling that part of her soul was finally mended after it had been ripped away so many years ago.

"Yes, Mom. I'm real," Kayla said with a smile, the gravelly voice Sheree was accustomed to hearing come from her mouth replaced with one that eerily sounded identical to her own.

"We're still in a bit of shock," Mr. Hollins told Kayla.

"I know. And I'm not going to push it. I know what I've done, and trust me, I will be making amends for the rest of my life. I'm not asking for forgiveness, but…"

"I forgive you!" Brendon said, rushing over to give her a hug.

Kayla rolled her eyes and said, "Of course you do, Brendon. You're the only one who could stop me if I ever decide to go all evil again." Mr. and Mrs. Hollins had looks of paranoia. "Not that I'm planning on it! Jesus, Mom, Dad! It was a joke!"

Sheree was still furthest away from Kayla, not moving from her seat.

"Okay, so here is the deal," Kayla started. "Sheree didn't kill those guys who raped her, I did. Yeah, so, maybe I got a little out of hand, but I made a deal with myself—wow, that is really confusing to say out loud—to exact revenge on behalf of Sheree for what they did to her—sorry, it's still weird to have both of my halves reunited—and so I made sure they were left in a state where they were so fully violated that they'd take their own lives rather than live them out as the less than human worthless pieces of shit they were. And since I was a ghost when this all happened, they won't find any evidence to suspect murder or foul play. Win win."

"So what is stopping you from you?" Sheree asked, still seated and small and slightly afraid.

"I am. And this little brat," Kayla said, messing up Brendon's hair even more than it already was, Rex and Deschutes at her side without sounding any alarms.

Mr. Hollins, still in shock though it was starting to wear off, said, "I don't know whether I should thank you or ground you."

Laughter filled the room as Kayla found herself unprepared for her father's sarcastic wit, "Geez, Dad! I'm back from the dead for like five minutes and you already want to ground me?"

"Screw it, I don't care if it makes me a monster for saying so, but thank you for taking care of those boys," Mrs. Hollins said before going in for a hug.

"Mom," Kayla said through happy tears.

"One thing. Are you still a witch?" Mrs. Hollins asked, still holding her long lost daughter, unwilling to let her go now that she had finally built up the courage to be near her again.

"If I say yes, do you promise not to kick me out?" Kayla asked back.

"Promise."

"Yes."

"Figures."

Chapter 21
Promises

Sheree found herself where she usually found herself when she needed to work things out: Jeff's gravestone. She'd go there to be alone. She'd go there to talk to Jeff, even though the conversation was one-sided. Mostly. She'd go there when she needed to reevaluate her life. This time she was going there for forgiveness.

"I hope you understand that I need to work things out with Kayla," Sheree told the granite slab with JEFF MAINS etched into it. "I don't know if I can ever forgive her for killing you, but I hope you can forgive me for trying to."

A long pause.

Wind whistled through branches baring new growth.

Squirrels chased each other up and down tree trunks.

Finches and jays chirped and flirted and flitted in and out of the canopy.

A lone black spider crawled over Jeff's grave.

"Sheree," Kayla said quietly as she walked towards her sister.

"Kayla," Sheree said just as quietly as she sat in the mud.

Another long pause.

The wind died down.

The squirrels stopped chasing each other.

The finches and jays flew out of sight.

The spider continued to crawl on the gravestone.

"I am not asking for forgiveness. What I did is unforgiveable," Kayla told her.

"But in order for me to be okay with you being back, I have to forgive you."

Sheree couldn't let her eyes look into Kayla's.

"Take your time then."

"It's the only way I can move on."

"Hurry up then."

Sheree giggled and Kayla followed.

"I'm not ready just yet."

"I understand."

"But I promise I will be soon."

Kayla looked at Sheree, covered in mud and looking more pathetic than she ever could have imagined, and said flatly, "I promise that you and Jeff will be reunited," before turning away and walking back towards their house.

Their house.

Where they would live together.

As a family.

Was that a threat or an actual promise? Sheree wondered as she watched Kayla disappear through the front door of the Hollins residence.

The spider continued to crawl over the gravestone until Sheree crushed it.

Author Bio

Cory Blystone lives in Vancouver, Washington with his husband Greg, their dog Chuck, cat Dexter, and their flock of chickens named after *Buffy the Vampire Slayer* characters. When not in school and doing homework, he enjoys writing, drawing, painting, reading, quilting, gardening, making absurd videos for YouTube, reading, rapping, cooking, baking, oh, and reading. He also was the Managing Editor for Clark College's award winning art and literature magazine, *Phoenix*, for the 2015 edition where his hand can be seen on nearly every page. Literally. He drew or wrote every title, and wrote all of the writer's statements for the literary works by hand to give the magazine a personal journal feel. You can check it out at ClarkPhoenix.com.